Beautiful Decay

by

Sylvia Lewis

RP|TEENS
PHILADELPHIA · LONDON

Books published by Running Press are available at special discounts for bulk purchases in
the United States by corporations, institutions, and other organizations. For more information, please contact the Special Markets Department at the Perseus Books Group, 2300
Chestnut Street, Suite 200, Philadelphia, PA 19103, or call (800) 810-4145, ext. 5000, or
e-mail special.markets@perseusbooks.com.

ISBN 978-0-7624-4611-7

Library of Congress Control Number: 2012951788

E-book ISBN 978-0-7624-4837-1

9   8   7   6   5   4   3   2   1

Digit on the right indicates the number of this printing

Designed by Frances J. Soo Ping Chow

Edited by Lisa Cheng

Typography: Agenda, Adobe Garamond, and Respective

Cover Photography
Tree: copyright © spxChrome/iStock Photos
Flowers: copyright © Oleg Milyutin/Shutterstock Photos

Published by Running Press Teens
An Imprint of Running Press Book Publishers
A Member of the Perseus Books Group
2300 Chestnut Street
Philadelphia, PA 19103–4371

Visit us on the web!
www.runningpress.com/kids

To Erin,

who volunteered to beta read a story,
and has ended up beta reading a life. Neither I
nor this book would be here without you.

CHAPTER

One

There was a spider building a web outside my window, right on the other side of the glass.

It was tiny, which made sense; it was barely spring. Probably it just hatched. I guessed that it picked that spot because it was some tiny fraction warmer than the rest of the landscaping—the new, lime-green grass and the trees with only buds of leaves. It was just barely above freezing out there. The glass was icy under my fingers, even though my hands were gloved.

"Hi," I whispered to the spider. I traced its busy movements with one cotton-covered fingertip, drawing odd patterns in the condensate my breath made. It wasn't enough moisture to soak through the fabric, so it was safe. My nose was nearly on the glass. "I wish I could invite you in."

The spider made no comment, of course. It spun its web with a sort of frantic efficiency that seemed practiced, planned—like it was following a pattern, something hardwired into its tiny spider brain.

If I didn't get going, I wasn't going to have time to eat before I had to catch the bus to school, but I didn't want to leave just yet.

Odds were the spider would be gone by the time I got home in the afternoon. Right now, it was maybe an inch away from my fingers, if that—safe, on the other side of the glass, but still so close. It was rare that I got to be so close to another living thing. Sometimes, though, when I had the light on after dark in the summer, moths would come to the window.

"But, really, you wouldn't do so well in here. For one thing, Mom would freak the hell out and kill you like, instantly," I warned the spider. "And then probably bleach your dead body. Disturbing, I know, right?"

It kept spinning. Its limbs weren't even a full millimeter thick, and translucent. They caught the light.

"And that's assuming you survived me. I wouldn't want to kill you—I like you. But probably you're better off where you are."

There was a kid I'd never seen before in my first period Calculus class, and he tried to sit next to me.

"You shouldn't sit there."

The new kid gave me an odd look, but didn't move from the desk next to mine. "Why?" he asked. He sounded honestly curious, and he was eyeing my gloves.

He didn't look afraid, which was seriously weird. Most people are, more or less instantly. New kid wasn't big on self-preservatory instinct, apparently.

"I have a condition," I replied, picking at a loose thread on my left index finger and hoping he wouldn't turn out to be one of the morbidly fascinated types. I just *loved* those.

He was still just staring at me, frowning a little. His hair fell into his face. It was a faded, rusty sort of brown, like dead leaves, and his eyes were gray.

It made no sense, but his eyes made me think of the spider outside my window that morning. No, of the window itself—the way it smelled like rain and radiated an almost living chill. It wasn't a scary sort of chill—it wasn't like he had cruel, cold-looking eyes. If anything, he looked like a bit of a dork, with his messy hair and his puzzled expression.

Probably I was just freaking myself out—I wasn't exactly used to people wanting to be anywhere near me.

"Oh," he said finally, frown deepening. It made a little line appear down the middle of his forehead. "Really?"

"No, actually, I'm just a complete hypochondriac, but they like to humor me. Also I wear these 'cause they're just so damned cool." I wiggled my fingers at him, then ducked my head and began flipping through my notebook. My hair fell forward, hiding my face.

"Ah, right," he said. "Sorry. Didn't mean—"

"Whatever," I set my notebook aside, blank page at the ready, then pulled my textbook out of my backpack and slammed it down on the desk. People were staring, starting to whisper. Wonderful. "Just go away."

"I just meant—" He lowered his voice. "Is that what you have to say? To cover? Or do you really have some kind of medical condition too?"

I whipped around so fast my hair flew into my face, caught on my lips, and stayed there. "What did you say?" I asked incredulously. He couldn't possibly mean what it sounded like he meant.

"I can tell you're . . ." He leaned forward, and his eyes took on a conspiratorial glint. "You know." He waggled his eyebrows. "You have an . . . ability? And maybe also a disability, I guess, it's not like one rules out the other, but I wasn't trying to be an ass about it if you do."

Apparently he *could* mean what I thought he meant. I tried to come up with a coherent response to that; hell, I tried to come up with a coherent *thought* about that. Mostly I stared more.

"Oh, and I'm Nate," he added with a lopsided, self-deprecating grin. He held out a hand, offering to shake.

The speculative whispering going on around us exploded into outright alarm, some jock in the third row calling out, "Dude, you don't wanna—" while a feminine voice shrieked out a shrill, "Oh my *God*!" from the front of the classroom.

Mr. Wagner walked in then, interrupting all of them in his strident voice. "Okay, so today we have a new—gah!" he spluttered as he looked up from his class roster, rushing toward Nate and me with hands outstretched and waving. "No, no, no!"

Nate pulled his hand back slowly, frowning.

"Told you," I muttered. "I wasn't actually going to," I said more loudly for Mr. Wagner's benefit.

"No, no, of course not, you wouldn't!" Mr. Wagner came to a halt a few paces away. He laughed nervously. "I know how careful you are, just . . . phew! Just overreacted a bit, there, seeing potential catastrophe. Sorry, Ellie."

"No problem," I murmured. I didn't need to look back to know Mr. Wagner would be wiping his hands on his trousers. He did that when he had to stand too close to me. At the beginning of the school year I'd decided to watch and see if he did it any other time—he didn't, of course. Sometimes I'm just a masochist like that. I wanted to know.

"And you must be Nathaniel MacPherson," Mr. Wagner said. "Well, that wasn't quite how I'd intended to welcome you to the class, but . . . well, we'll need to find you a new seat . . . move some chairs around here. . . ." The teacher trailed off into subaudible mutterings, assessing the arrangement of the classroom.

The whole situation was inevitable, really—there were only three empty desks, and they were all in the back right-hand corner of the classroom, arranged around mine. Sort of like a moat.

"Nate," said Nate. I glanced up. He was watching me closely, face full of apology. I felt myself going red. The whispers were starting up again. I heard the distinctive click of someone texting—just great. The entire school would be talking about this by the end of first period.

"Hrmm?" Mr. Wagner asked, still surveying the classroom. His eyes kept darting uneasily back in my direction. He tucked the roster under one arm so that he could wipe his hands on his pants again. I wondered if he even realized what he was doing.

"I go by Nate," Nate repeated, louder, still watching me and looking miserable.

"Okay, Nate," Mr. Wagner agreed. "Er, Nate, maybe you'd better just go stand over by the door while we figure this out. You don't want to be . . . well, we don't . . . we give Ellie her space. She has a condition."

❧

My mother's car was in the driveway when I got home from school, which was just the weird icing on my humiliation-cake day. For about half a second I thought about ringing the doorbell, but then I just let myself in.

We nearly collided. She was hurrying toward the door with her head down, improbably glossy hair falling into her face as she dug for something in her purse.

"Mom!" I ducked sideways at the same instant she looked up and yelped. Her purse hit the floor with a jangle and a thud, and she flinched two steps back before stopping, eyes huge, one hand fluttering to her chest.

"Elizabeth!" She sounded out of breath. "Oh. You're home? Oh—I must be later than I thought."

She must have been because there was no way in hell she meant to be in the house while I was both home and awake. I just stood to one side of the door and said nothing while she retrieved her purse. Her hand shook as she reached back into it and pulled out her iPhone, showing it to me with a strained, shaky laugh.

"Found it!" she chirped, her voice going unnaturally high. "So I guess—I should get going."

"Okay." I stepped a little further to the side of the door, so she wouldn't have to pass too close by—unfortunately, she noticed.

"I'm going to a rally in the city," she blurted. "It's a take-back-the-night thing, because of what's been happening to those poor girls? The women's shelter organized it; it'll be a big group, totally safe, you don't need to worry, but I might not be home until late."

"Okay," This would be different from the norm how, exactly?

"We're hoping to raise awareness—sort of force the police to take notice, you know? If we get some press, they'll have to, even if it's *only* prostitutes—you know it wouldn't have gone on this long if it were any other demographic being targeted, so . . . it's something?"

I had no idea how I was supposed to answer any of that—the righteous indignation or the familiar note of helplessness in her voice. She wanted something, clearly.

"I'm just not sure what else we can do," she said.

You could take me, I thought. *I could stand on a street corner until I got grabbed, and once the guy touched me? Problem solved.*

But I wouldn't do that, because I could get caught, and I'd worry her, and I had homework.

"It's a good idea." I tried to sound supportive but mostly sounded impatient.

Mom smiled, though—quick and scared, but satisfied. "Thanks, honey." She started to edge past me sideways, toward the door, keeping a good three feet between us all the while—running into me like this must have really spooked her, or maybe she didn't believe her rally was quite as safe as she said. She never got close, but usually she wasn't so obvious about it. I took pity on her and headed for the stairs.

"Your grandmother called."

I paused, two steps up; that'd explain it too. "Yeah?"

Mom was halfway out the door, keys jingling in one hand, the other fussing with her hair. "Just remember to check the caller ID before you pick up the phone."

"I know." I tried not to roll my eyes. There was a shiny new Lexus sitting in the driveway that had been a sixteenth birthday present from a grandmother I'd never met. Even though Mom spoke to her regularly and didn't seem to mind the amount of money she threw our way, I was not to talk to my grandmother. My mom had reminded me of this at least twice a week since I developed motor skills sufficient to picking up a phone. She still thought I might someday forget and then, apparently, the world as we knew it would end.

Or at least I'd be somehow instantaneously poisoned by my grandmother's influence. Or maybe molested over the phone. I honestly don't know what the hell my grandmother did to my mother when she was growing up, but I was to have no contact. *Ever.*

Mom was still standing in the doorway, tucking her already perfect hair into place one more time and watching me.

"Have fun," I offered.

"Dinner's in the fridge, sweetie." Her voice was still an octave too high and her smile tight, and then she closed the door behind her.

Today was really weird, I typed into my Tumblr, and then paused, considering.

I didn't talk about my "condition" online—not in any detail. I had *friends* online, people who had never met me in person and thus weren't scared of me. On the Internet I wasn't Elizabeth Miller, dangerous freak—I was just another girl with a Harry Potter obsession who compiled epic lists of fanfic recommendations but was a little too scared to post her own stories. I had a tendency to rant on the general uselessness of the human race, or maybe the evils of reality TV. Online I could be something like normal. Geek normal, anyway.

I said I had a medical condition that meant I couldn't be close to people physically, that's it, the end, and in cyberspace there's no reason for anyone to disbelieve me.

Unlike at school.

Every school record documenting my "special needs," the accommodations my mother had doggedly negotiated, said just the same thing: immune disorder. It made a nice, scientifically explicable story—gave all the sane adults who sat on the school board and taught my classes something to tell themselves that let their tidy worlds go on making sense. That didn't mean any of them really believed it, much less my fellow students. Even with all my mom's efforts—the gloves, and the cover story, and changing schools six times before I hit junior high and finally developed a little better self-control—I'd just had too many accidents. Out in the real world, my freakishness was an open secret, and my chances of ever being any kind of normal were pretty much nonexistent.

Sometimes I wished I could just upload myself into my computer and cease to physically exist at all.

Weird as in sucked even more than is typical, I went on typing. There's a new kid in two of my classes, math and Western Civ. He—

He what? Tried to be friendly? Caused an enormous scene in first period Calculus that resulted in the majority of the senior class spending their lunch hour trying not to let me catch them staring?

All true. All entirely beside the point.

He *knew*, somehow, that I didn't just have a medical condition—he called it an *ability*. He didn't seem scared.

The problem with having friends is that it gets tempting to tell them the truth. The problem with telling the truth is that it makes people think you're crazy, and then you don't have friends.

He tried to shake my hand, I concluded with a weary, sick feeling in the pit of my stomach. So I was omitting things of

significance; those things didn't define me. I was just . . . general-
izing. Translating my experience into less threatening terms. The
explanations were predictably awkward and, of course, public, I
added. Did I mention it sucked?

So you want to find me shiny new fic and make it all better,
don't you? I tacked on the end.

I hit the CREATE POST button, then minimized the window
and started my Western Civ homework. Within five minutes there
was an email alert in my inbox telling me I had a note from
"caffiendgrl"—Mackenzie.

Mackenzie and I "met"—in the virtual sense—in the comments forum of a fanfic archive about three years ago. We could
finish each other's sentences within the week. Instant connection.
That doesn't happen to me in person, probably because people
don't generally talk to me at all. I'm not sure who or what I'd be
if it hadn't happened with Mackenzie—I had other friends, sort
of, in a way. I guess. Maybe more like acquaintances. I think
there's the real possibility I'd have ended up one of those kids who
shows up to school one day with a machine gun. Not that I'd need
the gun.

Awww, *hugs*, wrote Mackenzie. Don't worry about it,
sweetie, boys suck anyway. If he's enough of a douche to have
made a scene? So not worth your time.

I hadn't said that I wanted to be spending time with Nate; I
hadn't mentioned what he looked like, or that he'd made me
blush. I wouldn't even have *noticed* what he looked like if I hadn't

been thinking of providing Mackenzie with entertainment. She was physically incapable of discussing a guy without assessing his romantic potential (most fell sadly short of her standards). Left to my own devices, I wouldn't have even considered him that way.

Well, not much.

Not seriously.

Of course Mackenzie could pry that smidgen of interest out from between the lines of a few sentences worth of bitching. The simple fact that somebody out there in the world knew me that well made me feel a little better, even if it was someone three states away who I'd likely never really meet.

Sorry I cannot feed your dementia today, Mackenzie concluded, but I can find no new fic. I suck muchly.

I reblogged and replied, You totally suck beyond all sucking. No idea why I put up with you.

Three hours and twenty-seven increasingly surreal and sarcastic comments later, I was still the only one home, and I was getting hungry.

The house echoed as I clomped down the stairs. It was getting dark. I hadn't bothered to turn on any lights but mine, but outside the floodlights had come on. They glared in through the oversized front windows, painting the living room in geometric swatches of blue shadow and yellow light. The only things out of place were my backpack, slouching open and lumpish near the door, and the coat I'd flung over the arm of the faux leather sofa. The glass sur-face of the coffee table gleamed, not so much as a speck of dust obscuring its brilliance.

The refrigerator was stocked with plastic-wrapped dishes labeled with the date, contents, and preferred method of reheat-ing. It was all home-cooked; Mom didn't work. She couldn't when I was younger; there was simply no way I could be put into daycare when I was little. By the time I learned to control myself a bit better I was old enough to be left home alone. She could have gone back to work, I suppose, but that would have cut into her obsessive cleaning time. Instead she volunteered at night—soup kitchens, a crisis hotline, teaching adult literacy at the community college. It was all very rewarding and socially responsible, and it gave her a good reason to be elsewhere when I was home and awake.

Dad, I could pick out of a lineup if I had to. Probably. He lived here, but he was home even less than Mom, working seventy and eighty hours a week. He was a lawyer. So was Mom, once upon a time.

When I was done eating, I put my glass and utensils—every-thing that had touched my lips, my tongue, any bit of bare skin—directly into the Tupperware tub waiting in the sink. It was already filled with bleach water. At some point after I'd gone to bed, I knew Mom would come home and wash my dishes—she and Dad never ate in the house, and thus used no dishes. She'd wait until I'd left in the morning to leave her bedroom. By the time I got home again she'd be out distributing blankets to the homeless or something, and everything would be back the way I'd found it this afternoon. Sterile. It was sort of like having obsessive-compulsive elves.

After dinner I made my way back upstairs, into my bathroom. It, too, smelled of bleach. A pair of flip-flops waited for me by the door so that my feet wouldn't touch the tile floor; Mom had a thing about grout. It was porous. She wasn't convinced it was ever really clean. I could have told her it was pretty danged close to totally devoid of bacterial life, but that was exactly the sort of thing that made her voice go all funny. I tried not to say stuff like that.

I threw my clothes into the hamper, gloves and all, and slipped my feet into the sandals, avoiding the mirror as much as possible. I knew what I'd see—too much limb and not enough of everything else, all of it paler than pale. At least I didn't have pimples; I didn't get infections of any kind. As a consolation prize for normalcy, it sucked pretty hard, but it was something.

The shower itself was all gleaming glass and steel, the fixtures soldered in place rather than caulked. Caulk got mildew stains. I turned the water on as hot as I could stand it, stepped inside, and closed the door. I braced my hands against the wall and let the water just pour over me.

Where my bare hands touched, the fiberglass began to darken with a fine film of mold. I watched it, knowing I ought to try to stop, to control it, but it had been a rough day and it just felt too good to let go. The stains around my hands darkened, thickened, were shot through with brilliant streaks of something that grew red—some kind of bacteria I'd brought in on my skin or my hair, I guessed. It didn't matter. It wouldn't hurt me, whatever it was, and I'd make sure I cleaned it up before Mom got home. For now, though, it was safe to give in just this little bit.

A fresh pair of gloves waited for me right outside the shower door.

CHAPTER

Three

The next day Nate sat in his newly assigned seat in Calculus, far away from me. Except for the slight increase in stares and mutters, things went pretty much back to normal.

The bell rang for the end of class while I was still trying to convince myself that normal was good, and I realized with no small amount of annoyance that I hadn't heard a thing Mr. Wagner had said in the last fifty minutes. That probably meant there was a homework assignment I was going to miss unless I stayed back to ask what it was—I certainly couldn't ask my classmates.

I shoved my book into my backpack, keeping my pen and notebook out, and found a corner to hover in as the rest of the class cleared. They gave me a wide berth. I tried not to be bothered as Amber, a girl who'd once thrown rocks at me and started the whole junior high in on calling me Mary (as in Typhoid), blushed and stammered her way through introducing herself to Nate. He looked sheepishly pleased at the attention, handing his schedule over for her to interpret. She was gesturing animatedly as they went past, presumably drawing him an invisible map to his next class. She had his rapt attention.

This, I told myself, was inevitable. Nate was cute. Amber was a piranha. If he fell for her sweetness and light act, he probably deserved her. And most importantly, it wasn't any of my business.

"Ellie?" I turned to see Mr. Wagner standing a few paces off, watching me with what he probably thought was a politely curious expression. It might even have worked if his eye hadn't been twitching. The rest of the classroom had emptied while I was busy staring after Nate and Amber from my place in the corner. I could just picture my own expression. In my mind's eye I was a demented caricature of envy, all huge eyes and bony, clutching fingers.

"Everything okay?" asked Mr. Wagner. He was fiddling with a piece of chalk, passing it from hand to hand. He wiped the empty hand on his trouser leg. It left a wide swatch of white. I felt a spurt of vindictive pleasure at that, but then felt immediately bad. It really wasn't his fault. He was trying.

"I didn't hear the homework assignment," I admitted.

"Ah," said Mr. Wagner, and frowned at me. He opened his mouth as if he would speak, but then closed it again, lips pursed, frown deepening. I understood his dilemma. If I were any other student, he'd scold me for my lack of attentiveness. I wasn't any other student, though. I was Typhoid Mary, and no one ever reprimanded me—I think the teachers' reasoning was about three parts pity to one part fear.

"I'm sorry," I said. "I know I should pay attention."

"Well," Mr. Wagner said awkwardly, "Yes." He spun the chalk between his fingers, passed it back to his left hand, and scrubbed his right. It made his pants almost match.

The combination of those smears of chalk and Amber and Nate and the hour I'd spent last night scrubbing down the shower all churned together in my stomach and made my voice sharper than I'd intended. "Can I have it? Or do I just lose the points?"

Mr. Wagner flinched visibly, dropped the chalk, and shuffled a furtive half step backward. There was sweat beading on his forehead. "What?" He gave a half-hysterical laugh. "No, of course not, Ellie, of course not! It's practice problems 3 through 18 on page 256, not that you need the practice." Another nervous chuckle. "But, more practice never hurt anyone, right?"

"Right," I agreed, and bit my tongue on the urge to tell him his acting skills needed practice. His next class was beginning to trickle in now, freshmen, all staring at me in bug-eyed fascination. I noticed that no one was taking my seat; I wondered if anyone else sat in that chair all day.

"Let me get you a pass for your next class," Mr. Wagner offered a bit desperately, and hurried off toward his desk. He bumped his hip on the corner of a desk in his clumsy haste and muttered a word that I'm pretty sure teachers aren't supposed to use in front of freshmen. He sounded scared and angry. I hugged my notebook to my chest, hands curled into fists. It pulled my gloves taut over my knuckles.

The final bell rang while I was still waiting; I'd been right, nobody sat at my desk. I wondered if Nate and Amber shared their next class. I wondered if they sat together. I felt all discombobulated and angry at the world and annoyed at myself for the pointlessness of that.

When Mr. Wagner handed over my late pass, my gloved finger just brushed his. All I should have felt was the faint pressure of contact. Instead my first three fingertips tingled and thrummed in response. A jolt of pleasant heat went down my spine, like swallowing something just a little too warm.

Oh *shit*.

Mr. Wagner jumped back as if he'd been burned, yelping something even less polite than what he'd said when he stumbled. I sucked in a panicked breath, eyes fixed on the hand I'd touched. He'd curled it into a fist and was staring at it, the bit of finger I'd touched hidden, as if he was afraid to look.

"I'm sorry," I whispered.

Mr. Wagner slowly uncurled his fingers. A bead of sweat ran down the side of his face. The top of his bald head gleamed in the overhead fluorescents, and I could feel the entire class watching us in unabashed horror. I crumpled the pass in my hand, curling my arms around my notebook and my body. My fingertips still burned, and now they itched, too. On some horrifying, instinctive level, I wanted to reach out and let go. Some voiceless thing at the base of my skull didn't like holding back. I was starting to shake.

Where I'd bumped Mr. Wagner's finger there was a cluster of tiny red bumps, like pimples. I exhaled; that didn't look so bad to me. I didn't see any cuts or scrapes or torn nails, and whatever I'd caused to grow hadn't eaten through his skin.

Mr. Wagner didn't seem to think so; he made a whining sound like a frightened dog. He'd gone alarmingly pale.

"You should go wash your hands," I suggested, trying to sound calm and reassuring. It came out choked and quivering. "I think it'll be fine. I'm sorry."

My fingers felt like I'd stuck them into a bucket of needles. Needles full of stinging, itching things. My reaction was all out of proportion to the degree of temptation, I knew. Mr. Wagner's fingers just couldn't be that dirty. The man was a neat freak. No, this was about me—me and my nerves and my stupid, stupid obsession with a new kid who'd said two kind words to me.

Mr. Wagner was still just staring dumbly at his hand. The class full of freshmen was staring at me. Someone whispered, "Holy *shit*," in a voice that sounded high and frightened and very young.

"I thought she couldn't do that through the gloves," another small voice said. I didn't look for the speaker; that'd just terrorize the poor kid. If I looked at him, he'd probably expect me to come crawling in through a crack in his window at night and give him the plague—and with that darkly ridiculous thought, I began to calm down.

Maybe it's weird that having the entire room on the verge of complete hysteria steadied me, but it did. Hell, I'd been handling my mother's germophobe freak-outs more or less since . . . forever?

"Mr. Wagner," I said, more clearly. His eyes snapped to mine.

He was probably a good foot taller than me, and I'm not especially short. There was something just absurd and pathetic about this huge, balding, middle-aged man staring at me like I was the boogeyman. Probably it should have made me feel worse, but it had the opposite effect. If I had to be the adult here, that was okay. I was good at that. "Mr. Wagner, you need to go wash your hands," I enunciated slowly and deliberately.

For a moment, it looked like comprehension wasn't happening. Then he nodded furiously and took a step toward the door. Unfortunately, that also brought him closer to me. He seemed to realize that a second later and jerked back. I got out of his way, flattening myself to the wall. He scuttled around me, knocking into the nearest row of desks, apparently oblivious to the fact that there were students sitting at them. Then he was out the door, leaving me with a room full of goggle-eyed fourteen-year-olds.

I could hear his footsteps break into a run down the hall.

My mother had the delusional idea that by sending me to public school, she was giving me a "normal life"—that I could wear my gloves and have the same experience of growing up as anyone else. What I actually got was this: Mr. Wagner's second period class watching me like I might eat them. It was seriously, seriously tempting to say "boo!"

Instead, I said, "Take out your homework." They all leaped to obey, one kid in such a rush to extract his work from his bag that he knocked over his desk. I didn't think Mr. Wagner was really supposed to leave his class alone; maybe I should stay? Then again,

I probably counted as one of the bad things that could happen while he was gone.

So I left. I made it about halfway to Chemistry before the adrenaline rush began to wear off.

I detoured into the nearest bathroom and locked myself in the handicapped stall. It had its own sink, which I gripped until my hands ached while I tried to get my jagged breathing under control. Things like what I just did *could not happen.* I'd made it through four years now in the same school district. I hadn't had an incident like that—through the gloves—since Amber hit me in the back of the head with a rock during field hockey in ninth grade, after which it was decided, by consensus of the school board and my mother, that maybe I didn't really need to take gym. Every school I'd ever attended had reached that conclusion sooner or later—usually sooner.

My hands were starting to burn again. Shit, shit, *shit.* I ground my teeth and scrunched my face and inhaled and exhaled.

It wasn't working; I could tell by how lousy I didn't feel. The burning went from sharp and unpleasant to thick and liquid, like a hot bath, like sunlight on my spine.

I let my breath out in a long sigh and opened my eyes.

The sink was covered in black mold. It had spidered out along the grout and halfway up the mirror. There were tiny mushrooms sprouting from behind the mirror's edges.

I carried Clorox wipes in my bag. This was going to be a little more than wipes could handle.

The warmth slowly seeped out of my hands, leaving me feeling all sated and sleepy. My gloves were black at the fingertips and across the palms, slippery against my skin. I ripped them off and threw them into the basin. My thoughts slipped back to Nate. I wondered whether he'd still be trying to make friends with me if he'd gotten to see this demonstration of my "ability." I felt like the biggest, most pathetic moron in the entire world for even caring, but I couldn't just shut *that* off, either.

I wished, sometimes, that I could just be an outright monster—that I could stop caring at all what my parents or the other kids at my school or stupid fucking *boys* thought of me. Stop caring if I hurt them. Just rip my humanity off like my gloves, and not be afraid anymore.

I wondered if Nate the all-knowing knew *that.*

Then I grabbed my gloves out of the sink, threw them into the toilet, and held down the handle until it started to overflow. It was all I could think of to get someone to come clean the bathroom—someone with their own gloves, and galoshes, and lots of Lysol—before some poor kid with a normal handicap tried to use this toilet and caught whatever you catch from black mold.

I was resourceful, at least.

Maybe Nate liked resourceful girls. He'd get bored of Amber real quick, if he did. But that didn't matter. So what if I had one single redeeming feature that Amber lacked? He could pick any other girl on the whole planet, and she could touch him without hurting him. I never could. End game.

On Friday, I had a girl thrown at me in the hall.

At first I couldn't see who had done the shoving; I was too busy trying not to trip over the sprawl of tattered black skirt and unfortunate dye-job that was suddenly in front of my feet. It was crowded, and it wasn't easy to avoid her without bumping into someone else, which would have been equally disastrous. There was momentarily a lot of cursing from everyone in a five-foot radius—except, of course, the giggling girls off to my right who'd done the pushing in the first place.

It took only a few seconds for all disinterested parties to clear the area, and then Goth Girl and I were alone in a rare little bubble of open space in the hall. I spun around—and to my absolute lack of shock, there was Amber, looking prim and innocent, flanked by another two girls on each side. They looked like an advertisement for some snotty retail chain, right down to the superior looks on their faces.

"Oops," said Amber.

"Watch where the fuck you're going," spat the Goth girl. "Bitch."

She was talking to me, not Amber.

Her eyes never left me as she scrambled awkwardly to her feet, tripping twice over her artfully ripped skirt. Her black-lined eyes belonged on some trapped animal—too scared to be anything but mean. I couldn't help watching as she stomped her way around me—way, way around me.

I should have known better than to be surprised by things like that. There was a reason I wasn't part of any of the assorted social fringe groups around here.

"Well, that wasn't very nice," said Amber.

I glared. She smirked. So did her whole little clique, like maybe they were actually, literally controlled by some sort of hive mind. It was almost funny, except for how it really, really wasn't.

What if I'd actually touched that girl? Tripped and fallen on her? Flung my hands out to break my fall and—

"I think she was scared of you," Amber observed, oh-so-sweetly.

She could have just killed that girl—at the very least, gotten her very, very sick. And it would have been my fault. And she didn't care even one little, tiny bit.

Amber wasn't anywhere near as scared of me as she should have been, and I really, really wanted to correct that. For a moment I seriously considered it; could I, without putting her in the hospital? However much I couldn't stand her, the idea of really hurting *anyone* on purpose made me queasy. The sad answer was that I probably couldn't just give her a rash and a good scare, not when I was this worked up. I'd been here before, thinking I could just defend myself, that I could stop, but I never could.

But what if she did it again? What was I supposed to do, just let her use me as her go-to threat until I actually did give some poor dweeb or Goth kid some kind of flesh-eating infection? Was *that* right?

Amber's smirk was faltering, just a little, as I continued to stare—but then she spotted something over my shoulder, and her face brightened. "Nate!" she called out, and shimmied her way around me—not touching, but deliberately close. She threw me a last, vindictive grin over her shoulder.

Nate stood a ways down the now emptying hall, frowning as Amber ran up to him. He was watching me, not her. I couldn't read his expression at all.

I turned my back—the wrong way to get to my class, but like hell was I walking past them. I could feel his frown following me off down the hall.

I came home that night to an acceptance letter from Penn.

I sat at my dining room table for a long time just holding it, my eyes darting between it and the handwritten note my mother had left on top of the envelope. The unopened envelope—she'd been completely sure it would be an acceptance. She was right, but that wasn't the point.

"Congrats, Sweetie!!!" read the note. *"There's ice cream in the fridge for you!!! Chocolate chip mint!!!"*

Little creeping black lines were starting to feather out over the paper from my sweaty fingertips. Damp gloves just don't work that well. I watched the mold crawl out over the classic font, the bold letters telling me all about the wonderful opportunities a prestigious university like theirs could offer me. How wonderful my life was going to be from here on out, because I was one of the chosen—smart enough to get in, rich enough to attend. Of course the letter didn't say quite that exactly, but it was the general gist. It was the third such letter I'd received so far, all of them Ivy League.

In the length of time it took me to realize I'd started crying, half the paper had turned black and it had started to crumble. I let it drop from my fingers. Left it where it fell.

Mom would see it there, and she'd hate that I'd left something contaminated on the table, and she'd fret and scold and reassure me that of course I could live in a dorm. Get a job some day.

Have a real life.

The worst part was that she believed it.

❦

I told Mackenzie about the girl in the hall, and Nate and his stares. I did not tell her about Penn. Amber had long since earned the title Supreme Bitch-Queen of Hell—SBQoH for short, and once you've come up with that one, there's really no improving on it— but she'd yet to have reason to rant about Nate, which gave her room for creativity.

He's a spineless slag. A ho with all the depth of a pie plate, Mackenzie wrote in instant message. If he wants the SBQoH, let him have her. Get over it. Better yet, take it as a compliment that he hit on you first, before he realized knowing you might actually involve work. Means he thought you were hotter. An ego boost is about all a guy like that is worth anyway. Consider him used up.

He wasn't hitting on me, I replied, flipping through my Western Civ textbook, pretending to study. He just sat at the only empty desk in the room and said hi. He was just treating me like a human being, that's all.

If I write you fic myself, will you cheer up? Mackenzie demanded. Name your pairing—just no Draco/Hermione, okay? There's only so much I can take before needing the brain-bleach.

You wouldn't do it for me? I teased.

You're gonna make me cry, Mackenzie returned, complete with a line of little sobbing smileys running across the screen.

I sent her a smiley batting its eyelashes as reply.

I hate you, she said.

LOL, I typed back. Okay, okay—you do realize I'm just screwing with you? Geez, since when do I like them together anyway?

Since you're evil, said Mackenzie, and want to traumatize me for life.

Just so long as you realize that, I answered, smiling to myself. And . . . something with Snape? Snape and Tonks? Tonks who isn't married to Lupin yet, so it's not all morally questionable.

You are one disturbed human being, Mackenzie replied. I'll do my best.

There was a pause after that, during which I made an effort to actually read the textbook pages I was flipping. I got caught up in the assorted neuroses of ancient Roman emperors, and it was several minutes before I looked back up at the computer screen.

My hair's red again, btw, Mackenzie had written. Like, crayon red. I got sick of the blue. Wanna see a pic?

Sure, I said. An invitation to share photos appeared in the IM box. I clicked it, and a picture of a grinning girl my own age appeared. Mackenzie had light brown skin with freckles across her nose and short, spiky hair the color of strawberry syrup. She radiated confidence, even in a two-inch-tall webcam capture.

Coolness, I told her. I like it.

Thanks! Now you do yours, she answered, with a smiley that looked like a little devil. You are so a purple girl. Darkdark purple. You'd like it, I promise.

Sure, I said, right after I get that lobotomy.

I so wish you lived closer, Mackenzie typed back. No smiley; I don't think there is a smiley for wistful.

Me too, I lied.

M r. Wagner wasn't back in class until the following Monday. He ignored me completely, as if by refusing to look at me he could make me cease to exist. The rest of the class alternated between staring at him and staring at me, gauging my reaction. I did my best to disappoint them by way of total indifference; it wasn't like Mr. Wagner had ever been one of my favorite teachers. In a way honest terror was an improvement over false civility.

At lunch, someone threw a grape at my head.

I spun around.

Daniel Latham, wrestling team captain and host of nigh-weekly keggers, was staring at me from two tables over. He was surrounded by a gaggle of similarly gawking friends, Amber among them. They collapsed into guffaws and giggles when they saw me staring back.

Over the hunched shoulders of the ducking, laughing grape-throwers, I saw Nate seated next to Amber. He was still sitting up straight, watching me. He was frowning. Our eyes met for half a second before he turned to Amber. They were too far away and the cafeteria was too noisy for me to hear what exactly was being said, but he didn't look happy. Amber turned toward him so that all I could see of her was shoulders and shiny, perfect hair, but the shoulders looked tense.

Daniel sat up, reached across the table, and gave Nate a teasing shove. Daniel was smiling, but it wasn't a particularly nice smile—more of a *play along or else* sort of expression. Nate stood. So did Amber, clinging to Nate's arm with one hand and gesturing pleadingly at Daniel with the other. Several of Daniel's friends were getting to their feet as well.

I looked back down at my lunch, feeling the back of my neck going hot. Nate could not possibly be picking a fight with Daniel Latham over the throwing of a grape. He hadn't said two words to me since that first day. He had no reason to be offended on my behalf.

I heard footsteps approaching as I drew angry swirls of ketchup all over my plate with a burnt French fry. A moment later a tray clattered down onto the table across from me. My head shot up and my stomach sank—I just knew who it would be, and I was right.

Nate was sitting across from me.

If sitting next to me in Calculus class was taboo, sitting with me at *lunch* was about ten bazillion times worse. Lunch involved *food*.

"Hey," said Nate, as if nothing out of the ordinary were happening at all. His face still held the remnants of an angry flush.

"What the hell is wrong with you?" I demanded.

He shrugged. "Realized I was sitting at the wrong table."
Then he grabbed a fry off my plate.

"Don't!" I yelped, reaching out to stop him. I caught myself
before I made the mistake of actually grabbing his hand. He
paused, and then we hovered that way, a frozen tableau, my fingertips less than an inch from his. "Don't," I repeated, more quietly
but also more desperately. "I touched that."

For a moment, I thought he was going to do it anyway. He
looked furious, and though I understood his anger was *for* me and
not *at* me, it was still unnerving. Gradually, his expression gentled.
He gave me a little nod of acknowledgment—what he was
acknowledging, I wasn't quite sure—and placed the fry back on
my plate.

"Okay." His voice was full of deliberate calm. "I'm not trying
to freak you out."

"You can't sit here," I insisted. "Did you not notice that no
one else is sitting here?"

"I noticed," Nate said, righteous indignation furrowing his
brow once more.

"Why don't you go adopt a puppy or recycle your soda can or
something?" I snapped. "I don't exist just so that you can feel like
some great philanthropist for associating with me."

Nate's frown deepened; he looked like he was considering his
next words carefully. I made a show of ignoring him, picking up
a French fry and swirling it through the ketchup without any
real intention of eating it. My head was tilted down so I wouldn't

have to look at him, and my hair wanted to fall into my ketchup-smeared plate. I shoved it behind my ears. Nate sat there, presumably watching me, though I wasn't about to look up to find out.

"Why are you still here?" I finally grumbled.

"Because I don't like people who get off on tormenting other people," Nate said.

"I didn't say you had to go sit with Amber." I kept my eyes on my plate. "There's a pretty wide range of possibility between that crowd and me."

"You're the bottom rung of the social ladder." He didn't sound happy with this conclusion.

"I'm what you land in when you fall off the social ladder," I corrected.

"Some people around here should get beaten with that ladder," Nate said darkly.

"No, they shouldn't," I sighed. "At least, not on my behalf. Not that they don't suck, and if you want to get all pissed off about how your average geek or Goth kid gets treated around here, fine, whatever, be my guest, but you can't get pissed off at them for how they react to me. It's not their fault that I scare the crap out of them."

That was, perhaps, a little more magnanimous than I really felt, particularly where Amber was concerned, but I didn't want to encourage him. It was obvious Nate was well on the way to casting me in the role of poor innocent victim, and being pitied was worse than being ignored. There was some dignity in life as a loner, at least.

"You don't scare me," Nate said quietly.

I felt my entire face suffuse with heat. There was something in the way he said it—something almost tender.

"Then you're an idiot." And I got up and left.

I should have remembered that I'd have to face Nate in Western Civ. He smiled; I ignored him, taking some of the most diligent notes of my already pathetically studious life. I left as quickly as I could when the bell rang, not wanting to see if he'd follow, maybe strike up a conversation, generally make the mistake of treating me like a normal person. Because I was not normal, not in any way. Some days I wasn't even sure about the "person" part.

I had to go down a floor and into the opposite wing of the school to get to the library. I had a study hall next, instead of gym. Amber caught up to me a few feet past the stairwell, falling into step beside me as if we were friends. I didn't have to look back to know we had a small herd of her clones following us.

"What?"

"You're very rude." Amber's voice was syrupy sweet, her frown exaggerated to the point of ridiculousness.

I didn't respond.

"So I think Nate likes you," she confided in a very loud whisper.

She'd have to peel off at some point. She probably didn't care about being late to class, but eventually I'd get to the library, and they wouldn't let her in without a pass. I walked more quickly.

"Do you like him?"

"Go away."

"If you don't, you should tell him." I could have gagged on the false sweetness of her tone. "I mean, it's not very nice of you to string him along."

Two right turns and a long stretch of south wing hallway to go. She wasn't even doing anything that bad. I repeated this to myself, counting down the doorways we passed, as my fingertips started to tingle and burn.

"But you're not very nice, are you, Mary?"

Her horde snickered behind me. Oh goodie.

"I tried to tell him about you, but he didn't believe me. I had to explain your name and everything. The school he went to before never studied Typhoid Mary and all that; I think it wasn't a very good school. He's sort of underprivileged, really."

He didn't believe her? Bullshit. He'd known about me the first time he *saw* me, which meant he was lying to Amber. Which meant . . . I didn't know what, as far as he and I were concerned. The thought didn't make me calmer. We turned the first corner. She seemed to be taking my ever-increasing pace as a challenge.

"Did you think you had a chance with him, because of that? That no one else would want him because he's poor? Because you know no one would want you if—"

"Why do you think I *care*?" I snapped. One more corner to go. My hands were clenched in fists at my sides, the fabric of my gloves digging into the skin between my fingers. It hurt, and it distracted me a little from the electrified sensation in my fingertips.

"Frustrated?" Her sympathetic smile could have stripped paint. "It must *really* suck, *never* being able to have a boyfriend."

"Fuck off."

"*So* rude," she tsked. "That's why you don't have any friends, you know."

I stopped dead, and when she stopped too I stepped in front of her, right in her face. It was a bad idea. A really, really bad idea. My hands felt like I was holding live wires. "No, I have no friends because I'm a dangerous freak, remember? Typhoid Mary?"

She blinked narrowed eyes at me; her whole little clique was watching us with bated breath. Every passing body in the hallway slowed a little and stared.

There was a reason Amber was queen bee, and I wasn't—because she was good at these situations. It took her about two seconds flat to recover her composure. Then she just shrugged and smiled sweetly. "Well, you said it, not me. You really shouldn't be so down on yourself."

I blinked, and blinked again, and wished all the scathingly witty words that I knew would come to me later would come *now*. That just for *once*, I could say the perfect thing to cut her down. The way a normal person would. I didn't want her scared of me like I was some sort of boogeyman—I wanted her scared of me because I was smarter and stronger and just goddamn *better* than her.

And I stood there and gaped like a fish while she raised a brow at me, triumphant in her shiny hair and her peachy lipstick and her herd of easily impressed minions.

I all but ran the rest of the way to the library, stomping to the farthest corner I could find and flinging myself into a chair. My bag skidded off across the carpet. I breathed, my burning hands clenched on the table.

What the hell was wrong with me? I wasn't this person—this pathetic little kid who couldn't hold it together. I hadn't been this person in years; I had been doing so well.

But I wasn't doing well now. The tingling in my fingers peaked and changed, turned warm and pleasant. Satisfied. The table blackened under my hands, then grew puffs of mint green lichen. The wood cracked and curled, coming apart in a series of ever widening fissures.

It was sort of pretty, like an old log in the middle of a forest. It made me think of the *Lord of the Rings* movies. Watching those movies was about as close to real woods as I'd ever gotten. I stared at the table that was, really, the rotting corpse of a dead tree, and thought, *I want to run away. I want to hike through forests and mountains and fight orcs and sneak into Mordor, and if I died, at least it wouldn't be here.*

In five minutes there was only a thin sliver of varnished surface left at the edge of the table, beneath my elbows. In the center of the table was a hole, its edges jagged, black and green and trimmed in jutting shelves of yellow fungus.

I collected my bag and moved to the other back corner, on the other side of the library, and hoped I'd be long gone before anyone found the mess.

CHAPTER

I got called out of seventh period health class (oh, the irony) to go to the principal's office.

Principal Warrick was aging and gray with bushy eyebrows and thin lips, and though his expression was friendly enough, everything about his posture was rigid.

"Thank you for coming, Miss Miller," he said, as if I had a choice.

I gave him a noncommittal sort of smile, sat in the worn office chair across from his desk, and waited.

"So," he began, steepling his hands. He had flabby hands, with arthritic knuckles; the overall effect was trollish. "You know we take your special needs very seriously."

"Thank you," I said flatly.

"We've had a few issues with campus . . . er, cleanliness, I guess, in the last few days. Mold issues in one of the bathrooms. A table in the library that must have had wood rot issues for a while and no one noticed until today, so . . ."

He waited for me. I returned the favor, keeping my face as blank as I could. I probably looked all sullen and delinquent;

maybe I should have cared.

"I understand that sort of thing could, um . . ." He cleared his throat, gave me a pointed, questioning sort of look, and waited. Was I going to be the one to finally say it out loud?

No, no, I was not. I wondered if he was.

"Could be a problem, with, um, your immune condition," he concluded, a bit belligerently, once the silence had stretched on long enough to prove that neither of us was budging.

We were sticking to the official record. Cowards—both of us. "I'm fine."

"Yes. Well." He glowered at me from under his improbable eyebrows, and rearranged some papers on his desk. This wasn't the first such conversation we'd had over the past few years. The mental gymnastics of dealing with my "condition" while never, ever admitting the reality of it made him twitchy—but not quite uncomfortable enough to overcome the dogmatic denial. Principals of high schools in upper middle-class suburbs do not believe in girls with supernatural powers, even if one attends their school. Maybe especially if one attends their school.

"How are you liking your senior year, Miss Miller? Everything going well?"

"Can I go?" I asked.

He glared, but he said, "Yes, I suppose, if that's—"

I walked out of his office while he was still speaking—he wasn't really saying anything anyway.

There was a card waiting for me on the dining room table when I got home. It said, *"Brown—way to go, kid!"* and was signed simply, *"Dad."*

Not "Love, Dad," which was probably good, or I might have rotted the house down. At least I *had* gotten into Brown—three weeks ago. He wasn't wrong, just late. And there was a $500 Amazon gift card inside it, so that was something. Maybe in another month or two, I'd get another gift card for Penn. Maybe another month or two after that, I'd actually see him. Maybe he'd even say hi.

What do you buy for $500 off Amazon when you kinda want to burn down everything? I asked Mackenzie.

Lighter fuel, she responded. Duh.

⸙

The next day Nate sat across from me again at lunch. I moved to the farthest end of the otherwise empty table. Every kid there watched in unabashed, morbid fascination. Nate gave me a long, unreadable look, followed by a nod that was almost a bow. Then he moved to the other end, as far from me as he could get while still sitting at the same table. He sat there and ate his cheeseburger. We didn't speak at all.

He's going to drive me into complete and utter psychosis just by sitting there, I told Mackenzie. I'm going to be driven insane by the nefarious act of *sitting.* How is he driving me so nuts without even doing anything?

He's male, you're straight, said Mackenzie. Do the math, sweetie.

On Thursday he showed up with a dandelion in a Dixie cup on his lunch tray. He sat it in the middle of the table, then took his now-usual seat at the other end. I stared at it. He took an enthusiastic bite of his grilled cheese and ignored me.

"What the hell is that?" I finally asked. He looked up, chewing, his expression the picture of confounded innocence.

"It's a flower," he said, mouth full, then took a long swig of soda.

"Why is it on—" I almost said "our table." "What is it doing here?"

He shrugged.

"Hey, MacPherson!" Daniel Latham shouted from behind me. I grimaced, but refused to turn around. It made my shoulders twitch to have him at my back after the grape incident, but if he wanted to throw things at me he would do it whether I saw it coming or not. They'd just think it was funnier to hit me in the face—also getting hit in the face was more likely to hurt if he decided to throw something more substantial.

Nate kept on eating his grilled cheese, playing deaf.

"MacPherson!" Daniel called again.

The rest of the cafeteria was getting quiet.

"I just wanted to know if you and Mary here were a thing. 'Cause y'know, she's a hot property. If you're not staking a claim there, man, I might want some of that myself."

The set of Nate's shoulders went rigid. He looked over at me questioningly. I shrugged. The only thing unusual about this scenario was Nate, sitting there trying to decide if he needed to defend my honor.

"Why is he calling you Mary?" Nate asked. His tone was just a bit too casual, as if he knew he wasn't going to like the answer. "Your name's Ellie, isn't it?"

"Yes." I lifted a spoonful of my tomato soup and eyed it doubtfully, then let it drip back into the bowl.

"So why is he calling you Mary?" Nate pressed.

"Hey, MacPherson, I'm talking to you." Daniel's tone had gotten deeper, uglier.

"He's ignoring you," Amber's voice chimed in, egging him on. *Bitch*, I wanted to say, but instead just dropped my spoon into my soup and resigned myself to the fact that this was going to end badly. I ought to have known better than to get soup, and red soup at that. It was just tempting fate to get something so splatterable.

"Why are you calling her Mary?" Nate asked, directing the question over my shoulder.

Amber giggled. "Remember she's . . . ," she trailed off. I could picture her shrugging prettily. "You know? Like Typhoid Mary? I told you it means—"

"It means," Daniel interrupted, "that if you try to do her she's gonna rot your—"

"Stop it." My voice sounded raw, and louder than I'd intended.

There was a moment of utter, dead silence. Amber gave a nervous titter.

"Aw, c'mon, Mary," Daniel persisted, "I'm just trying to explain to MacPherson here why it's important to practice safe—"

Nate stood up, the motion sudden and violent, and knocked over his soda can in the process. Cola spilled out over the table, hissing and fizzing. I was still hunched in my seat, staring into my bowl of congealing tomato soup.

It felt cowardly and weak and wrong to just sit there while Nate walked around me, but it's what I did, still trying to figure out the right thing while he disappeared behind me. His footsteps went a little further and then stopped. I heard creaking benches and rustling clothing and a rising tide of whispers from all around the cafeteria, and knew I really had to turn around. I didn't want to. I did it anyway, hands balled into fists to stop them from shaking.

Nate was standing in front of Daniel, too close for it to be construed as anything but antagonistic. Amber stood to Daniel's right, their usual group gathered around them. The usual group consisted of a number of guys a lot bigger than Nate, including Daniel. They were similarly built, both lean and lanky, but Daniel was a couple inches taller and had a wrestler's spare musculature. Nate was just skinny. This wasn't going to be pretty. My eyes darted around the room hoping to see a teacher, but they must have all been on the other side of the cafeteria, out of earshot.

"Her name's Ellie," Nate said levelly.

"I'll call her whatever the fuck I want," Daniel responded.

"Hrmm," said Nate, as if this presented an interesting intellectual conundrum. Daniel looked nearly as incredulous as I felt. What was he doing? "Let's arm wrestle for it," Nate suggested.

Daniel blinked at him. Amber scoffed; several others in the group laughed outright. Nate held out a hand.

What the *hell* did he think he was doing?

Daniel stared for a long, disbelieving moment, then shrugged. There was a nasty glint to his eye as he offered up his hand. Nate took Daniel's hand, and for a moment a mean, triumphant little grin took over Daniel's face. The muscles of Daniel's arm bunched beneath his shirt and their clasped hands jerked just a fraction of an inch backward, toward Daniel's body, as if he'd meant to grab and pull, hard—maybe to throw.

Whatever Daniel intended, it didn't happen. He stumbled, just a little, caught in thwarted motion. His grin faltered, then disappeared completely.

Amber watched him. Her expression went from amused to uncertain to worried as Daniel's face drained of color.

"Hey!" That was one of Daniel's wrestling team buddies—Greg something. "Hey, man, what're you doing to him?"

Nate had shifted so that I could no longer see their hands, only his back, but I could still see Daniel's face. He was going paler and paler, his eyes widening. Whatever Nate was doing, Daniel's face said that it hurt. Nate just stood there, the line of his back and the set of his shoulders betraying nothing. If he was straining, making any effort at all, I couldn't tell.

"What the hell are you doing to him?" Greg demanded, shoving his way closer to them as if he wanted to intervene. He stopped short.

Daniel made an inarticulate, choking sort of sound, somewhere between a cough and a moan.

"Dan?" Amber asked. She moved as if she'd lay a hand on his unoccupied arm, but then stopped, fingers curling away from him. She shivered. Her eyes flashed to Nate. "Whatever you're doing, stop it!"

"Ellie could hurt you all if she wanted to, couldn't she?" Nate asked. My stomach flipped over. I was suddenly glad I hadn't touched my soup. "She's Typhoid Mary, right? She's dangerous."

"You need to back the fuck off, man," said Greg, but his voice shook. Amber looked to be on the verge of tears. Daniel said nothing; I didn't think he could speak. He was looking down to where Nate held his hand with something like terror in his face.

"She's a freak!" Amber blurted out, sudden and shrill. "You're both freaks!"

"Yes." Nate turned toward her. "But maybe you should be nicer to the freaks." He looked back at Daniel. I couldn't see his expression, only the back of his head, but the gesture itself was pointed.

No one said anything. The tension held about two heartbeats longer, then Nate let go of Daniel, putting both his hands up in the air and backing up slowly. I got my first good look at Daniel's hand as Nate backed away around the table. I didn't know what I'd expected—bruises, maybe, from an abnormally strong grip?

His hand looked even whiter than his face, the skin wrinkled and rubbery around the joints, the fingernails blue. It looked *dead*. He instantly pulled it in against his chest and then cradled it there, his whole body shaking. As I watched it flushed an angry red, as if the blood was rushing back into it. Daniel looked up, and our eyes met.

I've seen my share of scared people. Daniel was several steps past scared and well into the territory where madness and gibbering is a real possibility.

"S-sorry," he said, then swallowed. "Ellie."

"It's okay," I managed to choke out.

Daniel nodded rapidly, then stumbled off toward his usual lunch table. Most of his crowd followed him in a frightened, protective knot, but Amber hovered. Her face had gone blotchy red. Her lips quivered.

"Freak," she hissed, and then darted off after Daniel.

I turned slowly back around in my seat. Nate was mopping up his spilled soda with a napkin. The dandelion in its little paper cup was starting to droop.

"What the hell was that?" I asked. "What did you *do*?"

"I told you. I don't like people like that." He picked up the remains of his grilled cheese; it dripped cola. He grimaced and let it drop back to the plate. It landed with a sodden splat.

"I meant—" I stopped and swallowed hard. I couldn't believe

I was about to ask this of someone else. I hated, *hated* this question, but I was freaked out. Badly. "What are you?"

He gave me a long look. It started out frustrated, but slid gradually toward challenging, ending in a crooked grin. "I asked first."

Then he got up and took his soggy lunch to the trash can, dumped it, and left.

W ow, said Mackenzie. That's really. Um. Wow. Huh?

Yeah, pretty much, I typed back, cringing. I'd told her almost everything that had happened today at lunch—everything but the really important part.

He'd asked first.

I didn't know what the hell I was supposed to do about that. Mackenzie couldn't help me with that, not unless I was willing to admit my own freakishness to her, and I really, really wasn't. She had no good reason to take such a confession as anything other than evidence of a psychotic break, and I didn't think I could survive Mackenzie deciding I was crazy.

So what do you think he did? Mackenzie asked. Some sort of Vulcan death grip thing?

No clue, I responded.

Huh. Wow, Mackenzie repeated. I am so jealous. My life is so boring.

I snorted. Oh, the horror.

Oh, bite me, Mackenzie said. You have boys with super-powers defending your honor, and I'm stuck here still trying to write your fic. I giggled. Seriously, why do you get all the fun? she insisted.

The universe likes me better?

Bitch, grumbled Mackenzie. So are you gonna go out with him?

I choked on my giggles. What the hell? Go out with him? Since when did he ask me out?

Oh please, Mackenzie scoffed. He brings you weeds in a cup—and the jury is still out as to whether that's really cute or just really pathetic, incidentally. He sits with you every day. He gets defensive of you. And last but not least, he tries to impress you with his freaky action hero powers. Guy wants in your pants.

Maybe it was just some martial arts type thing, I protested. Like, some way he grabbed his hand that did some . . . nerve . . . thing?

Stop wrecking this. You are going to let me think your boyfriend has superpowers until it is conclusively proven otherwise, Mackenzie pronounced.

He's not my boyfriend! I protested. Seriously, Mack, I can't *have* a boyfriend. No touching, remember? She might not know the real reason why I couldn't touch, but she knew that much—enough to know better than to think I could ever have a relationship.

There was a long lapse after that message.

Sorry, I typed. I don't meant to be all woe-is-

That's why God invented latex, Mackenzie replied, along with

a little devil-faced smiley, before I could hit enter on my apology.

I backspaced over what I'd been saying and sent only, !!!!

What? said Mackenzie. Just saying.

I am not going to—just no! Not happening! I sent.

shrug said Mackenzie. Just a suggestion. So are you going to ask him what he did? With the weird death grip that you are not going to explain away as some sort of martial arts skill?

Dunno. I wanted really, really badly to tell her the rest of it—the "he asked first" part, and the "I have comic book villain powers" part.

The "what if I'm not the weirdest or most dangerous person I know anymore?" part.

I think you should, said Mackenzie. I mean, even if it doesn't go anywhere latex-requiring (though I still think it could if you wanted it to), this is . . . I mean, how often does something like this happen?

Never? I ventured.

Exactly. This is it. This is your official letter from Hogwarts, hun. You run with it or you end up an extra.

I grinned in amusement—of course Mackenzie would think of the situation in those terms—but I also felt increasingly unsettled. Geek-friendly analogies aside, she wasn't telling me to blow it off like I'd thought she would, and unfortunately, she had a point.

You know you're mixing your metaphors, I observed, with the "extra" thing. Am I supposed to be starring in a film about fake people with superpowers, or living in a world with real people with superpowers? Because I don't think the real world has extras.

Screw that, said Mackenzie. You know what I mean. If you keep trying to ignore him, sooner or later he's going to have to take a hint, and then he's gonna go away, and you're never going to know what was up with him or what could have been up with the two of you, and your life will just go back to normal.

I stopped smiling. My life wouldn't go back to normal—my life had never been normal. It would just go back to being . . . whatever it had been.

Also, the real world *so* has extras, Mackenzie argued. That loser I went to the fall formal with? Totally an extra. The people on those makeover shows? Extras.

I burst into snorting laughter all over again. You are such a dork.

And I need to live vicariously through your torrid love life, Mackenzie replied, which sent me into fits of indignant sputtering. Don't let me down.

"Amber was right."

I dropped my tray down onto the table directly across from Nate. He watched me over a slice of pepperoni pizza, caught in the process of taking a bite. His hair was falling into his upturned eyes; it was cute. It was infuriating.

"I'm pretty much a walking plague. I can't touch people. Ever."

He chewed and swallowed. "Okay."

I stared at him. He stared back at me. I sat, collapsing onto the little cafeteria stool in a discombobulated huff. "Okay?" I demanded.

"What?" Nate asked. I glared. He shrugged.

"Fine." I started eating my hamburger, trying to ignore the sensation of being watched. It wasn't just Nate—I was pretty sure the entire room was staring at us—but I was used to the rest of it. It was Nate that mattered, and the fact that his staring mattered pissed me off.

A drop of mustard dripped out of my burger and onto my hand. I dropped the burger onto my plate, cursing in disgust at myself. Nate leaped out of his seat. As I watched, incredulous, he sprinted to the counter, grabbed an enormous stack of paper napkins, and jogged back.

"Here." He held out the napkins. I just kept on staring. Nate's face slipped into an apologetic, lopsided grin. He shrugged again; it seemed to be his default response to everything.

I reached out very carefully and took the napkins. "I really, really don't get you." I ducked my head and began scrubbing at my glove. I paid that task so much attention you might have thought it was rocket science.

"You're welcome," said Nate, as he slid back into his seat.

"Don't be an ass; you're actually doing okay here at the moment." I hoped my scraggly hair was enough to hide my blush. I really, really hoped Mackenzie was right and he was interested, or I was going to sound seriously pitiful—a blustery, clueless, desperate sort of pitiful. I could think of few things worse.

"I am?"

I didn't answer him, and couldn't make myself look up. He *sounded* interested, but also a bit amused. I fussed obsessively with my glove until I'd turned every napkin he'd brought me into a shredded mess, the remains of them forming a small mustard-stained mountain to one side of my tray.

"Doesn't count, by the way," Nate said. I did look up then. There was a definite challenge in his voice.

"What doesn't?"

"Telling me you can't touch people. I already knew that. That's not an answer." He took another bite of pizza.

"You are such an enormous poser," I hazarded, feeling brave for a moment before I had to stare down at the disaster zone that was my lunch again. I picked my burger back up and took a huge chomp—look at me, I can be affectedly casual too.

"I'm a what?" Nate asked.

"Fake," I said, mouth full. "Being all shrugging and cool. Like you never even heard of being nervous, like you're not even trying. You're so trying."

"To act cool," Nate repeated. "Because I'm what, trying to impress you?"

"I said that I didn't get you."

"Consider it mutual." He sounded a little unsettled, maybe even annoyed. I wasn't sure how I felt about that—somewhere between triumphant and nauseous.

"Can't ever cut your hair short," Nate tossed out. "Then you might have to look at people."

"Screw you," I retorted, hair still hanging down over my face, and took another bite of burger.

He was quiet. It took me a couple seconds, but I eventually got it. Screw you—right. Can't do that. As Daniel Latham had so helpfully pointed out yesterday, there was no such thing as safe sex with me. I did look up then, pushed my hair back and everything. I have some pride.

"Go on," I dared him. "Say it."

"No," Nate said flatly.

"Whatever."

"Okay." Nate nodded agreement, as if my flustered nonresponse had been a request. "I can stop screwing around, if that's what you want."

"I don't want anything."

"Now who's full of it?" Nate pressed. I scowled at him. "If you're what I think you are," he said, "then what I am is the opposite of you."

I blinked. I considered. I finally said, "What?"

"I think what you do, the whole 'walking plague' thing?" He waved his hands around in the universal gesture for unnecessary drama. "I think you're a—" He frowned. "A person who can work with life."

"What were you really going to say?" It was easier to address the hitch in his elocution than the idea itself. Work with life? What the hell did that mean?

"A term you probably don't know. I'm not being cryptic on purpose, I swear. When I first met you I thought—well, I could tell what you were, sorta, and I thought you'd know what I was too. I didn't realize you weren't—" He stopped himself. "Whatever. Later. I'm not trying to be some know-it-all jerk."

"You just do know it all." My sarcasm sounded strained even to me.

"I know more than you, about this, for the moment," Nate said levelly. "Are we back to taking cheap shots?"

I felt about ten years old and, for a moment, I really didn't like him at all. I wanted to tell him to go to hell—except that I wouldn't mean it. Mackenzie was right. Even though he was pissing me off, I didn't really want him to go anywhere. That probably meant I had to tone down the defensiveness a little. "No." I exhaled shakily. "Sorry. It's sort of automatic."

He shrugged—awkwardly this time, as if he didn't know quite what to make of me being nice. That made two of us. "Yeah, I'd guess it would be."

"We're so not going to be speaking at all if you're going to go all pitying on me," I warned him, then stopped, paused, breathed. Not defensive—right. "You said you're the opposite of me. Explain that."

"I'm—" He stopped, pressed his lips together, and actually looked uncertain for a moment. "Can I show you instead? I think the term for me is something you're gonna know, but probably not in a good way, and it's . . . it can be cool, okay? Let me show you how it's cool, rather than just freaking you out."

"Okay," I agreed uncertainly.

"It may still freak you out," he added. "You don't seem like a screamer. You're not, are you?"

"What the hell are you gonna do that might make me scream?"

"Just let me show you." Nate stood, pushing up with both hands on the table—he had disconcertingly adult-looking hands, long fingers with lots of knuckles. Very male hands. My heart was pounding so hard it felt like I might be sick as I watched him walk over to the nearest trash can. He ducked down, looking between the can and the wall, and came up scowling. He looked frustrated. I didn't get it.

Nate crossed the room to the next trash can. He had an audience, but he didn't seem to care. He bent over and grabbed something from the floor behind the can, then made his way back to me. His hands were cupped around his mysterious find, and he looked equal parts determined and uneasy. Heads turned as he passed. I wondered just how flashy a demonstration he had in mind, hoping desperately for something low-key.

"You're not scared of spiders, are you?" Nate asked as he sat back down.

"No. Actually, I kind of like them."

"Okay. Okay, that's cool." He nodded, as if needing to affirm for himself that he should be doing this—whatever "this" was going to be. He pushed both of our trays out of the way and leaned across the table, his forearms laid flat on the surface and his hands at the center between us. Very carefully, he pulled them apart so that I could see what lay in his cupped palms. It was still hidden from the rest of the room.

It was a dusty, dead spider.

I just blinked at him, nonplussed. "Okay."

"Watch," Nate ordered softly, and his voice sounded strange—too calm and sort of hollow. He sounded just like he had when he did whatever it was he did to Daniel Latham. I watched, feeling a thread of icy uncertainty weaving its way through my gut.

For a few seconds, nothing happened.

Then the spider twitched.

I told myself that I'd been wrong, as it pushed itself up on seven unsteady, translucent legs, that it hadn't been dead. It was just sort of sick and skinny, that's all.

It flexed its legs uncertainly, stretching out each small limb as if uncertain how they worked. It was missing the last joint on two of them.

Bugs and spiders can survive freezing and starving and all sort of things, I thought, can't they? It was a little worse for wear, but not dead, I told myself. It couldn't be dead.

It stood up as fully as it could, and I realized that the entire back half of it, the bulbous bit that made the silk, was gone.

Could a spider survive without that? What was that part called, anyway? We learned that in biology class at some point, I was sure—what grade was that?

I started giggling.

"Giggling," Nate observed, as if cataloging that fact. His voice sounded a little more normal, but still oddly detached. "No screaming. That's cool."

"That's *dead*." I jerked my chin at the spider. "And it's climbing up onto your thumb."

"Yeah," Nate agreed, and gently knocked the spider back into the cup of his hands. It tipped over and landed on its back, flailing. Nate nudged it carefully back to its feet with the tip of his thumbnail. The way he handled it seemed almost affectionate, tender. The spider trembled. "Go ahead," Nate murmured to it.

It bit into his palm. I hissed and flinched. Nate didn't react at all. As I watched, the spider . . . filled out. Its missing back end and broken-off legs grew out of the remains of the rest of it. It lost some of its translucence. When it let go, leaving a tiny, bleeding pinhole in Nate's skin, it looked like what I'd initially tried to convince myself it was—a spider on the verge of starvation.

The edges of my vision were going a little hazy.

"Breathe," Nate suggested, eyes still on the spider.

I sucked in a shaky breath. The feeling like I might faint receded, but my heart galloped even faster.

"Okay," Nate said softly to the zombie spider. "That's good. You can go. Sorry." He stroked its back with the tip of his thumb as if it were a tiny little cat. It stood there and didn't seem to mind.

Then it disintegrated back to its original state, fell over, and lay still like good little dead things should.

"Okay." There was a definite edge of hysteria to my voice. I didn't normally squeak like that. It wasn't very dignified; maybe later I'd care. "Okay then. So . . . okay. Okay. What the hell?"

Nate cupped his hands back around the remains of the spider and watched me, assessing. Whatever he saw on my face made him look glum and suddenly tired. "Well, I think it's cool." He hitched one shoulder disconsolately. "Would it have been cooler if I'd found a dead mouse or something? I couldn't have done that here in the cafeteria, but maybe if it'd been something cuter. . . ." He let it trail off with another dejected shrug.

I floundered for something to say. "I don't think a dead mouse would have better," I finally managed. "I mean, I'm not scared of mice either, but . . . yeah. No."

"Butterfly?" he asked hopefully. "I could do butterflies."

"What the *hell*?" I repeated. I sounded a little more like myself, and was damned proud of that.

"I'm pretty sure you're a viviomancer," Nate said. "Somebody who can work with life—I mean, maybe I'm wrong, I've never met one who wasn't trained, but it makes sense with you making stuff—germs—go all nuts. It's a really rare ability, much less common than what I am, but it fits."

"And you're . . . the opposite of me," I repeated back his earlier words in dawning horror. And I'd thought what I had was bad.

"Don't freak at the term, okay? I'm not some batshit insane megalomaniac, which seems to be what Hollywood thinks we are."

"We?" I prompted.

"I'm a necromancer," Nate said, words spilling out in a nervous rush. "I work with death."

CHAPTER

Seven

I drifted through the rest of the day on autopilot, until I found myself standing in front of my dining room table, looking at all three of my college acceptance letters. Brown, Harvard, Penn— my mother had lined them up neatly side-by-side and left a note on a piece of cute little silver-edged stationery in the middle, below the letter from Harvard.

"Decision time is creeping up! So exciting!!!!" read the note. She'd left space at the bottom of the note, and a pen.

I started laughing more than a bit hysterically. Sooner or later I was going to have to deal with the fact that my mother really, honestly expected me to go off to one of these schools in the fall—but not now. I didn't think I could fit my thoughts on the matter on the end of a four-by-six sheet of gilded paper, anyway— I wasn't sure there was enough paper in the world to fit all the reasons why my mother was being delusional about my nonexistent bright future.

I left the whole little presentation untouched and went up to my room. I couldn't think about it now; there just wasn't room in my head.

There was a term for what I was. I had a rare ability, but not so rare that Nate hadn't met someone else like me before—someone trained. Someone who didn't go around wearing gloves, petrified of bumping into someone in the hallway and giving them some flesh-eating disease.

Oh, and also, Nate could raise the dead.

Maybe that should have disturbed me more. I was aware of being really pitifully self-centered in my reactions, but I couldn't help it. Okay, yeah, the zombie thing was freaky—but the little hints he'd dropped were freakier.

Technical terminology. Training. That oh-so-casual use of the word "we."

There wasn't just *one* more person in the universe as weird as me; he'd implied that there were *lots*. He'd made it sound like some kind of secret club. He'd expected me to know things that I didn't—had expected me to be one of them.

I'd never been one of anything in my life. Just the possibility that I could be made me feel like someone had taken the entire world and shaken it, then dropped it on its head a few times.

I sat at my desk for the better part of an hour without even touching the computer; I think that was some sort of personal record.

What the hell was I going to tell Mackenzie?

I sighed, then reached out to jiggle the mouse. The computer began whirring and beeping its way back to wakefulness. I flipped through my Chem notebook until I found the page with the night's assignment and realized that I was going to need my periodic table chart—which was downstairs, in my backpack. I went off to retrieve it, the computer still doing its thing.

When I got back upstairs, periodic table in hand, instant messenger was already running and there was a message from Mackenzie waiting for me.

You're torturing me, Mackenzie typed. It's like, four o'clock. Why do I not yet know how things went with Nate?

I frowned at the computer, setting my periodic table aside and sitting down slowly. I was pretty sure I'd shut instant messaging down before I left for school in the morning.

Elle? Mackenzie typed. Helloooo, I so know you're there! Spill already!!

Oh well, maybe I'd forgotten. It wasn't like I didn't have reasons to be forgetful of late. I typed back, What's in it for me?

You will so be the evilest person in the history of ever and be destined for the lowest, darkest ring of hell if you do not tell me what happened, right now! Mackenzie responded.

We talked, I said evasively.

AND?!? Mackenzie responded. Did he explain what he did?!?

No, I said, wincing. It wasn't a lie, not really—I still didn't know exactly what Nate had done to Daniel Latham. We talked about other stuff, I said, and then, sure this would distract her, I spilled mustard on myself and he went and got me the world's visible supply of napkins. Like, jumped up to go get them.

Awww! said Mackenzie.

Yeah, I admitted.

There was a little pause, then, Are you really not gonna tell me what you talked about?

I squirmed, fingers hovering, feeling like the biggest coward in the world.

Seriously? Mackenzie demanded when I hadn't replied in several seconds. Oh come on!

There was another long, uncomfortable pause. Is it weird that I didn't need to see or hear her to know she was hurt? The little blinking cursor in the IM box looked disappointed and accusatory.

I just—I began typing, even though I wasn't sure how the thought ended. Mackenzie cut me off before I had the chance to figure it out.

I mean, you're allowed to have couple secrets, but I can't believe you're gonna do this to me. This sucks. I'm your best friend, right? Best friend trumps all. You haven't even known him two weeks.

We're really not a couple, I typed back. I mean, there's been no official asking out.

There was a long, extremely pointed pause.

Not the point, huh?

You think? Mackenzie responded.

You're gonna think I'm crazy, I typed, sweating. It wasn't like I hadn't lied to her before, both outright and by really extensive omission. She thought I had an immune disorder, for God's sake.

If I could lie to her about the nature of my entire existence, I could lie to her about Nate.

Except that I couldn't. Those other lies were old, told before I knew her well. This would be a new lie, and a whole new level of betrayal.

Give me some credit, said Mackenzie. I cringed. Then I thought of the perfect stall tactic.

My computer's being weird, I typed back in a rush.

What? said Mackenzie. Oh come ON, if you sign off now I'm really, actually gonna be pissed at you. At least tell me you're not gonna tell me; don't give me some computer-issue crap. Your computer is fine.

No, seriously, I think I might have a virus. My fingers stumbled over themselves so that I had to go back and fix my typos before I hit SEND, holding my breath and hoping the message got to her before she had a chance to get any angrier. I couldn't deal with the idea of Mackenzie being genuinely angry at me. Messenger started itself. It was weird.

She didn't respond for an awful, queasy long time.

Oh, said Mackenzie, and nothing else.

Fine, I'm freaked out about all this with Nate and I don't really want to talk about it, I confessed. It's not you, it's just . . . lemme sign off and run a virus scan and then I'll get back on, okay? I'm just not talking about this if some hacker somewhere might be recording my every keystroke.

It's probably nothing, Mackenzie said. Your computer, I mean.

Yeah, but still. It's making me even more freaked out than I already am. I'll be back in like, two hours, okay? I held my breath. As excuses went, this one was obvious with a side of pitiful, but there was a grain of truth to it. I hoped Mackenzie would accept that smidgen of veracity.

I guess, said Mackenzie. I don't get why you're making a big deal out of something like that. Computers are just weird sometimes.

She wasn't buying it, but at least she didn't seem mad anymore.

My computer does that all the time, okay? Forget about it.

I'll be back in two hours, I persisted. I had no idea what I was going to tell her then, but at least I'd have some time to think about it. Please don't be mad?

Okay, said Mackenzie, fine, whatever, forget it. Run virus scan. I'm gonna go run to the drugstore, my hair's fading out and I'm in danger of looking like Strawberry Shortcake very shortly. What do you think of plain old black? I think I might go black for a while. Black's classic, right?

Sure, I typed, feeling off-kilter and traitorous and awful. We'll talk later?

Later, said Mackenzie, and then she was gone.

———✥———

Usually, when I hear the door open downstairs, that's my cue to pretend to be asleep, or really engrossed in homework, or anything that gives me a good excuse to avoid actually having to talk to my mother.

Not tonight. I shut my notebook and headed downstairs. I was just stupid like that sometimes.

I stopped on the last step, watching my mother shake the rain from her coat and hang it neatly on the coat tree by the door. She hadn't seen me yet, and she looked thin and tired and beautiful. I looked a bit like her, in the way a cheap knock-off looks like a designer bag. Mom had a sort of brittle grace. I was just gangly and sad, and I doubted it was a matter of growing into my features. I'd seen pictures of her back in college, before she had me. She was even prettier then.

And back before I found the Internet, she was the only living person who'd say more than three words in a row to me. We used to talk, sort of, from a distance. I couldn't remember a time before she was terrified of me, but I could remember believing she could fix almost anything—anything but me. I guess I wanted that, just for a minute or two, delusional though it might be.

Of course, I couldn't actually tell her anything about my surreal and traumatic day. I tended to hedge around the subject of Mackenzie—Mom knew I spent a lot of time online, but I think it would unnerve her to know that I thought of someone I'd met there as an actual, trustworthy friend. Mentioning Nate would be an even bigger disaster.

That didn't leave a lot that I *could* talk about, I realized. Possibly this was not my best idea ever. Probably I ought to just go back upstairs and grow up. I was too old to be wanting my mommy.

I stayed where I was a second too long. She looked up and jumped halfway out of her skin.

"Hey," I said, scuffing my toe against the slick linoleum step.

"Elizabeth," Mom exclaimed, eyes rounding. I watched her face shift from startled to afraid to concerned, and I thought nastily that maybe it was a good thing she never had the chance to work in her profession. A lawyer ought to have a poker face, and Mom's expressions were a guided tour to everything in her brain. Right now she was wondering if she was morally obligated to step closer to me, then feeling guilty for the fact that she really, really didn't want to. "Is everything okay?" she asked, still standing just inside the door, voice rising in pitch as she spoke. Her slender hands wrapped around themselves and clung until the knuckles went white. "Did your grandmother call again?"

Of course she'd go there immediately.

"No. And it wouldn't matter if she did, because I'd let the phone ring. Really, I'm not going to forget."

She smiled. "Of course you won't, sweetie, I just worry."

Understatement of the next several millennia.

"Did you see the note I left you? Have you thought about it?"

"Yes. No. I mean—where were you, soup kitchen?" I asked.

"What?" Mom asked blankly, then scrunched her eyes shut and shook her head, trying to orient herself. She opened her eyes and met my gaze with obvious determination. I looked down at my feet, dragging my toe along the floor. It left a faint smudge, but it wasn't growing anything. I didn't know why, but it's mostly my hands I had to worry about.

"No, voter registration," Mom replied belatedly. There was a heavy pause. "We'll have to get you registered pretty soon," she offered, faux cheerful and pathetically awkward.

Right. Voting. That was up there on my list of priorities, really.

Mackenzie was turning eighteen next week, I remembered. She was having a real party, just like a real person, but we'd also planned a synchronized movie marathon over the weekend.

I could not be screwing things up with Mackenzie. I just couldn't be.

"Is everything okay?" Mom asked, still from across the room. She frowned and tucked her hair behind her ears. It was a little frizzy from the rain, but not so that you'd notice if you weren't looking for something to make her human. Mostly it was long and dark and shining, and I doubted it'd dare to be out of place.

"Everything's great," I choked out, then ran back up the stairs.

Her voice followed me up the stairs. "We need to talk schools this weekend, sweetie, you need to make a decision!"

I made a mental note to have a headache all weekend. The way things were going, I might not even have to lie.

When the virus scan on my computer had finally finished—it took closer to four hours than two—Mackenzie wasn't online anymore. I'm dyeing, proclaimed her away message, with a winking little smiley.

I didn't hear from her for the rest of the weekend.

At lunch on Monday, I sat down across from Nate. I didn't fling my tray down on the table, and I didn't say anything biting and witty. I just sat. When he smiled at me around a mouthful of tuna hoagie, I smiled back.

And then we didn't talk, at all, for the longest five minutes in the history of ever.

Why had I thought things would be easy now? Somewhere in the back of my brain, behind the weirdness of keeping things from Mackenzie (or rather, Mackenzie knowing that I was keeping things from her), behind the approximately two billion questions I had about the existence of others with "abilities" like mine, I'd been counting on this, at least, to be easier. We'd had our big reveal, and if I wasn't exactly sure where we stood in romantic terms, I was pretty sure Nate liked me. Not *liked* me, maybe, but just . . . liked me. And I liked him.

I'd treasured the idea that having broken the proverbial ice, maybe I could just sit at lunch and make pointless conversation with a friend, just like everyone else in the world.

What the heck did everyone else in the world talk about, anyway?

It's a stupid expression, when you think about it, "breaking the ice"—I mean, what happens once that ice is broken? If we're talking real ice, there's generally water under it, and if it breaks, you fall in and drown.

"So I was thinking," Nate said, his eyes on the bag of potato chips he was struggling to open and not on me, "that we should do something sometime. Hang out or something."

"Hang out?" I repeated back uncertainly.

The bag of chips split all the way down both sides. Day-glo orange Ruffles went flying everywhere; Nate swore viciously. He tried to throw the bag down onto his tray, but all the indignation in the world isn't going to make an empty foil bag a very effective projectile. It sort of fluttered. He glared at it murderously.

"Yeah." He picked sour-cream-and-cheddar chips out of his bowl of chili. "Hang out. Like normal people or something." He gave up trying to salvage his lunch, shoved the tray to one side, and dropped his head so that the heels of his hands dug into his eye sockets. "Forget it. Stupid idea."

Okay then.

"Is, um," I stumbled, mentally kicking myself—I'd just been congratulating myself on having a real, live, in-person friend, hadn't I? This wouldn't be hard if it was Mackenzie. "Everything okay?"

"Oh yeah," Nate responded, forehead still cradled in his hands. "My life is just fucking awesome." He sighed, as if trying to exhale all his problems—whatever they were, not that I had any idea. Maybe I'd been a little overly optimistic in categorizing us as friends already.

"Oh." I clutched my knees beneath the table. "Wanna talk about it?" It seemed like the thing to ask, at least hypothetically, but it came out sounding awkward and forced and pathetic, not at all like I actually cared. Mackenzie and I had passed the "wanna talk about it" stage years ago—if something went wrong in her life, I knew all about it in excruciating detail before I had time to notice that she was upset.

Also Mackenzie had never looked like that, all bony shoulders and hands with too much knuckle and unwashed hair and seriously, since when was that sexy? Scruffy hair? I was falling for *scruffy hair*?

Nate lifted his head, blinking at me in bleary embarrassment. "Sorry."

"It's okay. Just . . . bad day?" I hazarded.

"Yeah. Really not your problem, just . . . family stuff. I'm probably going to have to ditch the rest of the day."

"Oh," I said blankly.

"My mom's sorta got issues. It's just me and her, so . . ." He let it trail off, shrugging again.

"Your parents are divorced?" I asked. That seemed like a reasonably neutral question—something a friend should know, at least in general terms, asked in such a way that he could answer "yes" or "no." I wasn't asking for any prurient details. I felt all proud of myself for about a second and a half.

"My dad's dead," Nate answered.

Well, crap. I tried not to cringe visibly. "I'm sorry."

"Was years ago." Nate picked up the remains of the potato chip bag and began tearing it methodically into shining strips of foil. "You know, in my head, this conversation was a lot less pathetic."

"Talking about your family?"

"Me asking you out."

"Oh." I felt a rush of heat up the back of my neck. "You know I can't really go out? I mean not . . . out. I can't do movie theaters and stuff like that."

He gave me an unimpressed look."If you don't want to go out with me, you can just say so."

"I didn't say that." My face was on fire. I felt my fingertips beginning to tingle, and pushed back on the sensation ruthlessly. It made me sick to my stomach, but I didn't care. I was not going to start rotting my lunch tray in the middle of this moment. Just was not going to happen.

"I was thinking I'd ask you over to study or something." Nate said, shredding the foil bag and not looking at me. "It wasn't really my best plan ever, because that'd involve you having to meet Mom, and that's . . . yeah. But last night just really sucked, and when things suck I get impulsive, and I've wanted to ask you out pretty much since I met you, so I thought, 'Screw it. Ask her.' Or something like that."

"You're sure you want me in your house?" I asked doubtfully. "Touching stuff?"

"Yeah, I'm pretty sure about that. I'm not sure about you sounding like that about it, though."

"Sounding like what?" I asked, faintly indignant despite the way my head was spinning.

"All *calm*, and doubtful. Like you're not sure this is a good idea but it's not like you really care." He tossed aside the shredded scraps of the chip bag and pressed his hands over his eyes again. "Fuck, forget that, I'm being an ass."

He sort of was, but what I said was, "You look really, really tired." How had I not noticed how tired he looked when I first sat down? I'd been so wrapped up in my happy little fantasy of having a fellow freak friend that I'd forgotten to pay attention to said fellow freak when he was right in front of me.

He snorted. "Yeah, I—" A cell phone began ringing under the table. Nate swore and ducked down to grab his bag.

"Hey," he answered, grimacing. I couldn't hear the other side of the conversation, but whatever was being said didn't improve his mood. "Okay, just—" he tried to say, but the person on the other end of the line cut him off.

"Okay," he repeated, voice going low and soothing. "It's okay. You just—okay, that's good. Keep doing that. I'll be there in half an hour, okay?"

Another pause.

"Because I'll have to stop at the store," he explained, in the sort of tone one uses with frightened animals. "It won't do any good for me to come straight home. I'll be quick. Very quick. I'm leaving now, okay? Right now. Bye."

Nate ended the call and looked at me, expression bleak and frustrated.

"So now you're definitely ditching the rest of the day," I guessed. I refrained, just barely, from asking the approximately eight hundred new questions I had. "Go take care of what you've gotta take care of. I'll tell Ms. Petri that you're sick or something."

"Petri's . . . Western Civ?" He sounded lost and defeated and too exhausted to exist. His tousled hair wasn't making him look sexy anymore; it was making him look about twelve years old.

"Right. Western Civ." I didn't point out that Western Civ was the only class we shared after lunch period, and I really couldn't do anything about his other classes. "Hang on a sec," I said on sudden impulse, fumbling in my bag for a pen.

"I've really gotta go," Nate objected—but he waited. I tore half a sheet of paper out of a notebook and scribbled furiously, then shoved it at him.

"Here. I've got a phone too." I winced. "I mean, duh, every-body's got a phone, or at least everybody around here, so . . . yeah. You could call me, or text me or something—actually, could you text and not call? Because if my mom hears my phone ringing she's going to get curious because my phone seriously never rings. But text me, okay? If you need anything or you need to talk or . . . anything."

Nate looked down at the scrap of paper, then up at me. "Thanks. So, um—" His phone started ringing again. He scrunched his eyes shut and didn't answer it. "I've really gotta go."

"Yes," I blurted.

He stared.

"Yes, I'll—I'll go out with you. And I can come over to study. Whenever it's good, okay? Or . . . at least better? Whenever."

He broke into a wide grin that made me feel like my guts had gone hollow and I might just float up out of my seat. "I'll let you know when it's a good day." Then he left at a jog.

Mackenzie wasn't online when I got home, a departure from my usual routine that made me feel like throwing up. I made an attempt at doing my homework, but my concentration was shot. Mackenzie was still avoiding me. A guy had asked me out—for real, not as a prank or on a dare. The guy who asked me out *could raise the dead.* I was having some difficulty processing. After an hour or so of rereading the same equations five times and stumbling over problems that I'm pretty sure I could have solved easily in the eighth grade, I gave up and went back to the computer.

I read fanfic and took the time to leave detailed and eloquent reviews. I browsed through the blogs of some of my more casual acquaintances. I offered condolences on the death of someone's cat. Mostly I tried to remind myself that Mackenzie wasn't the *only* friend I had. I could just make a post to Tumblr about the whole being-asked-out thing, and I'd have a handful of congratulatory comments within minutes.

But none of them would be people I *really* talked to, about things other than movies and books and conventions I couldn't ever attend, and besides that, it felt all kinds of wrong not to tell Mackenzie first.

I checked my phone for messages probably about eight hundred times. By five o'clock I'd settled into an obsessive rhythm of checking phone, checking email, checking buddy list to make sure Mackenzie hadn't signed on to IM—lather, rinse, repeat until disgusted with one's self. I forced myself to go downstairs and eat something.

When I came back up, there was an IM from Mackenzie waiting for me. The time stamp said it had been there about fifteen minutes.

So, I suppose there's stuff I don't tell you either, it said.

Hi! I typed in a rush. Are you still there? I was downstairs, I'm sorry.

There was a long, stomach-dropping pause. Then, Hey.

Hey, I typed back. My fingers felt clumsy and awkward on the keys. So . . .

So . . .

There was another long, uncomfortable silence.

I'm not just saying that to be a bitch 'cause you won't tell me what's up with Nate. Another pause, then, Okay, so maybe I am.

I'm sorry. I felt sick.

Still not going to tell me? she asked.

I wanted to. I really, really wanted to. But what I typed was, I just can't.

She said nothing for a full two minutes.

I don't mean can't like vow-of-secrecy can't, I clarified desperately. I mean just can't, okay?

Another three minutes went by before she said, Okay.

Okay?

This sucks. I mean really, seriously, this blows. But yeah, okay. If you can't talk about it, you can't talk about it. I actually really, really get that. Is the whole subject of Nate off-limits?

No? I was unnerved. This wasn't like her.

All right. So, talking about Nate is okay, just no talking about Nate having weird and freaky abilities, is that about it? I don't push on that subject, we're okay?

No, we were not okay—it was absolutely and utterly not okay that there were things I didn't know about her. Significant things she was keeping from me that were making her so weirdly understanding. We were supposed to tell each other everything. But saying any of that would make me the world's biggest hypocrite.

Yeah, that'd work. I paused, fingers hovering over the keys, but finally just repeated, I'm sorry, all rushed and fingers shaking.

Okay. Mackenzie didn't acknowledge my apology. Okay, good.

I know words on a screen can't really sound like much of anything, but I'd swear she sounded no happier about this arrangement than I was.

So, still friends?

Well, maybe. My stomach dropped right through the floor for half a second before she went on, I'm not sure I can forgive you for not intervening on that whole dyeing-my-hair-black deal. Seriously, Elles, it is your job to stop me when I lose it like that.

It turned out all green? I guessed.

Yes! And not a good green. Pause. You think I should do it green? I'd have to bleach it. It's all going to fall out and I'll be bald.

How 'bout streaks? I suggested, trying to ignore the uncertainty that remained in the pit of my stomach.

Green streaks? asked Mackenzie.

How 'bout . . . red streaks? I offered.

Ooooh, red and orange and pink streaks! What about that? Would that be cool, or too out there?

Go for it, I said, and let her ramble on about hair and color and the intricacies of outward representations of personal identity—things that mattered a great deal to her, and were mostly mysteries to me. I wondered if Nate would like me with purple hair. It was almost an hour before she wound down, and I got around to telling her that he'd asked me out. She squealed and congratulated and made all the appropriate lewd comments, and it was almost as if things were actually okay.

Nate wasn't in school the next day. I worried, and checked my phone a few thousand more times, and endured a predictable degree of heckling in regard to the absence of my boyfriend. Of course, they meant to be facetious and cruel—no one knew he'd asked me out. That was fine with me. My coupled state still seemed improbable and very strange, even to me. I was good with having a little time to figure out my own reaction before I had to face anyone else's.

I felt caught in an odd sort of limbo between Nate and Mackenzie. Something was finally going amazingly, incredibly right for once in my life, but at the same time, everything else was falling apart.

I made the deliberate decision to enjoy being a girl with a boy who liked her and ignore the rest, just for one day. Trying to actually have a relationship with someone I couldn't even touch was going to get complicated fast, but it wasn't yet, and it was pretty rare that I had a good reason for giddiness. I was going to be giddy, damn it.

When Amber deliberately bumped my desk on the way out of

Calculus, knocking my notebook to the floor, I smiled at her.

"Fucking freak," she snarled. I kept smiling. She scurried off. Being a little scary fit my mood just fine.

On Wednesday morning Nate was back, looking alarmingly used up and gray. He plunked down next to me in Calculus and said, "I lost your number," before I could say hi, or ask what was wrong, or give in to the foolish temptation to reach out and just brush the hair out of his eyes. Maybe I could do that with the gloves on if I was sure not to touch his skin, only his hair.

"S'okay." I shrugged, casting a nervous glance around the classroom. Mr. Wagner hadn't arrived yet. The rest of the class was still trickling in past us and, of course, staring. "You should probably go sit in your not-near-me seat, though, or Wagner's going to have a panic attack."

Nate managed to look even more exhausted. "Yeah, probably." He sighed and pushed himself back out of his chair as if he were ninety and arthritic.

"Wait." I reached for him. I caught myself in time, but not before he—and everyone else—had seen my grasping hand, my too-bony fingers in their white gloves curling in on themselves and clutching in frustration. There were gasps and whispers and nervous laughter.

I pulled my hand protectively in to my chest. Nate just hovered, watching me, one hand on the desk and shoulders hunched. He looked *so* tired. *The hell with them,* I thought, suddenly furious almost to the point of tears. *The hell with all of them.*

"Are you okay?" I asked, very determinedly ignoring the fact that everyone was listening. They were pathetic, and that was not my problem. Nate looking just about ready to keel over *was* my problem, I thought, surprised at the ferocity of feeling that accompanied that conclusion.

"Yeah." Nate shrugged and gave me a lopsided half of a smile that didn't look particularly okay to me.

Then he reached out and tucked *my* hair behind *my* ear.

I assumed the rest of the class reacted, but I didn't hear them. I didn't hear much of anything, see much of anything. For a flinching fragment of a second, the entire world narrowed down to the sensation of his fingertip just brushing the tip of my ear.

He pulled his hand back and gave it a very cursory examination. It looked okay, I thought, not daring to breathe. I didn't see anything wrong with it. It was mostly my hands I had to worry about. I didn't think I'd ever infected anything with my *ear* before.

I knew that no one besides my mother had ever intentionally touched me before. I could still feel the ghost of that faint touch, was suddenly aware of my left ear to an unprecedented and completely ridiculous degree. The back of my neck was hot. My heart was pounding so hard it almost hurt.

Nate held his hand up for me—and our horrified audience—to see. "All good," he said, and went to sit down across the room.

—❧ 3 ❧—

"You really can't do that," I told him the minute we sat down at lunch.

"Do what?" Nate asked, as if he didn't know.

I glared at him and mumbled, "Touch me," wishing it didn't sound so much more intimate than it had been—for him, anyway. It was presumably no big deal for him to touch people's ears. That it had felt one step shy of losing my virginity in the middle of math class to me was just a function of the weirdness of my existence.

"You can't do that. It's not safe," I said, though I had the feeling that I wasn't succeeding in hiding my reaction at all.

"My risk to take." Nate held my gaze. He still looked like hell, but he looked like *stubborn* hell. "Unless you don't want me touching you."

"No, I just—I—don't do that in *math class*, okay?"

He grinned a very unrepentant grin. "Got it." He gave me a little deferential nod.

"Seriously, are you okay?" I blushed at the look he gave me—okay, so it wasn't the most subtle change of subject ever. I was still genuinely concerned. "You looked like roadkill this morning."

"Thanks."

"Seriously," I repeated.

"Yeah, things are pretty much status quo." He paused and looked momentarily uncertain before continuing in far too casual a tone. "Actually, I think things are probably calm enough that you could come over this afternoon if you wanted. I talked to Mom about it. She wants to meet you."

"Oh." I had to fight the urge to blush again, and possibly giggle. My ear was tingling. "Today? That's—"

"You need to tell your parents where you'll be?"

I stopped, and for a moment had nothing to say, though I felt all my giddiness draining away as reality seeped back in. In its place came a sort of sober determination.

"No." Mackenzie might miss me, but I could just text to let her know what was going on. My parents, on the other hand? As long as I got home before eight or so, my parents would never notice I was gone. "No, I can do today. Today's good."

———❦———

Nate parked behind the church next to the school because he didn't have a parking permit. He drove a battered old sedan that still smelled like the previous owner's cigarettes. His car made me think guiltily of the Lexus that had been sitting in my own driveway for almost two years, untouched.

It took almost twenty minutes full of awkward silence to get from the high school to the neighborhood where Nate lived. The area was all older houses with faded siding, strip malls, and sad-looking diners. This was as close as we got around here to having a wrong side of town. I'd bet the median income in Nate's neighborhood was still way over the national average, but we were a long way from where I lived, and it just added to my uneasiness.

"I gave the school a fake address," Nate said, jerking my attention away from the window and the neighborhood outside.

"Couldn't afford to actually live in a good school district, and my grades suck but I still have this delusional idea that I'd like to go to college, so I figured, better school. . . ." He shrugged, eyes glued to the road.

"Oh." I winced. I hadn't meant to embarrass him. "Sure. Makes sense. Where'd you apply?"

He said nothing; I glanced sideways at him.

"I'll probably take the fall semester off and work." He didn't look at me as he spoke. "Or I'll find someplace that does last-minute admissions or something, I don't know, there just hasn't been time."

He hadn't applied anywhere.

I thought about my three acceptance letters and my mother's increasing impatience for a decision, and wished I could just give them to him.

"I hear more people are doing that," I offered, though I'd heard no such thing. "Working first, I mean. Makes sense, to save up some money."

He gave me a doubtful, sidelong look, but he smiled—a wry sort of smile, like he appreciated that I'd tried. I flushed and went back to looking out my window.

"It'll work out," Nate said, with a mutinous sort of conviction. "I'll figure something out."

"Sure." I watched the neighborhood go by, the houses getting older and less well-kept the further we got into the development.

He pulled into the driveway of a split-level with beige siding and a tiny lawn that had been trimmed so short it almost killed it, the grass coming up in little yellow-green clumps of stems. The evergreen shrubs were cut into obsessive-compulsive squares. There was a pot of wilting pansies hanging next to the door.

"Mom, we're home!" Nate shouted as we stepped inside.

It was cool in the house, not much warmer inside than it had been outside, and it echoed. The room we'd entered contained a threadbare couch, an ancient-looking television, and not much else. I could see into what I'd guess the builders had intended to be a dining room. It contained a plastic kiddie table in bright red and a kitchen-style chair with one leg held together by duct tape. Drips of something dark stained the chair and the carpet all around the odd little setup.

The air smelled just faintly of mold, which ratcheted my level of nervousness up by several points—just great.

"Mom! Company's here!" I heard someone stirring upstairs. "Here," Nate said. I turned and saw him holding out a hand for my coat. His was already hung up inside a linen closet that rattled with empty, mismatched hangers. There were spiderwebs drifting out of the upper corners, but no spiders that I could see.

I shrugged awkwardly out of my coat and handed it over. Nate looked absurdly solemn as he shook it out, searched the closet for the nicest hanger, and then carefully arranged the sleeves. He shoved the other dilapidated hangers and his battered jacket out of the way as he hung it up, so that it dangled unmolested in its own empty little space.

I considered pointing out that I usually just flung it over a chair, but didn't—it was sort of nice that he cared.

"Hello!" chirped a feminine voice behind me.

That voice was bright and chipper enough to make me wince. I didn't want to turn around—for this one second, Nate's mom sounded happy to see me, and I wanted to hold on to that for as long as possible.

Then I turned and saw Mrs. MacPherson.

I gaped. My stomach dropped so hard it felt like it hit the floor. I locked my knees against the urge to back away and ran through a laundry list of reasonable explanations for what I was seeing. Bad lighting? Weird skin condition? I'm dreaming? The closer she got the more obvious her actual condition became.

Maybe it was the shock of it, but I suddenly felt like laughing. I contained myself, but it was a close thing.

That's probably not the most normal reaction to seeing a dead person sashaying across the room toward you, but then, I've never claimed to be normal, and Mrs. MacPherson was really, obviously, definitely not amongst the living. I wasn't quite sure what to make of that, but I did know that it meant at least one thing conclusively—Mrs. MacPherson's existence was stranger than mine. She had no room at all to throw stones.

"You must be Ellie," she gushed. She held out a gray-skinned hand for me to shake, grinning like I was rock star and she was my biggest fan, and didn't flinch even a little. There were dark stains under her chipped fingernails, but only at the corners, like she'd tried to clean them up. I looked to Nate, biting my lip—I knew better than to shake hands with living people, gloves or no gloves, but this situation was a new one for me.

Nate scrunched his eyes shut and pressed the heel of his hand into his forehead as if he had a sudden headache. Mrs. MacPherson's blue-lipped smile faltered when I hesitated, cloudy eyes rounding as if she might cry. If you could get past the grayness and the pallor, she was a very pretty woman, small and blonde and oddly innocent-looking.

"You can shake her hand." Nate sounded somewhere between resigned and mortified. "You won't hurt her." So I did; her skin was cold and rubbery. She smiled brilliantly.

"Mom, I thought you were going to do your makeup," Nate said in weary admonishment.

"Oh!" Mrs. MacPherson exclaimed, jerking her hand back out of my grasp and staring at it, aghast. "Oh, I was! I forgot! Oh, Nathaniel, I'm so sorry!" She turned to me. "But—it's okay, isn't it? You're special like my Nathaniel. God gave you a gift. You're a safe person."

"Special doesn't mean safe, Mom."

"She's not safe?" Mrs. MacPherson's eyes went even rounder, filling up with tears. "I'm sorry, I didn't mean—don't hurt her, okay, Nate? Please? God doesn't want you using your gift to—"

"No, Mom, I'm not going to—Ellie's safe, okay?" Mrs. MacPherson's bloodless lips pressed together, her whole face wobbling, on the verge of a breakdown. "Sorry," Nate amended, his voice growing more gentle by deliberate increments. "I'm sorry, Mom, I'm not angry at you. You didn't do anything bad. Ellie's a safe person."

"God doesn't want you to hurt anyone," Mrs. MacPherson persisted in a tiny, choked whisper. "Jesus says to turn the other cheek, Nathaniel. Even if people want to hurt us. God didn't give you that gift so that you could—"

"Okay!" Nate interrupted sharply, then inhaled deeply. "Okay. Right. I'm not hurting anyone here, Mom, Ellie's my friend."

"But that man back in—"

"We'll talk about that *later*, okay, Mom?" Nate said. "It's okay. Everything's okay."

"Everything's okay," Mrs. MacPherson repeated back.

"Everything's okay," Nate affirmed. Mrs. MacPherson's face relaxed somewhat. She stopped wringing her hands.

"Just because I tell you someone's special or different, though, Mom, that doesn't mean they're safe."

If I were him, I think I would have left things at "everything's okay," but mostly I was busy staring in morbid fascination at Mrs. MacPherson's hands. Deep purple marks twined all around her knuckles where she'd been twisting them together, and the skin remained pulled and bunched to one side. It looked a bit like modeling clay. I wondered how long it would take to go back to whatever passed for normal.

"You can't assume stuff like that, okay?" Nate was saying. "You just can't, or I won't be able to tell you about the people I meet, and then—" He paused and swallowed hard. I wrenched my eyes away from my study of his mother's hands to look at him. Nate suddenly sounded just as potentially tearful as his mother. "I wanna be able to tell you things so you can help keep us safe, okay, Mom?"

"Of course, sweetie." Mrs. MacPherson frowned gently. She reached out one modeling-clay hand and ruffled Nate's hair. "You're such a good boy."

Nate just closed his eyes and stood there, looking acutely miserable.

"God will keep us safe," Mrs. MacPherson assured him.

Nate's mouth tightened into a grim line.

"I'll keep us safe."

"Oh, honey—" Mrs. MacPherson began.

"We've gotta go get started on our homework." Nate shook her hand off. Mrs. MacPherson turned back to me as if just remembering I was in the room. She looked confused for a moment and went back to smiling delightedly.

"Of course you do!" She clasped her hands together and beamed at me. "How about I make you some snacks? Do you like chocolate chip cookies? Fresh from the oven!"

"Sure," I agreed. "No such thing as bad chocolate."

Her grin quirked up at one side, suddenly wistful. "Oh, I miss chocolate."

"Did you eat today, Mom?" Nate asked sharply.

"Mmhmmm," Mrs. MacPherson agreed absentmindedly, still watching me. "Everything you left in the fridge. You're such a good boy, providing for me—and you're such a pretty girl, aren't you?"

"Thank you," I said awkwardly. I'm not pretty. Maybe something like "striking" or "memorable," but not pretty.

"Everything?" Nate demanded. "You mean—*everything*? Seriously?"

"I get so hungry," Mrs. MacPherson said to me, shrugging apologetically. "You must be hungry so much too, growing girl—look how thin you are. But so pretty, with all that hair—oh, Nathaniel, she's such a—" She turned toward Nathaniel, but he was stomping past her, deeper into the house. He disappeared around a corner, and a moment later I heard the distinctive sound of a refrigerator door being opened, then things rattling and clinking into each other, then swearing.

"Nathaniel Patrick MacPherson, you will not use that language in my house!" Mrs. MacPherson called after him.

"You ate everything." Nate came back around the corner looking flabbergasted and grim.

"God hears you using those words, Nathaniel," Mrs. MacPherson admonished. "And a gentleman doesn't speak that way in front of a lady."

"Right," Nate agreed distractedly, looking at me. "Listen, I'm really sorry—um, about everything—but I've gotta go out to the store, and it's better if I go earlier, so I'll drive you home, okay? I can call you later or something."

"Oh, don't be silly," Mrs. MacPherson argued. "I'm fine. You go to the store tomorrow."

"We've got nothing at all in the house, Mom," Nate countered.

"I'm fine!" Mrs. MacPherson insisted. "I'm going to bake you cookies."

Nate grimaced and rubbed at his forehead again.

"I could come with you to the store," I suggested. "We'll just run out quick and then we'll come back and work on Western Civ. I can do the Calculus myself after I go home."

"Pretty *and* practical," Mrs. MacPherson said approvingly. "You be real charming to this one, Nathaniel. You are a Christian, aren't you, dear?" she asked me.

"Uh—" I stammered.

"Right. We should go." Nate stormed past his mother. "Now." He grabbed his coat with one hand, making all the empty hangers rattle, and my hand with the other. I didn't even have time to flinch at the shock of contact before I was being dragged out the door. My coat was left behind.

"Drive carefully!" Mrs. MacPherson called after us, leaning out the door to wave.

"Get back in the house, Mom!" Nate shouted back, wrenching open the passenger side door of the car for me and storming around to the other side. Nate got into the driver's seat and slammed the door as I scanned the street nervously. There was an elderly man out raking his lawn three doors down, but he didn't seem to be paying us any attention. When I looked back up at the MacPherson home the front door was closed, and it was just another tired-looking house on a run-down block.

CHAPTER

Nine

"So." I was still fastening my seat belt as we peeled out of the neighborhood at speeds that threatened to break the sound barrier. "Mom's a zombie."

Nate shrugged.

"You weren't going to tell me?"

"Not yet," he said.

"Why?"

"It's sort of embarrassing?" Nate growled.

I had nothing to say to that. We skidded out onto the main road through town.

"Wanna tell me what happened?" I asked, as we flew around another corner. That was nice and open-ended, and even sounded sort of considerate.

"No," Nate snapped. "She was drunk when she died," he went on anyway, glaring at the meager afternoon traffic as if it had personally offended him. "Oh, come on, asshole," he barked at the car in front of him. "Move!" When it failed to respond immediately, Nate whipped around it, tires squealing. "Like, absolutely shit-faced. That's why she's like that—she's stuck exactly how she was when she died. I can keep her that way, no rotting or losing limbs or any of that Hollywood shit, but I can't make her better than she was."

"Ah." I'd asked, but I had no idea what to do with the information.

"The religious crap came after. She's bored, she's stuck at home watching TV all day, starts paying attention to the whack-job televangelists and decides I'm some sort of fucking—oh, come *on*!" he shouted at another car, pounding a fist against the steering wheel.

I thought of something useful I could do; I could offer to drive. If I had a license, that is. It crossed my mind that we might be safer with me driving regardless. We came to a screeching halt a few inches from the bumper of the car in front of us. It had dared to stop at a red light.

"Fucking asshole," Nate growled, fuming for a long moment before looking sideways at me. He winced at my expression. "Ah, sorry. I should possibly calm down."

"Green light," I pointed out. He turned back to the road and revved the engine, but with less manic enthusiasm.

"It's okay," I said as we turned into the grocery store parking lot. "You got blindsided—weren't planning on having this conversation with me today. I get that."

"You're okay with that?" he asked, searching for a parking space. "I mean, I was going to let you think she was alive. Possibly for months, if not indefinitely." He found a spot and pulled in neatly.

"I lie to everybody every day." That wasn't exactly an answer, and the look Nate gave me said he knew it. He shifted the car into park and just kept on giving me that look.

"Okay, so it's different," I admitted. "Not in that . . . not as different as your mom's thinking, okay? I think possibly we should hang out a bit more before we start picking out the white picket fence and all, but . . ." I shrugged. "It could be different."

"I'd like us to be different," Nate offered cautiously. "I mean, hell, if you can react like that to my mom? I mean, *not react* like that, to my mom? That makes you officially the coolest person in the entire world."

"Can I ask one more thing?" I hedged, resisting the urge to duck my head. No guy had ever called me cool before, let alone the coolest person in the world.

"Sure," Nate agreed.

I hesitated. Part of me wanted to let it go and not wreck the moment, just enjoy the fact that I'd found someone who liked me and whose life was weird enough to make mine look normal. I couldn't quite make myself do it. "What was your mom talking about, with you hurting someone?"

Nate's face twisted like I'd punched him in the stomach, then went hard and angry. "You can't ask *that.*"

"Okay," I blurted. "Okay. That's fine."

"No, it's not," Nate said. "Look, are you sure you don't want me to drive you home now?"

I thought about it pretty seriously for a second; this was not a good situation. This was scary, and I didn't need him. I was fine before.

I *wasn't* fine before. I was lonely and miserable before.

"You wouldn't hurt somebody unless they were trying to hurt you," I ventured. "You or somebody you cared about." Nate glared at me, but there was no way I could just let this go, and apparently I wasn't willing to just let *him* go, either. "Right?"

"What if I said wrong?" Nate asked. "What if I said I'd hurt someone if I had to, to get something I needed? Something I wanted?"

"Then I'd say you should drive me home," I answered, proud of how unequivocal I sounded despite the shaking of my voice, "and then stay away from me."

"I'm not giving you the third degree. You're just as scary as I am, and I'm not making you give me a rundown of your working moral code."

"You can if you want," I offered. "Throw me some hypothetical situations."

"Suppose someone didn't want to hurt *you*," he said, "but they wanted you to hurt other people. They wanted you to do . . . really bad stuff. And they weren't leaving you alone."

"I'd . . . ," I faltered. "I'm sorry, but can you make that a little less hypothetical? I know it's probably not my business, but if I'm going to be okay with all of this, I need to know what's going on."

He sighed. "Yeah, okay, I guess that's fair. My dad was like me—could raise the dead. The people he worked for want me to do the same sort of work he did, and it's—he wasn't a bad guy. My dad. It was one of those things where it was what his dad did, and his dad's dad, and he started when he was younger than I am now and it was really good money and he just sorta never thought about it, I guess. Anyway, it's not the sort of thing you get to just walk away from, so if they can't get him back, his son will have to do, y'know?"

I didn't know. I didn't know at all.

"Basically they're a bunch of total bastards who don't compre-hend the word no, and they won't leave us alone. So we move around a lot—which is the other reason the school doesn't have my real address. They wouldn't want to grab me at school, in public with all kinds of witnesses. If they track me that far, they'll go to the fake address—and hey, normal people will live there, and hopefully they'll just think they got the wrong MacPhersons, for a while, any-way. It's not like it's that unique a name. So yeah, we hide, they catch up, I do what I have to—which sometimes means hurting people. If you can't deal with that, I'll really, really get it. Just tell me now."

"What did your dad do for them?" I asked, having visions of terrorists with zombie armies. If there were people out there doing things like that, I'd know about it, right? Everybody would know. Zombie armies are a little hard to miss. "I mean, what do they want you to do?"

"You don't want to know. Seriously, just—bad stuff. Leave it there."

"Okay."

Nate sighed. "Could you not do that?"

"Not do what?"

"Be okay with things that aren't okay, just because I'm being a cryptic douchebag about them." He scrubbed at his eyes with the heels of his hands and stared hard at the steering wheel. "I'm sorry, it's just—I don't like talking about it. I don't like thinking about my dad like that."

"Can you just tell me that you wouldn't hurt someone unless you had to?" I asked quietly. "That it's a last resort, whatever, you know what I mean."

"Yeah." He stared hard at the steering wheel. "Seriously, I'm not some psycho. Just . . . these aren't people who are going to respect me using my words. And Mom's . . . the way she is, screwing with her, that's like picking on the retarded kid, y'know? You just don't do that." Then he looked over at me and slipped into a grin. "I can also get kinda protective of my friends. Especially my girlfriend."

He looked pleading and desperate and like he was trying very, very hard not to let me see it. Something in my stomach wobbled and clenched. The back of my neck felt warm. "Okay. That's . . . that's okay, I guess. Can I ask something else?" I sounded a bit squeakier than I'd really intended.

"I guess," Nate answered, grin slipping.

"What are we buying for your mom to eat?"

He relaxed visibly. "That's an easy one. Meat. Lots and lots of raw, bloody meat."

"These cookies are awesome." I tried to scoot a piece of torn note-book paper under one so that I could pick it up without touching the plate.

"You don't have to do that," Nate commented.

"Yes, I do." I had the paper mostly under a single cookie.

"Seriously, I don't care," Nate insisted. "You've got gloves on already, and I'm really not that worried about it."

"That's because you've never had an antibiotic-resistant infec-tion." I bit my lip as I creased the paper down the middle with my thumb and first two fingers and snapped my wrist back, all in one quick motion. The cookie jumped and rolled obligingly down my impromptu paper chute into my hand. I grinned in triumph, holding my prize aloft for him to see. "Also I'm getting good at this." I took a bite.

"Hey, whatever makes you happy." Nate smiled and shrugged. "Just saying, you don't have to—necromancers don't get infec-tions."

I blinked at him. "Seriously?" I said around my mouthful of cookie.

"Seriously," he agreed. "I've never even had a cold."

I chewed and swallowed, because it gave me time to think. "Me either." I tried very hard not to wonder if that meant I could touch him.

"Animals don't like me either. Except scavengers. I had a pair of pet rats once." He sounded wistful. "Rats are cool."

"I've never had a pet. . . .You think that—the not getting infections—that applies to stuff like what I can do? I mean, you said you'd met another viviomancer."

"Yeah," Nate said, but he looked uncertain.

"So, could they . . . ?" I couldn't think of a way to finish the sentence that wouldn't sound just wrong.

"She. My dad's . . . coworker, I guess, Audra. She was around so much I started calling her Aunt Audra. She'd pick me up and spin me around the room sometimes. I was little. But she didn't have any problem touching whoever or whatever, so I dunno. She'd . . . been around a while. I honestly don't know how that'd go, with you. I'd guess it'd depend on who's stronger, whether my immunity would cancel out your ability. I'm willing to test it."

My heart was suddenly pounding so hard I could hardly hear over the rushing of blood in my ears. "That's—I'm—"

"—not," Nate finished for me, with a smile and a shrug that said that was okay. "That's cool. Whenever."

My face felt like it might burst into flames, and I couldn't have managed a coherent reply if my life depended on it.

"Really, it's fine. Just wanted you to know the offer's open, whenever you're ready." And he shrugged again.

I stared, and struggled to get my brain to reconnect to my vocal chords, and finally managed to get out, "You really need a couple more mannerisms." It wasn't the sophisticated reply I would have liked, but at least it was sort of witty.

"Why?" Nate asked. "Shrugging's good. It's all-purpose."

"I'm going to start keeping count of how many times you do it in an hour," I threatened, regaining my composure by inches.

He shrugged at me, and I snorted, and suddenly found that I couldn't stay unnerved around him if I tried.

We were sitting on the floor with our backs propped up against the side of his bed, Western Civilization textbook open between us, next to the plate of cookies. Nate's room looked like he'd attempted to clean up for the occasion, maybe, sort of, but that only meant that the clean and dirty clothes had been separated into different piles, one on the floor, one on the haphazardly made bed. A clunky, ancient-looking laptop sat up by the pillow, the power cord dangling off over the side.

Stacks of boxes and heavy black plastic trash bags spilled out of the closet. One of the bags had been ripped open, and I could see that it was filled with odds-and-ends sort of clothing—snow boots, rollerblades, a ski jacket. Most of the boxes seemed to contain books—I even spied a dog-eared copy of *Harry Potter and the Prisoner of Azkaban* peeking out from under a pile of comics. It was a long way from the sterility I was used to at home, but I hadn't accidentally rotted anything yet.

"You know, in theory, I already studied this stuff." Nate nodded down at the textbook. It was open to a page full of essay questions. We'd split them in half. Change up a few words, and Ms. Petri wasn't likely to notice the similarity in our answers. Technically it was cheating. I'd never had someone to cheat with before.

"We did Mesopotamia to Rome in ninth grade, back where I went to school before," Nate was saying. "Which makes it sort of messed up that I don't know half of this stuff. Mind if I flip back a couple pages?"

"Sure." I popped the last of the cookie into my mouth and picked up my notebook. "Well, it was ninth grade, right?" I offered. "Probably wasn't as in-depth."

"Well yeah." Nate thumbed back through the chapter, "but that's not what I mean. Some of this stuff's just totally different."

"It's subjective?"

"It's made up," Nate countered. "Totally twisted to the author's perspective, and just about everybody who was actually there is dead now, so who knows which author got it right? If any of them did. It's all a lot of bullshit."

I opened my mouth to reply to that but then stopped short, thought a moment, and finally said, "Just about everybody?"

"I keep forgetting how much you don't know." He winced almost instantly. "And hopefully you'll keep forgetting that I keep saying asshole-ish stuff like that."

"So there are people still alive from when there was a Roman Empire?" I pushed. "Seriously? How? I mean, are we talking vampires or something?"

He just gave me an abashed sort of look.

"Vampires? Seriously?"

"I was actually thinking wraith," Nate said, ducking his head and acting really, really focused on the textbook. "But yeah, vampires would fit the bill."

I just blinked at the side of his head, once again completely at a loss as to what to say, if for very different reasons. Nate just kept on flipping textbook pages, ignoring me.

After a long, awkwardly silent moment, he sighed loudly and said, "Okay, so, fair warning, I suck at explaining this stuff. Necromancy 101." He sounded frustrated, almost angry, but he was glaring at the door, not at me. "There's a couple different ways to make a lich—L-I-C-H," he spelled out. It sounded like he was saying "lick," and my eyebrows were somewhere near my hairline. "Undead. Walking corpse. Whatever. First, easiest thing—you just use your own power to keep it up and shuffling—and it's nobody, it's a machine. Totally obedient. Whoever it was, their soul stays wherever it went—and no, I don't know that one. They can't remember. Anyway, you can do that with pretty much any dead body coherent enough to function—head has to be mostly intact, though. The zombie movies get that part right."

"Oh," I said. Well then. That was . . . well then.

"I was accidentally raising dead birds and bugs and stuff by the time I was ten. You kinda can't help it if you've got the ability, but they tend to go back to being dead pretty quick. And they crave blood," Nate said. "It's a hell of a lot of work to keep them going without it. If you feed them, though—living blood especially, though the dead stuff still works, sorta—it pulls the spirit back to the body. A lich that's been fed living blood is pretty much who they were before they died."

"So . . . your mom?" I prompted uneasily.

"Had living blood, yeah." I felt a rush of adrenaline start its way up the back of my neck before he added, "Mine."

"Oh." The adrenaline retreated a little, settling at a level that just left me queasy.

"You don't give a lich only dead blood," Nate said. "Not unless you're one shitty excuse for a necromancer. For a human being. Any kind of blood makes it easier on the necromancer, lets you keep them around longer with a hell of a lot less effort, but you need living stuff at least once to really bring them back. If all they ever get is dead, they're like . . . I don't even know. They're there, totally aware, but they're trapped in their heads. Can't disobey, can't even really act on their own. It's a fucking cruel thing to do."

I didn't say anything. Apparently the nothing I said was pretty loud because Nate added, "They only really need living blood once, though. After that, the dead stuff . . . it's not really what they want, but it takes the edge off. It's better than the alternative, right?" He tried to make it sound light, half-joking. His voice cracked. I stared, leagues away from coherent speech, let alone being able to feign nonchalance.

"I found her at the bottom of the stairs." The defensiveness in his voice took on an angry edge. "You know, you see somebody lying there on the floor not moving, you run up and you grab them."

"Sure, anybody would—"

"You try to pick them up, shake them, get them to wake up. It's not really a voluntary thing, you just do it, and . . . I guess she had a glass in her hand when she fell." He gave a bitter, snorting laugh, and shook his head. "Of course she did, right? So there's all this broken glass and I'm not paying attention to it and I cut my hands all up and she wakes up and there's all this blood around and I'm a fucking moron, because when she starts moving I'm not thinking, 'Oh, hey, I just raised my mother's body,' I'm thinking, 'Oh thank God, she's okay. She wasn't really dead.'"

I felt like I might throw up.

"If she hadn't done that—" Nate stopped, licked his lips, pushed his hair out of his eyes. He was looking everywhere but at me, and I couldn't seem to stop staring at the side of his face. The dark circles under his eyes. The way his Adam's apple bobbed in his throat as he swallowed three times before he could talk again. "That's how we got on this topic, right? Permanent forms of undeadness. Forget vampires, we don't have anything to do with them, that's like . . . I dunno, a virus or something, there's all these theories, we don't actually know how they work. But we can make wraith."

"Like . . . ghosts?" I asked, focusing hard on the technical and not the slight rasp Nate's voice had developed.

"Those exist too," Nate said and sighed, sounding about a thousand years old himself. "And are fucking obvious about it, generally, so the fact that most people think they don't is just further evidence that it's really time for something new to evolve and replace us, because humans suck. Anyway, with a wraith—you pull the spirit back at the same time you're raising the body. No blood involved, just a bunch of power and terrifying levels of skill, 'cause like I said, we don't really know what happens to dead souls that don't stick around. We can't just reach through the ether and grab one."

"But the body, once you start to raise it, it kinda . . . wants its spirit back, creates a pull, and if you know what you're doing you can sorta follow that pull and . . . pull more, I guess. Direct it. Or something. I've never done it." His shoulders hunched inward. It wasn't really a shrug; it was more like he was bracing himself against a blow. "My dad didn't get around to teaching me that. He called it an art, though, making wraith. If you do it right, the soul settles back into the body and the body adapts and you've got something like a person, but a lot more permanent. They look a little freaky, but they don't crave blood and they don't need the guy who raised them to keep them going—you can still control one if you've got the strength, they're still dead, but you don't have to in order to keep them unliving. If you're trying to keep somebody around for any length of time, postdemise, that's the way to do it. Trying to keep a regular lich around without turning them into a wraith, it . . . it doesn't work that well."

"What happens, with a regular lich?" I knew I shouldn't ask— knew it was a terrible, awful, cruel thing to ask—but I couldn't not. "Why can't you keep them around?"

"They get needier," Nate answered. "And needier, and needier.

Like a fucking black hole, sucking everything in until it doesn't matter what you throw at them, blood or power or whatever. They're still a dead body walking around, and eventually, they stop walking around. They go back to being just dead."

I couldn't begin to think of what to say to that. If it had all been abstract theory, it might have just been really nifty, but the problem was that it wasn't abstract at all—and in context, it was too awful for words.

"That's all so oversimplified it's ridiculous," Nate added, his voice sounding even more hoarse and strained, "but that's the general idea."

He paused again. I could feel the tension in him, and wished I could think of something, anything to say.

"I would have tried," he finally said. "I don't really know why the hell I'm telling you all this, but since I seem to have lost the ability to shut up, you should know that—that I would have tried, or I would have let her go. If I couldn't, I didn't mean to make her—I didn't mean to leave her like this. But once it was her? I couldn't—I just couldn't. And once they've tasted blood, it doesn't work anymore. Making a wraith, I mean. It won't work. If there's some way to make her a wraith now, I don't know it."

He stopped, and the room went very, very quiet.

"So yeah, vampires and wraiths and shit." Nate slammed the textbook shut and surged to his feet. "More things in fucking heaven and earth, right?" He stalked around me, stepped over the textbook and plate with its one remaining cookie, just a pair of legs going by. I stayed huddled where I was, my back pressed into the side of the bed. The bed creaked as he sat down on the other side.

"I'm sorry." It was trite and pathetic, but all I could come up with.

"Not your fault." He would have been a disembodied voice, but the bed behind me moved when he moved.

"I didn't mean that kind of sorry," I said. "Just . . . sorry." The bed shifted and creaked, just a little, only an echo of him. It was almost as if we sat back to back, and it was strange and stomach-churning and intimate.

"I know. It's not your problem. I mean, you've known me what, three weeks? I didn't mean to dump all this shit on you."

"What did you mean to do with me?" I asked, made brave by the fact that I couldn't actually see him. It was almost, almost like talking online to Mackenzie, except for that subtle movement against my spine. "Why'd you tell me that first day that you knew what I was? That doesn't make any sense, if you were running away from something. Shouldn't you have been keeping a low profile?"

"I thought you'd know," Nate said. "I could tell what you were, sort of—I mean, not that you were a viviomancer, but just that you had some kind of ability. If you'd been brought up with it, you'd be able to tell that about me, too. And if I couldn't hide, then I figured it'd be better to know where you stood, just have it all out in the open. If you were gonna be a problem, I wanted to know that right then and there, so we could take off again."

"Oh," I said, trying for cool disinterest but unable to keep from sounding disappointed. That was really not the answer I'd been hoping for, and I wanted to kick myself for the hoping.

"But then you didn't know anything. You didn't even know what *you* were, let alone me. You wore freakin' gloves all the time, and everybody treated you like shit."

"You felt bad for me." My voice cracked. I wrapped my gloved hands around my knees. The bed shifted. I imagined he might be turning, leaning back, staring down at the top of my head, but I didn't twist around to see.

"Yeah, a little," Nate admitted. "But mostly I felt impressed as all hell with you."

"Why?"

"Because your life just fucking sucked." The bed bounced like he had flopped down on it. When he spoke again his voice was right behind me, right over my head. "And you didn't feel sorry for you."

"Oh." I didn't think that was all that accurate. I felt sorry for me all the time. I just didn't go around being all emo about it. I'd never thought of that as in any way impressive.

"Are you pissed at me?" Nate asked.

"Why would I be?"

"Because I was going to lie to you and not tell you stuff I probably should have told you." I could feel his shrug in how the bed shifted against my own shoulders. "And now I can't seem to stop telling you shit you probably don't even want to know."

"I want to know," I insisted.

Something crashed downstairs. The bed jumped as Nate sat up.

"Mom?" he called out. I twisted around to look up at him. He was frowning worriedly. There was no response from downstairs, just another crash, then a tearing sound. A wild, keening wail followed, building in volume and intensity as it went on.

Nate swore, then jumped down off the bed, right over me. "Stay here," he ordered. I stayed, staring, as the door closed behind him and his footsteps pounded down the stairs. That one long shriek grew louder, more despairing.

"Mom!" Nate's voice came muffled up through the floor, somewhere below me and to the left—the kitchen?

He had an *Avengers* poster on the back of his door, torn in multiple places and patched together with Scotch tape. The screaming hadn't stopped.

"Mom!" I heard shuffling, a bang like someone had run into a wall. *"Mom!"*

The scream stopped. I stared at the metallic lettering of the poster and clutched my knees until my gloves pulled taut between my fingers, digging into my skin.

"It's okay, I've got it," Nate was saying, his voice low and soothing. "Look, I'm getting it right—"

He was cut off by a furious shriek. It sounded more like a sound a big cat might make than anything human. I heard him swear, and then there was more shuffling and the thump of unbalanced footsteps, like struggling. Something tearing, then hitting a wall.

"Jesus, Mom, give it back!" I couldn't tell if he sounded more angry or more frightened. I pressed more tightly back against the bed until the bed frame dug into my spine. Nate's plain blue bedspread draped down around my shoulders. It still smelled new, like plastic packaging.

More sounds of struggle, then running footsteps, off to the right, toward the living room. "Just gimme a fucking second!" Nate shouted, definitely more scared now. Another indignant scream, and a wooden-sounding crash. My mind's eye dredged up the image of the already once-repaired kitchen chair in what should have been the dining room. Then the sound of Styrofoam ripping again.

"Here!" Nate shouted. Shuffling steps, moving toward his voice. "Here's—that's right—there you go."

The screaming tapered off into a muffled, garbled sound that was almost words, then quiet.

The bed frame creaked with my shaking. I was going to have a bruise across my back where I'd pressed against it. I noticed that one corner of the torn poster was signed in heavy black Sharpie. I couldn't make out the name.

Downstairs there was shuffling again, then normal footsteps, then calmer sounds. Plastic on plastic, maybe a drawer sliding. More sounds of ripped packaging. The refrigerator door opening and closing. Water running. Footsteps coming back up the stairs. The door opening.

I was still staring, bug-eyed and heart pounding, when Nate

came back in. There were bloody handprints on his shirt—two on his chest, like a shove. One handprint twisted around his arm. Little splatters of blood down his jeans. His hands were mostly clean—he'd obviously washed them, but he'd missed a watery trace of red under one thumb.

"She gets shaky," Nate said, standing in the doorway, two spots of color high on his cheeks and the rest of him deathly pale. "Has trouble opening doors and drawers and packages and stuff if she lets it go too long, which she always does, and then she can't get at something to eat right away and she gets . . ." He trailed off, then shrugged. His shoulders shook. I swallowed and tried, tried *so hard*, to think of something to say.

Nate just watched me, color receding from his cheekbones until he was just ashen and frail, too thin for his bones. "I should take you home," he said, voice devoid of all inflection.

And because I'm a coward, I answered, "Okay."

"You mind if I change my clothes?"

I shook my head rapidly. Nate walked around me to the other side of the bed, smelling like raw meat as he passed. I stayed where I was so I only heard him as he pulled his shirt off over his head, unzipped his jeans and kicked them away, rummaged in the pile of clean clothes on the bed. My heart hammered at the thought of him just on the other side of the mattress with no clothes on. Downstairs it was still unnervingly quiet.

I heard Nate pull on a new pair of pants and do up the zipper. Down in the dining room, Mrs. MacPherson began to sob. Nate sighed, then walked back into my field of vision.

"Stay behind me, okay?" He opened the door and waited with his back to me. I looked down at the one remaining chocolate chip cookie, sitting there on its pretty white plate, and pushed myself shakily to my feet. I followed him down the stairs. He didn't turn around, hadn't looked at me since changing his clothes. He was wearing an oversized green T-shirt. It had stains too, faded splatters that looked many times washed.

Mrs. MacPherson sat wedged into a corner in the dining room, the pale, exsanguinated remains of what had been a T-bone steak discarded on the floor beside her. Her lips were bright red; her chin was smeared with blood. Her bloody hands were clutched together, trembling on her knees, as she chanted, "Jesus help me, Jesus help me, Jesus help me," over and over again between hiccuping sobs. A pile of meat on Styrofoam packing trays sat next to her, right on the already splattered carpet, the plastic shrink-wrap torn away. It was half of what Nate and I had just bought that afternoon.

The last step creaked as I stepped off it into the room, and Mrs. MacPherson stopped praying. She looked up, and her eyes met mine. They were still milky pale, but clear and intelligent, and I froze.

"I'm taking Ellie home, Mom," Nate said, slow and soothing. "You've got more food right there next to you. I'll be back in—" He paused, then turned around to look at me. I dragged my eyes away from his mother. Nate gave a half-hysterical, self-deprecating little laugh. "I have no idea where you live."

I had to swallow twice before I could say, "Wrightstown. Over by the quarry."

"Okay." Nate turned back to his mother. She was still watching me. "I'll be back in about twenty minutes, okay? I'm going to lock the doors. You're okay, you've got plenty to eat right there."

"Jesus will protect me," Mrs. MacPherson said in a broken child's voice, her eyes never leaving mine. "God provides. God takes care of us." I could feel the demand in her gaze.

God didn't provide *me*, I wanted to tell her. I couldn't argue that Nate needed someone other than her to take care of him, and I cared about him, yeah, but this? I was still shaking, clutching my elbows and wanting to be absolutely anywhere but there.

"Right." Nate was clearly trying to stay calm, but an edge of anger had crept back into his voice. "That's fine. Just . . . keep praying or something."

"God provides, Nathaniel," Mrs. MacPherson insisted, her eyes boring into my skull, begging.

"I'll be right back," Nate repeated, then went to get my coat from the closet by the door. I tripped along after him, feeling Mrs. MacPherson's eyes on the back of my head all the way out to the car.

We were in my driveway by the time I gathered the nerve to say, "I thought you said they just went back to being dead if they didn't feed."

"They do." Nate stared hard at the steering wheel. He still

hadn't looked at me, not once in the entire ten-minute ride. "Just . . ." His voice caught, and there were too many emotions there for me to begin to sort out—fear and guilt and rage and grief. I think mostly grief. "Just not right away."

CHAPTER

Ten

So, Mackenzie asked the minute I signed on that night. Tell! Tell, tell, tell! What's his house like? And his Mom? And did anything that required latex happen? I'd emailed her from my phone right after lunch, so she knew where I'd been.

My fingers shook so badly I could barely hit the keys. I'd thrown up twice, and my stomach still felt uncertain. Tell me about the fic you're working on? I begged.

There was a silence. Then, What?

Please? I typed back.

That bad, huh? Do I need to kick his ass?

No. I shivered hard. Wasn't like that. It was just . . . bad, okay? His family situation is bad.

Oh, said Mackenzie. I'm sorry. You're still together, though? Or not so much?

I thought about how he wouldn't look at me for the entire ride home, and about how his mother had stared at me. How his mother, blood smeared down her chin, had decided God had provided me to take care of her son. I think so, I said. Then, stomach clenching painfully, I really like him, Mack. He's a fanboy and he's

geeky and he's deep and he cares about stuff and he's just . . .
I didn't know how to finish.

And his life is seriously fucked up, Mackenzie supplied for
me. I'm sorry, hun. *big hugs*

Yeah. I tried not to start crying.

So fic. Your fic, or the other thing I'm writing?

I started to type, whatever, but she replied before I could hit
SEND.

Stupid question. Your fic. So—how about I send you what
I've got so far? I think it's pretty hot, but we know that what I think
is hot and what you think is hot really don't so much exist in the
same universe, so tell me if I'm getting it right, okay?

Right then I wouldn't have cared if she sent me a story about
a hamster orgy, I just wanted a distraction, but I typed back, Sure.

You know I love you and I will seriously kick the ass of anyone
who screws with you, right? Mackenzie said. And if you love this
boy, well, we'll figure it out.

If I loved this boy.

It was too soon for that word, wasn't it? Surely any relationship that had yet to hit the one-month mark had to be casual,
right?

The horrible, drowning feeling in my stomach when I
thought about how he had refused to look at me didn't feel casual
at all. Nor did the urge to pull the keys to my pristine car out of
my jewelry box and drive back over there and . . . what? Kidnap
him, run away together, drive off into the sunset to somewhere

that we could both be normal and life wouldn't suck so fucking much? We'd be more likely to end up like Thelma and Louise going off the cliff. Also he'd never agree to leave in the first place.

Love you too, I typed back.

Sending fic now, said Mackenzie.

The next day, Nate said hello in math class first thing in the morning just like he always did, but his eyes didn't meet mine. At lunch he sat in his usual seat, picking at a plate full of fries and no main course. He was focused on his tray like it might reveal the meaning of life if he just stared hard enough, and didn't so much as glance over at me once. He looked angry, but I was starting to pick up on the fact that Nate looked angry a lot, even when he wasn't— when he was actually freaked out or embarrassed or overwhelmed. Today, I suspected all of the above.

Having a clue what to do about that would have been nice.

"You should meet my friend Mackenzie," I finally blurted out. He looked up.

"Yeah?" he said. "Where's she go to school?"

So apparently we were going to pretend that the whole scene at his house never happened. Okay then.

"South Hadley. It's in western Massachusetts." He looked confused, which I suppose made sense, given that was three states away from where we were in the suburbs north of Philadelphia. "I mean meet like, meet online? I saw you had a computer, so . . .

do you have Internet?" I couldn't imagine living without Internet. It suddenly struck me as weird that we'd exchanged phone numbers but not emails. I'd been keeping a careful distance from him more than I realized, not really wanting him to know about my online life.

That seemed petty and stupid, now, with what I'd seen of his life.

"Did she move?" Nate asked. "Like, she used to live around here?"

"No, no we just met online." I kept my chin up, refusing to be embarrassed. "She's awesome, though. You'll like her."

"Huh. We don't have Internet at the house yet. We did at our last place, but the rent's higher here, and—" He stopped himself.

"Oh," I said awkwardly.

"Our last place was an apartment, but Mom's gotten . . . we've got to have a house now, or people'd call the cops. And we're living off my dad's life insurance policy, until I can find a job." Nate looked halfway between embarrassed and defiant. "And I can't keep in touch with anyone anyway."

Why had it never occurred to me that he must have had friends before? People he'd had to abandon when he ran from whatever it was he was running from. I suddenly wondered if I even knew his real name, and felt caught between hurt at the idea that I might not and fear for him at the idea that I might. Would he know how to get a fake ID and register for school under a fake name? I wouldn't.

"Also I suck with computers," he said, shrugging. My stomach twisted. That probably answered the fake-name question. "I can work email, but that's about it. I'm a lousy geek." He grinned. It was a little strained, a little pleading, but genuine.

"You have a signed *Avengers* poster, you can't be that bad a geek," I pointed out, forcing myself to sound lighthearted. "Where'd you get it?"

He looked almost pitifully relieved at the change of topic. "You've heard of Comic-Con, right?"

Of course I'd heard of Comic-Con, and that was the end of any discussion of his finances, his unnamed enemies, or his mother.

For the rest of the week and into the next we played normal. He couldn't email from home, but he could text, and we did—mostly about mundane things, like homework or our obnoxious classmates, clueless teachers, and why the textbooks sucked. Every now and then, though, the conversation would veer in a more personal direction in spite of all the heavy subjects we were both purposefully avoiding. I learned that factory farming offended him and he wanted to go vegetarian, but thought it was kind of a lost cause when he had to buy so much meat for his mother. (I thought he should do it anyway, if it mattered to him—I'd never really thought about it seriously myself.) He hated hypocrites of any kind, and because of that, thought politics was mostly a waste of time. He didn't plan to register to vote. (I did, if only to appease my mother; he didn't make fun of me for it.) He'd played soccer as a kid and missed it, but really didn't care about professional sports (neither did I).

I imagined myself collecting these little bits of Nate and hoarding them, like a dragon on a pile of gems—and then I rolled my eyes at myself because really? Gems? But I wondered if he felt the same way about the things I told him. Did he care about my favorite ice cream flavor (butterscotch ripple)? Or that I'd lied and said I lost every English textbook I ever had so that I could keep them at the end of the year? He said that was cool—subversive. He'd asked me out, so he had to care at least a little, right? I thought he seemed interested, but I wasn't sure that honest, unfearful interest was something I could recognize.

Our first "date" was Mackenzie's idea. She and I watched TV and movies together all the time, synchronized over the Internet while we chatted, so why couldn't Nate and I have a movie date that way? Since Nate didn't have Internet it meant either texting until our thumbs fell off or a phone call, and Mackenzie talked me into calling him—even though I'd never called her. She said it was more intimate, and she had a point—that was exactly why it was also more nerve-racking. I thought of making it a comic-book movie marathon, remembering the comic books in bags strewn around his room.

If he gets weirded out that you like this stuff or wants to know why you don't want to watch a romantic comedy, you're morally obligated to dump him, no matter how much you like him, Mackenzie told me. Well, maybe not dump. That's sorta harsh.

But hang up on him, at least.

He won't, I answered her, with more confidence than I really felt. He isn't like that, he's just as big a geek as I am.

Even geek boys are still boys, and boys can get really dumb about what they want in the way of a girl. Trust me—voice of experience speaking, here, Mackenzie said. Just because he's all kinds of dorky cool doesn't mean he thinks it's okay for you to be. I mean, he asked if you'd heard of Comic-Con—HEARD OF COMIC-CON. That's a warning sign, dear. I'm just trying to prepare you.

He won't, I insisted.

He didn't—he said, "Huh—that's a really cool idea," and went to dig out his DVDs. The comic book theme was a good call. He didn't have an Amazon Cloud drive full of the genre like I did, but he had enough on disc for several hours worth of viewing.

We started with *Batman*. His ancient computer kept locking up as it tried to play his even more ancient DVDs, and then I'd pause my streaming video and he'd curse and apologize and I'd giggle.

I *giggled*. Since when did I giggle?

"So what are you wearing?" Nate asked, midway through *Batman Begins*.

I snorted. "Yeah, right. Try again."

"No, shit—no!" He sounded a little panicked. "I didn't mean it in a pervy way!"

"There's a nonpervy way to mean that?"

"I just meant, if this is a date, a first date, I just wondered if—you know, if you dressed up or anything."

I rolled over onto my stomach and blinked down at my phone—it was on speaker, lying next to my pillow, and at the moment it was being conspicuously silent. The movie kept playing across the room. I was wearing an oversized T-shirt with holes in it and a dragon on the front, and no pants. My underwear was probably two years old and had faded sailor stripes.

"Never mind, dumb idea," Nate said. "I don't expect you to dress up or anything. I like how you usually look. I like that you don't wear makeup."

My face heated, and my stomach wobbled. I grabbed the phone and switched the speaker off. "Did you?"

"What?"

"Did you dress up," I pressed, and bit my lip.

There was another long pause.

"I didn't, like, iron my shirt or any crap like that," Nate muttered. "But maybe I took a shower and there's some gel in my hair? It just seemed—I dunno."

"Tell me more about the hair," I teased. My face felt like it was on fire. If we'd actually been out together, I never could have been this brave.

"I look like a reject from a boy band," Nate grumbled. I tried not to laugh, and choked on my giggles. "Shut up! Okay, I lied. I was just trying to make you feel better because you apparently *didn't* dress up. Really, I look amazing. If you saw me now, your clothes would spontaneously fall off."

"Uh-huh."

"So what do you wear on the weekends? You don't seem like a tank-and-booty-shorts kinda girl."

That knocked me back a little—had he spent weekends with girls who dressed that way before? I twisted around to look over my own shoulder, at my faded underwear and my long pale legs with two days' stubble on them.

"Pretty much the same as what I wear during the week," I lied.

"You do know you're pretty, right?" Nate asked.

Am I so amazing that if you were here, your clothes would fall off? I wanted to retort. I wasn't feeling quite *that* brave, though, even with most of a county between us. "Thanks," I said instead, and, "You're—too. I mean, I think you're nice-looking. Can we watch the movie?" I faceplanted into the pillow. I hadn't meant to say that last part.

"Yeah, I like this scene—you like this scene?" Nate asked, and I couldn't tell if he really wanted my opinion or was humoring me. I managed not to blurt out, "What scene is it?"

"I haven't watched this in a while," I hedged. "I don't remember. I'll tell you in a minute."

"In that case, I'm gonna shut up so you can appreciate how awesome this is—which you will, because *you're* awesome."

My face was still buried in my pillow, so my lips caught on the fabric when I smiled. "Okay," I answered, and lifted my head to watch.

We got through the whole Christian Bale version of *Batman* that evening, all of the movies, and made plans for *Iron Man* next week. We talked—mostly by text, because voice calls still made me sort of nervous—every night that week.

Sometimes he would disappear midconversation, and when that happened I'd just very pointedly ignore the thread of queasy horror that wove its way through my gut. Maybe he'd just been distracted by something on the TV, or he'd fallen asleep, or something like that. Something normal. Something that wasn't his zombie mother degenerating into a mindless, feral state.

We stayed up until 3 a.m. on Thursday debating whether graphic novels would ever be taken seriously as a literary medium. (I said yes, eventually—Nate said no way.) I was exhausted in school the next day and had a headache from staring at my phone's tiny text screen in the dark, but I didn't mind at all.

I tried to see if Mackenzie and Nate could be introduced on the computers in the school library, but they blocked instant messaging. All I could manage was to relay to her what he'd said via text, while I talked to her on my computer at home.

He's got a dreamy voice, Mackenzie pronounced, after a conversation consisting entirely of second-hand text. Swoon-worthy, completely.

You are the world's most enormous dork, I replied.

So he doesn't? she asked, of course, because I'd walked right into that one.

His voice is fine.

Just fine, or fiiiiiine? she typed back.

I hate you, I replied, and I wished so hard it hurt that I could have this, just this, without all the messed-up parts.

Nate didn't invite me back to his house. He called me the next Saturday to say he couldn't spend the afternoon on the phone with me after all, and his voice sounded thick, like his nose was stuffed up—or like he'd been crying.

"Are you okay?" I asked. "You sound like you've got a cold."

"Yeah, maybe." He snuffled a bit; I wished I could see his face. Hadn't he said something about never getting sick? Maybe viruses were different. "I just need to spend some time on—just stuff around the house. Cleaning and crap, it's kinda gross here. I'm sorry. Next weekend, okay?"

From what I remembered of Nate's room, he wasn't exactly a neat freak—but then, I also remembered the way his mother had thrown furniture around, and the bloodstains on his clothes. "Sure," I said.

I ended up settling in for a *Harry Potter* movie marathon with Mackenzie instead. Since we'd both seen the entire series so many times we could recite the dialogue, this mostly involved the movies playing in the background while she IMed me ever more lewd and inventive ways I could be making Nate feel better. I retorted with links to the grossest and most graphic illustrations of her suggestions that I could find—and hoped my computer didn't catch a virus from all the highly questionable websites I was visiting.

OMG WHY would you post that? Mackenzie exclaimed, at

my latest find. Why would you RECORD that, in any way, at all?
Seriously, WTF, people SCARE ME.

Then my mom's thin voice came up the stairs. "Ellie? Can you
come down here, sweetie?" I jumped half out of my chair, my fingers tripping over themselves in my haste to restart my browser
and clear the history.

Ugh, Mom, brb, pause for me! I told Mackenzie, and went
reluctantly down to the dining room.

It was only my mother waiting—big surprise there. I could
hear my dad upstairs in his office. She had my college acceptance
letters spread in front of her, each one with a tidy stack of computer printouts compiled behind it—presumably lots of stuff I
already knew about how anyone with half a brain would kill to go
to any one of those schools.

"It must be hard to have so many good choices," Mom began,
smiling nervously.

"I don't have good choices." I hadn't really meant to say that.

"You have a preference, then?" Her chin tilted up, but her eyes
were still too big, her voice still too high. *You're scared of me*, I
wanted to say, *You're my own mother and you're so scared of me that
you're halfway to a panic attack over discussing my options for higher
education. What the fuck do you expect a dorm full of stupid kids to do
with me?*

"Mom—" I began carefully.

Her expression hardened. "You are going to college, Elizabeth."

Maybe she was a little more clued in to what I was thinking than I'd realized.

"How? Seriously, tell me that, how am I going to do this? It'd be one thing if we were talking somewhere I could commute, so maybe, *maybe* Penn, but a dorm? Really?"

"Yes, really." Her shaking hands started to make the papers rattle on the table. She clutched them together, fingernails digging into her knuckles. Her lips were bloodless. "You've made it through sharing public bathrooms at high school—"

"And that's gone so well."

"You've been accepted to the University of Pennsylvania, and Harvard, and Brown! It's gone amazingly!" I was surprised her voice didn't break the glass in the china cabinets. "You're almost there, Elizabeth!"

"Almost to what?" I threw up my hands.

"A life!" Mom said. It was somewhere between a whisper and a shriek—this tortured, hopeful sound that made me want to claw her eyes out, just to make it stop. "A normal life, like anyone else—"

"And when I get my normal life, with my normal job, and my normal house, are you going to follow me around and bleach all of that too?" I snapped.

She looked, quite satisfyingly, like I'd slapped her.

I stormed back up the stairs. Halfway down the hall to my room, my dad's office door opened and his head popped out. It was the first time I'd actually seen his face in over a month, and thus, enough to make me pause.

"Didn't go so well, huh?" he asked, giving me his best sympathetic smile. I guess maybe it got him somewhere in the courtroom. I bet juries full of strangers who didn't know him any more or less than I did just ate it up. "Be nice to your mom, she loves you."

I blinked at him in disbelief. He quirked a cheerfully pleading brow at me. I stomped away without saying a thing and slammed my door.

I put *Harry Potter* back on and chatted a bit more with Mackenzie, about everything but schools—what could I say to her when I knew she was going to school somewhere in New England—probably UMass—and if I went to Harvard, we'd practically be neighbors? She wouldn't understand why I didn't want that, and I couldn't tell her enough to make her.

I sent Nate probably a dozen texts—assorted, increasingly lame variations on a theme of "feel better"—but he answered none of them.

If he'd had a cold, it was completely gone by the time I saw him again at school.

"Do you ever think about whether you could do something like that?" I asked.

We'd squeaked the first *Iron Man* movie in on a Wednesday night, and now—Friday—we were almost finished with *Iron Man II*.

"Stick a hunk of untested, newly synthesized element into my chest? Um, not really?"

"Dork." I smiled into the phone. "No, I mean—" I wasn't really sure what I meant. We'd spent three semi-long-distance "dates" now watching movies about superheroes, and while those were some of my favorite movies, the way we'd accidentally focused on stories about other people with powers was messing with me a bit. I needed—I didn't really know what. Reassurance that I wasn't the only one who got a little weirded out by how people with strange abilities always, always turned into either heroes or villains?

Maybe I wanted him to tell me that I wasn't delusional for wondering why my life wasn't turning out that way, or for being a little afraid that it might yet.

"Ellie?"

"Being someone like that. Actually using your powers, openly." If anyone in the world was ever going to get it, it'd be him.

He was quiet, and my pulse thumped in my ears. On screen, things were blowing up.

"Yeah, I've thought about it," he finally said. "I don't think that kind of thing goes well in the real world."

"But you could—" I was momentarily stumped and racked my brain. "You could bring murder victims back so they could tell the police who killed them. Let them say good-bye to their families."

"Took you a minute to come up with something good I could do with my set of powers, didn't it?"

"No—"

"Were you thinking zombie armies? Because everybody thinks zombie armies."

"I'm not everybody." I winced—that came out harsher than he deserved, I thought. Or maybe it wasn't? I wanted him to know better, to understand why I'd get offended at being compared to the general population—but it was possible he didn't, and it was more than possible that I was expecting too much of him.

"You're not," Nate agreed before I could take it back, and I heard his sigh—could picture his hunched shoulders, his apologetic eyes and scowling face. "Sorry." A beat of silence, then, "That's not all I could do that'd be good."

"What would you want to do?" I asked quietly.

"Think about what I did to Daniel's hand," he said. "I pushed the life out of it—the spiritual energy. Like the opposite of raising the dead. Without that, everything, every living cell, it just stops. Think about that—I could do that to anything."

I did think about it, and it made me uneasy. It wasn't that far off from my own ideas on how I could use my powers, really, but he hadn't specified a target. He hadn't said he could take out bad guys—he'd said he could take out *anyone*. Was that what he wanted? To be the sort of boogeyman I'd have given anything *not* to be?

"That's good?" I asked, and tried to sound as neutral as possible about it. It came out a whisper, high and scared like my mother's voice got with me, and that really made me want to throw up.

"Think about how else I could use that, if I knew how." There was an urgency to his voice, like he needed my understanding just as much as I needed his. "Ellie, I could do that with tumors. Infections. I'm a walking cure for cancer. Every necromancer is."

That knocked every thought I had right out of my head. Then they came rushing back, so many possibilities, so many ideas I'd never even considered, all coated in guilt at what I'd thought of him. "Oh my God."

"Yeah," he agreed. "And you? A viviomancer? Think about what you could fix. Heart disease, birth defects, pretty much any wound. And forget that, think about other stuff—think about making crops grow with no chemicals. Regrowing rainforests. Hell, think about your bacteria and mold—they make medicine out of that shit. Think how much you could make in a day."

I could still hear the movie playing in the background. I wasn't looking at the screen anymore. I was staring blankly at my headboard. The climactic battle sequence was full of explosions and tense music. Something about that soundtrack playing through this conversation was abruptly hysterical, and I had to bite my lip not to laugh.

"You asked—did you ever think about it?"

"I thought I could be an assassin," I admitted. "Like, I could take out genocidal dictators and warlords. It'd look natural, like they just got sick."

"That too," Nate agreed.

"I like your idea better. I—you said there were other people like us, especially like you, so why don't they—*do* they?"

"Sometimes." He apparently understood the question despite my incoherence. "If it's necessary to interfere in mundane politics, to keep someone alive who they need or get someone out of the way who's a problem, mostly. Or for each other. But definitely not in the open."

"Why not?" I demanded. "I mean, I get that it would freak people out and way back when there probably would have been witch burnings but—now? Now I think people would get over it."

"Because they're powerful," Nate said. "Not like, abilities powerful, though that too—I mean like economically, politically powerful. Behind the scenes. And they pull some fucked-up shit to keep things that way—not just the shady influence shit, I mean how they make their money. They think they're better than ordinary people. They don't give a shit what they do to ordinary people. And if it were all out in the open, who they were, what they could do? That'd all fall apart. There'd be rules and regulations and Senate committees and boards and—the fucking Mutant Registration Act. You know *X-Men*?"

"I know *X-Men*," I agreed dazedly.

"We should watch that next weekend."

"You're a necromancer and you're not like that. So who are these people who—" I stopped myself. I wanted to bang my head against something at my own half-spoken stupidity. All I had at hand was my pillow, and that wasn't very good for head-banging. "The people your dad worked for. The people you're hiding from."

"Yeah."

"And if someone tried to—I don't know, go public, start healing people on the street corner, they'd—"

"They'd have a little 'accident,'" Nate said bitterly.

Did your dad have an "accident"? I didn't have the nerve to ask.

The credits rolled on the movie. I said nothing. He said nothing.

"That's *terrible*," I finally exclaimed. "That's—that's fucking *disgusting*. Do you know how much better the world could be?"

"Yeah."

"How much they could fix? We could fix? I could have gone to school like normal with everybody understanding and—God, I am the world's most self-centered, petty bitch."

"You're really, really not."

"They could *cure cancer*. And they *don't*. And they won't let anyone else!"

"I know."

"That's—that's an *atrocity*. That's pathetic, that's just—just *disgusting*. I keep coming back to that word, because it really fits."

"It's a good word for it," Nate agreed. "Elle?"

"Yeah?"

"I really want to kiss you right now."

"I—oh. What?" I stammered. "I mean—thanks? Not *thanks*, that's—God that sounds stupid, you know what I mean, I—don't do that!"

"Don't kiss you?" He didn't sound at all like he thought that was what I meant.

"I was being serious."

"I know. That's what made me want to kiss you. I don't mean because it was cute or some sexist bullshit like that, I mean because you really were totally serious and offended and righteous and—I liked it. You sounded ready to take on the world. You sounded—you make me believe you could do it. And then I want to kiss you."

"Oh."

"No pressure, though."

Oh, yeah *right.* He wasn't even in the same building and I could feel the pressure—but I believed that he didn't mean it that way.

"Maybe—soon?" I offered, my stomach tying itself in knots and my fingertips starting to burn. "If you're really, really, REALLY sure I'm not going to accidentally give you bacterial meningitis and herpes and the plague."

"What if I said I thought it'd be worth it?" he asked.

"I'd say you should think more of yourself." I hesitated, then added, "Because I do."

"I'll take that," he said, and there was something funny about his voice, a note there that I hadn't heard before. I wondered if I sounded funny too.

"Good," I said. "Now go find your *Avengers* DVD. If we can't save the world, we can at least watch it get saved."

—❦—

Nate disappeared for the rest of the weekend, and then wasn't in school Monday.

I tried to write this off as completely explicable for any number of mundane reasons. He had a cold—for real this time. He had a paper to finish. His practically fossilized car was acting up. I didn't want to nag.

By Tuesday I broke down and texted, Everything okay? I got no reply, and no sleep that night. Neither of my parents had spoken to me in a week—which meant things were pretty much back to normal on that score. The packets of college materials still sat on the table, slightly askew.

On Wednesday Nate was back, the left side of his jaw a mass of oversized Band-Aids, the sort intended for covering skinned knees. There was a bruise on the other side of his neck. He gave me half a rueful grin with the undamaged side of his face, then went and sat down without a word.

Mr. Wagner did a double take when he saw Nate. He seemed to hover on the verge of saying something, but instead launched into too jovial admonitions to take out our notebooks and put on our thinking caps.

I wanted to drag Nate out into the hallway right then and demand to know what the hell had happened, and if he was okay, and if there was something, anything I could do. I didn't think he'd thank me for causing a scene, though. I made a brief, half-hearted attempt to actually pay attention to the lesson. After about three minutes, I gave in to the impulse to stare fixedly at Nate's back, willing it to provide me with explanations.

Mr. Wagner dropped his chalk twice in the course of the class period. His voice kept getting louder and louder, until it cracked. He tried to cover it in a fit of coughing.

I wondered how I'd never noticed before what an utter, abject coward Mr. Wagner was—I'd known he was afraid of *me*, but I'd thought it was just, well, me.

But maybe it really wasn't me, I thought suddenly, watching everyone else watching Nate—whispering, texting furtively under their desktops. Mr. Wager ignored them, of course, because to scold them he'd have to turn around and acknowledge the situation, and that might have involved doing something other than copying his own notes onto the board. I leaped out of my seat the instant the bell rang, so quickly that the desk teetered. Nate didn't wait to say good-bye. I scrambled out the door after him, not bothering to wait for the room to clear. They could damn well get out of the way—and they did.

I caught up to him a little way down the hall. He didn't acknowledge me as I fell into step beside him. "What happened?"

"What're my odds on you believing I walked into a door?" Nate asked, trudging forward.

"Pretty much zero."

"Yeah, kinda what I figured." He grimaced but didn't say anything else. I just kept pace alongside him, periodically glaring at all the open stares. I wondered how long it'd take the school rumor mill to start churning out bizarre theories as to how I was responsible for his injuries.

"Isn't your next class the other way?" Nate grumbled.

I shrugged. He gave me a sidelong scowl.

"Taste of your own medicine."

He scowled harder. Then, with a wicked little gleam in his eye, he shrugged right back at me. "Fair enough."

I flipped him a middle finger. He grabbed at it and almost caught it. I was quicker, but not by much, and I almost bumped into a horrified freshman in my haste to evade him. He gave up, and I wrapped my arms around myself, hiding my hands under my elbows.

"So you walked into a door."

"Yep."

"Did you forget to buy the door its raw steak?" I asked.

"Something like that," Nate mumbled, glancing nervously around the hall.

I was so disgusted with everyone's gawking that I wanted to tell him it didn't matter what anyone else heard or what they thought, but I bit my tongue and forced myself to think before I spoke. Not all the teachers were as useless as Mr. Wagner, and the last thing Nate needed was someone in a position of authority overhearing something unfortunate. I needed to calm down.

"Actually, I tripped over a chair—really, I mean. Fell on my face. While trying to reason with . . . the door. The door wanted to go to the neighbors." He paused a beat. "You really can't reason with doors, you know, when they're being all . . . really door-like. But they look like what they were before they were doors, and it's just hard not to try. And then they try to dart around you all fast, and you fall over chairs."

I blinked. "Trees," I said after my brain had a moment to catch up.

I much preferred thinking of ways to continue the metaphor, as opposed to actually thinking about the situation he was describing.

"Trees?"

"What doors were before they were doors," I elaborated. "Doors are wood. So they were trees."

"Ah," said Nate, giving me a look that required me to stare down at my shoes and let my hair fall between us.

"So you were trying to restrain your door, keep it from going over to the neighbor's and munching on the trees," I tried to spell out the scenario, wanting to get an idea of just how badly he might be hurt under all those bandages, still unable to look at him. "And you tripped over a chair?"

It was horrifying enough as presented, but it didn't really add up. So he fell—he'd have bruises, in that case. Bruises don't need Band-Aids.

"Pretty much," Nate affirmed.

"Did you trip over a chair and fall on a steak knife or something? You've got an entire first-aid kit on your face."

"The door felt bad, and insisted on taking care of it," Nate said. "It's just rug burn. Not as bad as it looks."

Rug burn. That was plausible, wasn't it?

So why didn't I believe him?

"She's—I mean, the door's good now," Nate added. "All . . . firmly on its hinges."

"You could call me," I offered. "If it'd be easier with two people. I've got a car—no license, but I could work on that, and it's not like I'd care so much about a ticket if you were—I mean, if it were an emergency."

I did not want him to call me because his mother was losing

whatever little bit of sanity she had and needed to be physically restrained. His mother terrified me. I'd probably be useless.

I didn't regret offering.

I could feel him staring at the side of my head.

"Thanks," Nate said, trying and failing to keep me from hearing the rejection in his voice. "Really. You're awesome."

That, I thought he meant—I just kept shuffling along, face burning. So I was awesome. Great. Yay for me. I still knew he wasn't going to call, and if I really were half as awesome as he seemed to think I was, I'd be able to think of a way to help him. I didn't have the first clue.

The bandages were still in evidence the next day, and his eye was looking a little puffy. I forced myself to actually pay attention in Calculus anyway. I wouldn't help Nate any by flunking. I told myself I could worry at lunch.

He got to the cafeteria before me, and was already scowling at a dog-eared copy of the CliffsNotes to *The Grapes of Wrath* when I sat down across from him. He didn't have any food.

"You're not eating?" I stuffed a spoonful of apple pie into my mouth—okay, it wasn't the most mature nutritional choice, but it was comfort food. Looking at the way his left eye was starting to bruise, I wanted comfort.

He glanced up in a way that seemed almost guilty, then shrugged. "Not hungry." He tried to speak without moving his jaw. It made his voice come out all muffled and wrong. "Did you actually read this?" He nodded down at the CliffsNotes. "The book, I mean."

"Yeah. And trust me, you've got the right idea."

He shot me a pained-looking half of a smile, his lips holding to a tense line on the side of his face that had the bandages.

"You're not eating 'cause it hurts too much to chew, aren't you?" I demanded. "How bad *is* that?"

He shrugged. "Had worse," he said, but in the sort of carefully casual tone that meant he probably hadn't, really. There was something wrong with the shrug, too, a stiffness to the way he moved.

"Well," I started, then stopped, fidgeting with my gloves. "At least it can't get infected, right?" I asked, trying to make it sound like I was just pointing out the bright side and not trying to reassure myself.

Nate was conspicuously silent. My stomach gave an uneasy wobble.

"It can't, right?"

"Actually," Nate began, then winced. "Actually," he tried again, quieter and not quite so clearly, "there's an interesting exception to that."

"Which would be . . . ?" I prompted.

"Bites from undead things."

It took a moment for that to really process. For a few seconds, I wondered what sort of animal he'd accidentally raised from the dead. What really awful luck he was having, I thought, to need to restrain his mother and be bitten by some zombie animal all on the same day. Then logic kicked in.

Whatever had happened hadn't been just some shouting and shoving and Nate falling over a chair. His mother had bitten him. *Bitten* him.

"She doesn't know what she's doing when she's like that. Seriously, it's not her." He was going pale and sweaty. "It's my fault, I'm the one that raised her, I have to control her, or keep her fed enough that she can control herself, but she's getting hungrier and I lost track. I fucked up, so I got beat up, and she feels like shit about it, so it's just—it's just all fucked up." He looked up, his eyes catching mine with a desperate intensity. "It's not like she's doing it on purpose—it's like a person who has seizures. She's just really not there."

He hadn't said so, but in between the words was the admission that this had happened before—maybe not this bad, but it wasn't the first time. And he said she was getting hungrier.

"Anyway, I washed it out again this morning and I put some Neosporin on it." He glared at me, daring me to comment, to judge. I didn't know if that was what I should be doing or not. What was coming out of his mouth sounded an awful lot like the standard string of abusive-situation excuses—she didn't mean it, she's not herself when she does it, she's really sorry. And you're supposed to tell someone in that situation to get out, right? Get help.

I didn't think there was help for this, and I had the awful feeling that maybe he was telling me the literal truth—maybe she really, genuinely couldn't help it. He'd told me zombies weren't meant to be kept around so long. You turned them into something more permanent or you let them go, he'd said. He didn't know how to turn her into a wraith. Which left nothing I could possibly tell him to do.

"I'm sorry." I tried to keep my voice steady, and the words came out at barely a whisper.

Nate's eyes dropped away from mine and his hands tightened into fists, still clutching the edges of the CliffsNotes. For several long and miserable minutes, we were both silent.

"I hate this book," Nate announced, quiet and garbled again, in sufficient control of himself to try to spare his jaw. "I tried to read it—I mean, I'm not some shit for brains jock who has to read the CliffsNotes because they can't figure out the big words and the symbolism and all that crap, but I just fucking hate this book. It's depressing as all hell and it doesn't fucking quit, and it's not like you can appreciate the irony or the witty dialogue or *anything*, it's just beating you over the head over and over again with how much people suck and poverty sucks and greed sucks and nothing ever gets better, and hey, y'know what? Knew that. Thanks. Fuck that."

He shoved the thin book away across the table with sufficient force that it skidded to the edge, teetered there, then fell to the floor under the table in an ungainly flutter of pages.

"I liked *The Great Gatsby*."

He gave me a blank look.

"We're reading that next. I read it already—I mean, not for fun, it was summer reading for ninth grade social studies, 'cause this school system's too screwed up to figure out that if you're in the gifted program back in junior high you're going to read this book twice, so—it's better." I paused a beat. "Well, just as depressing, I guess, but not quite so . . . ," I floundered, gesturing.

"Soul-sucking?" Nate suggested.

"Yeah. More clever, less soul-sucking."

"Good quality in a book." Nate started, slowly and painfully, to reach for the CliffsNotes to *Grapes of Wrath*.

"I got it!" I ducked down and grabbed the book while he was still trying to bend under the table. "Here."

He winced as he straightened, looking as embarrassed as he was pained. "Thanks." It was distinctly resentful.

"You're *hurt*," I said.

"Really?" he shot back, but then flinched. As I watched, a dark spot appeared beneath the plastic of the bandage closest to his ear. All that talking had broken something open.

"So . . . that could get infected." I watched the dark spot expand. It looked sort of green, though I couldn't be sure through the bandage.

"Yep," he rasped out.

"Would antibiotics help? I mean, how does that work? The lack of immunity, I mean—is it like, zombie germs?"

Nate gave a snorting little attempt at a laugh, and began rolling the CliffsNotes up, first one way and then the other, attempting to get the crinkles out. "No," he said, speaking slowly and not very clearly. "Normal germs. It's just—" He paused.

"You could explain later. Like sometime when talking doesn't make you bleed."

"It's like . . . whatever it is that makes live stuff give me a wide berth normally?" He didn't acknowledge my protests at all. "Getting bit by anything animated that way, anything that keeps itself going on the same sort of power, it cancels it out. If it's a bad enough bite, it deadens everything for a while. Makes you powerless. This isn't that bad, though, it's just the spot where I got bit that's all mundane and helpless for the moment."

"Did you ever get bit that bad?" I kept my voice carefully neutral.

"No." Nate shook his head just a little. "My dad did once."

"Oh." I was taken aback. It couldn't have been his mom who bit his dad, because she hadn't been dead yet when his dad was alive. I wanted to ask more about it, but it really wasn't the time for that, and besides it really wasn't my business. "So, then antibiotics would work."

"Guess so," Nate said. "You've gotta go to a doctor to get antibiotics, though. Or order stuff off the Internet from China that might be cyanide cut with drain cleaner. Doesn't seem like a good plan."

He'd told me that a trained viviomancer could heal almost any wound; a fully trained necromancer could kill an infection. I guessed that even if he had known how, he probably couldn't have treated himself. I had no idea at all how to use my powers that way. It made sense in theory—all I had to do was make his cells, rather than the germs causing the infection, grow faster. Great theory. In practice, I'd probably rot off half his face if I tried.

But maybe there was another way I could help him.

"My mom has antibiotics," I offered quietly, "and this surgical soap stuff."

Nate gave me a questioning look. The dark spot on the bandage on his jaw had stopped expanding, but it was plenty big enough already.

"For some reason living with me makes her paranoid." I tried to make it a joke. The look on his face said he didn't find it all that funny, which it wasn't, and I just gave up. "She hoards meds, and she looks for doctors who'll give them to her without too many questions."

"Won't she notice if something's gone, if she's like that?"

Yes, she probably would.

"She's seriously got a lot of stuff," I insisted. "And we can take stuff out of the back of the cabinet that's about to expire—or I could open up capsules, put the powder in something else, put the empty ones back."

"Devious." Nate tried to make it sound teasing. It didn't work.

"It'll be fine." I don't know why anyone ever says that, really. The only time you say things will be fine is when you know they won't be, and everyone knows it. "You're not allergic to anything, are you?"

"No," said Nate, still hesitant. "Ellie—"

"Okay, so I probably won't accidentally kill you. That's good."

"Ellie—"

"What's she going to do, ground me?" I cut him off. "I don't care."

"You don't care if your mother thinks you're some kind of addict," Nate said doubtfully.

"Right, 'cause those antibiotics, they're the hot party drug," I snapped. "And really, no. I don't."

He didn't look like he believed me, which was perceptive of him.

"Okay," he finally sighed. "Fine. Thank you." He looked like he was struggling with something, and then said, "If we're going to do this, can we be thoroughly delinquent and do it now? I feel like crap. I really wouldn't mind missing the rest of the day."

That brought me up short. I'd never ditched so much as a single class in my entire life, let alone half a day of school. Would Mom be out of the house right now? It was only a little past eleven in the morning. I was pretty sure that was still obsessive cleaning time.

"Never mind," Nate said, seeing the look on my face. "After school's fine."

"After English class," I offered. It'd be about one thirty by then, and she'd be heading into the city. It was Thursday, which meant she'd be doing pro bono consulting at the women's shelter, and I was pretty sure that started in the early afternoon.

Pretty sure.

A tiny, wicked part of me almost wanted to know what she'd do if she caught me sneaking home in the middle of the day, and with a boy, but the rest of me didn't want to do that to Nate. One thirty should be safe.

"And hey, I could get on your computer and meet Mackenzie," Nate offered.

Mackenzie wasn't online when we got to my house, of course—Mackenzie was still in school. I tried not to be self-conscious as Nate took in his surroundings—the posh furniture, the raised ceilings, the surgical sterility of it all. The house echoed. I suppose it always did, but it didn't bother me when I was there alone. Showing it to someone else, it seemed simultaneously ostentatious and lonely. It also smelled just faintly of bleach, even out in the living room.

I didn't want to, but it was impossible not to compare my house to his. Nate was poor; I wasn't. I'm not sure why exactly that was embarrassing, but it was. I felt like I should explain how none of this mattered to me, but that would be acknowledging it, and I didn't have the nerve.

"We had a pool with a waterfall. When my dad was alive." He was looking out the bay window in the dining room into the backyard. No pool for us—a pool could not be sterilized sufficiently to please my mother.

"Oh." So he hadn't always been poor. It fact, it sounded like once upon a time, his family had been better off financially than mine—I mean, a pool with a waterfall? The remaining MacPhersons had fallen pretty danged far. I think that made it worse.

"It's okay to have a nice house," Nate told me. "I'd like to have a nice house again."

"Sorry," I said awkwardly.

"Eh, it's whatever. Doesn't matter."

We didn't talk anymore as I led him upstairs to my parents' bathroom. It was almost as pristine and gleaming as my own bathroom—but my father's razor sat on the edge of the sink. Mom had left a tube of mascara next to the mirror. There were two electric toothbrushes, a shower curtain printed with a pattern that looked like rippling water, and his-and-hers monogrammed towels.

I don't know why those towels and those toothbrushes bothered me so much, but they did. I clenched my teeth and jerked open the mirrored medicine cabinet, trying not to notice my own reflection. The inside of the cabinet was both as full as it could get and perfectly organized—dozens of little labeled bottles sat in neat rows on gleaming Plexiglas shelves. My mother had three bottles of surgical soap, two of them still sealed.

I'd known all that would be there, of course. The pills and the soap were the whole reason Nate was here. It shouldn't have been such a punch in the gut to see them, to have tangible proof of how much I terrified my mother—as if the ubiquitous bleach smell wasn't enough. It's not like this was news, but it was different with Nate there to see it. Everything I'd gotten so good at ignoring was suddenly brought into sharp, unforgiving focus, and for a horrible moment, I felt like I might cry. My fingertips were starting to tingle.

"Here." I grabbed the open bottle of soap and held it out to Nate. He took it without comment. I eyed the pill bottles, ignoring the pins and needles in my hands and the churning of my stomach and the sound of Nate's clothes rustling as he shifted his weight from foot to foot, clearly uncomfortable. I needed to think rationally, not break down blubbering. Definitely not rot my parents' bathroom.

This had sounded a lot simpler back at school. None of the bottles' labels said "antibiotic"—just the drug names. Were they all antibiotics? Did it matter which one I picked? The only antibiotic I could think of by name was penicillin, and there was nothing in there that said penicillin on the label. There were other things that ended in "-cillin," though—should I be grabbing one of those?

"We don't have to do this if you're not sure," Nate said quietly to the back of my head. "I'll be fine."

I didn't answer him, just picked up random pill bottles and searched labels for something to tell me which one would be right. Why didn't any of them say "treats infected bite wounds"?

Probably because a doctor was supposed to be in charge of dispensing them, and a doctor would know what she was doing, unlike me. Nate watched over my shoulder. Standing so close to him, I could feel the potential in it like a soft thrumming at the base of my skull, my fingers itching madly now, just this side of pain. There was potential there, lots of it.

A piece of me wanted badly to reach out for that potential, even though I knew that really wouldn't be a good thing for Nate.

I could stop myself from doing it, but I couldn't stop wanting it. It wasn't a rational desire, it was just reflex, like blinking or swallowing or breathing—but repeating that over and over inside my head didn't make me hate myself any less.

Nate didn't understand. My mother, with her stash of pills, she understood. I was a thing to be frightened of, a walking disease.

I bit my lip and shuffled through the bottles more anxiously, my burning hands shaking as I made sure to settle each one back down exactly as it had been, so my mother wouldn't know I'd been here. I didn't know what the hell I was doing. I was going to pick the wrong pills and hurt him. I was going to lose control and make the infection in his face go haywire. I was a screwup, a freak of nature, and my own mother kept rows upon rows of pills like talismans against me, stored in her pristine little bathroom with its matching monogrammed towels. I didn't belong in this room; I didn't belong in this life.

"Ellie?"

I could feel tears welling up behind my eyes, but I stubbornly refused to let them spill. There was potential on the bottles too—much, much less, but it was still there. And on the knob that opened the mirrored cabinet door, and scattered across the mirror, and the floor, and on Nate's skin and his clothes and his shoes and my shoes and the outsides of my gloves—right there on my gloves—

"Ellie, are you okay?"

I grabbed a random bottle of something-cillin from the back of the cabinet and turned around to face him. "Here." I thrust the bottle at him, my voice wobbling. I swallowed hard, once and then again, fighting tears, fighting the urge to just let go. Just a little.

Nate took the bottle, very carefully not touching my fingers at all. I clenched my jaw so hard it ached. I *would not cry*.

"It gets worse when you're upset," Nate said quietly. "Or scared. It's worst when you're scared."

"Yeah," I choked out. "It's like that for you too?"

Nate nodded. "We don't have to do this," he repeated.

"Yes, we do. Your face is all—I can tell it's—" I gestured helplessly.

"Ah. Right."

"It's not your fault. It's not this. I mean, not the stealing medicine? It's—I never go in here. They have matching towels." I scrunched my eyes shut. Why the hell had I said that? Could I sound more pathetic if I tried? I didn't want to open my eyes, didn't want to see how sorry for me I knew he'd look.

"On the plus side, they don't try to eat you."

I blinked and stared.

"They're normal," he offered. "They've got it easy—unlike you. I'm more impressed by the fact that you're not a serial killer than I am by their perfect little lovey-dovey bathroom."

"I don't think living with me is exactly easy," I responded.

"Too bad for them." Nate's voice was hard. I flushed and looked down. Knowing what Nate put up with out of familial loyalty, what could I say to that? They're doing the best they can? Not everybody is like you?

"You need me and my germs to go away for a bit, let you get it together?"

I took a deep, shaky breath. "No, I think I'm okay." I shoved my hair behind my ears and made myself look up. "There are Band-Aids and gauze and stuff in the hall closet, if you wanna clean that up?" I nodded toward the mass of bandages on his jaw.

"Yeah, that's the plan, huh?" Nate said, wincing again. "Really not looking forward to that. I don't suppose we can pilfer some vodka first?"

"Uh—"

"Kidding," Nate rushed to say.

"No, you weren't." I retorted.

"Okay, no, I wasn't," he admitted. "But probably not a good idea. Let's go get the Band-Aids and stuff, get this over with."

We ended up in my bathroom. Nate stood at the sink with a heap of first-aid supplies on the counter in front of him. I sat on the toilet lid, trying to hold myself together.

Nate had taken his shirt off to avoid getting it wet. He faced the mirror over the sink, his back to me. It let me see far too much of him. He was too thin, all ropey muscles and the sharp outline of ribs. His entire torso was bruised and scratched, and they weren't little bruises—these were huge, ugly, red-purple things that made me wonder if he'd broken some of those too-visible ribs.

He hadn't looked at me since the shirt went over his head. I hadn't said anything. I could see the muscles of his back move as he arranged things on the counter—ripped open a packet of gauze, squirted a bit of the surgical soap into a cup full of hot water. He was taking his time, delaying the inevitable.

Even with him looking so beat-up and pitiful, some part of me wanted to reach out and trace the line of his spine, to feel the tense muscles of his bony shoulders move under my fingertips. I kept my hands on my knees, ignoring him, ignoring my itching fingers.

Nate hissed as he began pulling the bandages away from his face. I stared hard at his discarded shirt, lying in a heap on the floor by my feet. The uncovered wound smelled, a sour-sweet smell like spoiled meat—not a good sign. It made me feel sick and a little light-headed, but it also pushed the pins-and-needles burning in my fingers from distractingly uncomfortable into downright agonizing. I was sweating. I could taste it at the back of my throat, cloying and enervating, making the hairs on my arms stand on end.

I heard him drop the old bandages into the trash can. The soap solution made a sloshing sound as he swirled a gauze pad through it. Nate breathed, too fast and too shallow, as he brought the gauze to his face. He was in pain; it radiated off of him. The used gauze went into the trash, every crinkle and drip loud. Nate tore open another gauze, repeated the process.

I could feel his heart rate accelerating. My eyes followed the gauze as he tossed it away. It was smeared with blood and something else—something sickly yellow that pulled at me, whispering possibility. I was going to have bruises where I clung to my knees.

He tore open yet another gauze. His heart hammered and his stomach clenched, but I knew that cleaning the wound out was doing some good. The feel of overwhelming, tingling potential wasn't so concentrated now; it was about evenly distributed between the bite and the trash can. I could still feel how much the bite hurt, though.

I sucked in a breath. I wasn't just imagining how it must feel. I could actually feel it myself. I could feel *Nate*, just as much as I could feel the infection.

At least, I thought I could. It was strange, different from the affinity I usually felt for simple things like bacteria, or mold. There was nothing simple about this. I felt him turn in response to my sharply indrawn breath, felt his ribs protesting the movement, felt his face throb, felt *him*, a hazy second set of perceptions that fled as I tried to bring them into focus. I'd never sensed a person that way before—I'd never even sensed an animal or an insect or a tree that way, nothing that complex.

"Ellie?" Nate asked.

I looked up. He hadn't rebandaged his face yet. There were a perfect set of half-moon tooth prints at the edge of his jaw. The flesh around and between them was swollen and angry red. The wound was ragged, torn flesh dangling. It leaked a clear fluid tinged with blood and yellow pus.

It was like my vision narrowed down to a pinhole. All I could see was that trickle of blood and, in my memory, his mother's blood-smeared chin. Every other perception, natural or otherwise, washed away in a cold rush.

"You okay?" Nate asked. His voice sounded far away and hollow through the sudden rushing sound of my own pulse in my ears. My blood. His blood. *His mother's bloody chin.*

I gagged, slapped a horrified hand over my mouth, and fled.

I waited in the living room, sitting on the couch with my knees pulled up to my chest, not caring what my mother would say about shoes on the furniture. I wrapped my arms around myself and tried to stop crying.

About twelve eons later, Nate came down the stairs. He had the bathroom trash bag in one hand, neatly tied off. His face was all bandaged up and tidy again.

"Trash?"

"Out by the garage," I said to my knees. "Around the side in this little lattice thing."

"'K," Nate said and vanished out the front door. He reappeared a few moments later, hands empty. He loped past me into the kitchen without comment; I heard water running. He was probably washing his hands. I focused on breathing, curling tighter into myself when I heard his footsteps approaching again.

He knelt down in front of me so that I had no choice but to look him in the face. "I scrubbed the sink and the counter and the floor, and I put the soap stuff back in your Mom's cabinet where it was. I shoved the trash under some other trash that was in the can outside. I think our tracks are as covered as they're gonna be."

"Thanks," I croaked and wiped at my face. My gloves were cold and damp and gross. "You didn't have to do that. I'd have cleaned up."

He shrugged and kept watching me.

"Sorry."

"For what?"

"Being a big spaz?" My voice cracked.

He reached up to push my hair behind my ears. I pulled away. "Don't."

"Shut up," he said softly. "It's fine; I'm fine. I'm sorry I made you cry."

"Not your fault," I whispered. His hand lingered on the side of my face, bare fingers on my skin. I could feel him again. It was clearer this time, less confusing. He felt warm, warm and bright. I could feel what remained of the infection in his jaw, too, but it was somehow easier to ignore.

"Want to run away and join the circus?" he asked. "I think we could put together a pretty good act, you and me. There have gotta be some good old-fashioned freak shows left somewhere, the political correctness police can't have gotten all of them."

I gave a watery little giggle.

He cradled my jaw in both hands. I clung tighter to my knees, the sense of him as a living thing burning in my mind, tangling up with the very physical warmth of his thumb brushing across my cheekbone, smearing the tear tracks. "I'm gonna figure out how to fix her," Nate said, voice low and solemn. "I'm gonna figure out how to fix *all* of this. And then you and me are going to graduate, and we're gonna go off to college and get an apartment together, and we're gonna have matching towels, okay? We're gonna have a whole fucking closet full of matching monogrammed towels. Got it?"

His hands were so warm, and he was so alive, and I just wanted to sink into that warmth and cease to exist. I wanted to believe him so, so badly.

"Got it," I repeated back, almost inaudibly.

"Good," said Nate.

You need to call the police, was the first thing Mackenzie said after I'd related a very carefully edited version of the afternoon's events. Seriously. That's way beyond not okay.

I can't, I replied, rather miserably, and wished I could explain in a slightly less-carefully-edited way, so that she'd actually get it.

So convince him to go to the hospital, and then they'll call the police. Then you're not the bad guy.

I don't care if I'm the bad guy, it's not that, it's just complicated. I scrubbed at my eyes with gloves that were already a little damp and a lot disgusting. I'd been crying on and off for the better part of the evening. My nose was running, my eyes were puffy, and I'd run out of tissues. Getting more would mean going downstairs looking all sobby, and considering my mom had come home half an hour ago, that was out of the question.

It's always complicated, Mackenzie retorted. I mean, nobody grows up saying, "Gee, when I'm a parent, I think I want to beat the shit out of my kid on a regular basis." You don't get there 'cause your life *doesn't* suck. It's still not okay.

Not that kind of complicated, I typed back.

There was a long, awkward pause, during which time I gave up on sniffling and wiped my running nose on the back of my seriously repulsive glove. Something began growing in little abstract, fractal swirls of mustard green on the fabric, but I didn't have the heart to do much more than glare at it. My self-control was officially shot for the day. I was going to have to bleach the keyboard later.

Oh, Mackenzie finally said. Right. That other kind of complicated that you don't want to talk about.

I'm sorry. Several of my keys began sprouting a fine haze of red mold, thickest around the vowels, where my fingers landed most.

No, I get it, Mackenzie replied. I seriously hate it—I mean loathe with the fiery passion of a thousand burning suns, hate it, but I get it.

Dramatic much? I asked.

Always, she responded, with a little smiley that started with a single quotation mark, like a face with one eyebrow raised. So—no police?

I started to type out my agreement but then I stopped, fingers hovering over keys that were still growing an ever-thicker layer of putrescence. I knew Mackenzie—I was as certain of that as I was of anything. I *knew* her.

And I knew that it made no sense, no sense whatsoever, for her to let something like this go.

I couldn't shake the feeling that her easy acceptance of my secrets was just *off*. Wrong. That maybe I *didn't* know her the way I was so certain I did.

That maybe the one reliable, good thing in my life was just as fucked up as everything else.

And right then, at the end of the day I'd just had, I just couldn't deal with that.

You shouldn't be okay with this, I typed out, quick, jabbing at the ENTER key before I could lose my nerve.

It took her several eon-long seconds to answer. So you want me to go all drama queen on you? I could swear the words looked incredulous. Demand you reveal all?

Well, no. But . . . yes? Because that would be like you?

Gee, thanks.

You know what I meant, I pushed. I mean you have a low bullshit tolerance.

And you wouldn't be playing bullshit games with me, Mackenzie answered. I know that. You wouldn't be doing this just to be mysterious or some crap like that. You're freaked out.

Yeah, well, you're freaking me out more, I admitted.

There was another long pause.

Okay, Mackenzie finally replied. Okay, yeah, I can see that. I'm sorry, but I'm not sure what else to do.

I could sympathize because I didn't know what else to say, where I'd wanted this conversation to go or even why we were having it. I just knew that I'd used up my ability to play normal sometime around noon, and it was creeping up on midnight.

Downstairs I heard the front door opening and closing again. My father called out a greeting. Mom answered from somewhere upstairs, down the hall. Her footsteps padded softly past my door and down the stairs.

Do you want to tell me? Mackenzie asked.

No, I didn't. And yes, I did. The mold on my keyboard was starting to fill in the spaces between the keys, and my right glove was almost entirely green.

Yeah, I answered on the third try, after two shaking attempts to type that didn't actually result in a comprehensible language. My parents' hushed conversation carried up through the floor, but I couldn't make out words—just voices.

I can pretty much promise you I won't think you're crazy, if that helps, Mackenzie offered. Also you're making me feel absolutely like pond scum.

My fingers paused over the keyboard. I frowned in confusion. What? Why? The conversation downstairs had tapered off, and I heard footsteps coming back up the stairs.

Because you're brave, Mackenzie answered. You're all kinds of brave that I'm not.

Why do you think—I started to type.

My doorknob creaked.

Mom—sorry, bye! I typed in a rush, then clicked the little X at the top of the instant messenging program right before the door opened a crack.

"Elizabeth?" A pale sliver of my mother's face showed through the narrow gap.

"Yeah?" I swiveled in my chair and tried to keep as much of

my hair over my face as I could manage. I really, really hoped she didn't want to talk colleges again. That was just going to end badly for everyone involved.

My mom pushed the door open a little more, enough so that I could see all of her silhouetted against the hall light. It was dim in my room, lit only by my desktop lamp and the glare of the computer screen. Mom had a sheet of paper clutched in both hands in front of her—just the one, so not my collection of acceptance letters.

She stared, and I knew that my hair wasn't covering my puffy eyes and my red nose—it certainly wasn't covering my rotting glove. I hoped that she couldn't see around me to the mold-encrusted keyboard. The paper crinkled where her fingers curled into it.

"I—I wanted to ask you about something." Her voice rose in pitch and tapered off in volume as she spoke. A piece of her hair fell loose from its tidy updo and hung down in front of her eyes—just like mine did, I realized, only hers wasn't a knotty mess.

"What's up?" I tried to sound casual and unconcerned but managed only an annoyingly revealing croak.

"This—" She gestured vaguely with the piece of paper, but came no further into the room. The paper made a dry rattling sound in her shaking hands. "This is our cell phone bill. There are a few very, very long calls on here, and an enormous number of text messages that I don't recall sending, and neither does your father, so—"

I took pity on her and interrupted. "Yeah, that was me."

She stopped, her mouth hanging open a moment before she snapped it shut and swallowed rapidly. "Oh. Well. That's—well, that's—who are you calling?" She didn't bother to sound other than terrified. As far as she knew, I didn't have friends—hadn't even tried to make friends since about third grade.

"Someone in my Western Civ class." I shrugged. I think my shoulders shook, but it was hard to tell with how hard the rest of me was trembling, and my mother didn't seem to notice. "Group project. We can't get together, so . . ." I let it trail off into another wobbly shrug.

"Oh," Mom repeated. "I thought I'd worked that out with the school, that you couldn't do things like that, you shouldn't have to—"

"It's fine," I cut her off. "Really."

"Right," Mom tried for a smile and failed just as miserably. "You're such a trooper—you're probably doing all the work, aren't you?"

"No," I said, maybe a little too quickly, feeling a spurt of entirely irrational indignation on Nate's behalf. There was no group project and Mom had no idea who we were even talking about, but still. "No, the guy I'm working with, he's pulling his weight. It's really okay."

"A boy," Mom said carefully. "It's a boy you're working with."

Crap.

"Yeah." I hitched one shoulder again.

"Elizabeth," Mom began. She stopped. Her hands clutched at the cell phone bill until it tore, loudly. She jumped and began smoothing the paper compulsively. "Ellie, sweetie, you know you can't—"

"Yeah." I could feel tears gathering again behind my eyes. I had my hands clutched together in my lap, and I felt the decay spreading from one glove to the other, out onto the leg of my jeans. It gathered in the germs and spores it found along the way and grew in wild, fractal swirls of exuberant potential. I didn't have to look down to know that—I could *feel* it, and besides that, I could see my mother's face. She was going paler by visible increments.

"Yeah, I know. I can't—with a boy. Ever. I get it."

"Okay," Mom said. Her whole body was shrinking away from the doorway, but she hadn't actually taken a step back. "I love you, sweetie." Her voice was whisper thin.

"I should get back to my homework," I lied.

"Of course," Mom answered, and shut the door behind her with deliberate care. I heard her footsteps retreating down the hall, then the stairs. My father's voice again, from the living room. My mother responding. Her voice was still high, uncertain— she laughed a little. My father said something incomprehensible, but the tone was reassuring. Then the TV turned on, drowning them out.

I pulled off my now thoroughly decayed gloves and threw them across the room, trying to swallow down a sob as I stalked over to the stack of fresh gloves by my bedside and used one to blow my nose. It blossomed a purulent yellow where my fingers touched the cloth. I perched on the edge of my bed and left black mildew hand prints where I braced myself.

I needed to get back online—Mackenzie was undoubtedly waiting for me. We were in the middle of quite the important, scary conversation.

I didn't think I could have an important, scary conversation tonight—I was having a hard time just breathing. I crawled into bed bare-handed and with my clothes still on, curling into a ball and clutching my pillow, trying to ignore how it turned pungent and black and how the foam collapsed under my fingers.

Eventually I fell asleep.

By morning the top half of my bed had been reduced to what looked like either compost or a crime scene, but that was more annoying than startling—I'd done that before. The swatch of pale green that wavered in front of my bleary eyes, though—that I wasn't expecting. It swayed from the faint force of my breath as I tried to blink it into focus. It had sprung up where my left hand had lain on its side through the night, my palm cupped around it, right in the middle of the worst of the rot.

Eventually my eyes decided to forgive me for all the previous night's crying and function, and the little green blur solidified into something I could recognize. I sucked in a breath, held it, and stared.

There was a tiny seedling growing out of what had been my pillow, its spindly leaves so bright green it almost hurt to look at it. It was an oak—a tiny, frail little start of a tree.

CHAPTER

Fourteen

dug the tree out of my ruined mattress with my bare hands, a little creeped out by the feeling of dirt and roots and fibrous mattress filling against my bare skin. My hands felt weird, almost
raw, without the gloves, and I could swear I felt the little tree in the
same sort of vague, intangible way I'd sensed Nate the day before.
I had no idea what I was going to do with it, but I knew I couldn't
just leave it there. I headed downstairs with the tree's roots cupped
in my hand, feeling a wobbly, nauseous sort of vindication in the
fact that I was leaving a fine trail of crumbling dirt and half-
decayed mattress bits behind me as I went.

I stopped at the bottom of the stairs. The kitchen light was on.

It finally clicked in my still shell-shocked and sleepy brain that
it was considerably earlier than I usually got up. It was still full
dark out, cold and silent except for the shuffle of feet on the
kitchen floor, around the corner, out of sight. My dad hadn't left
for work yet.

I considered going back upstairs, but then he walked into the
darkened dining room. I must have made some sound, because he
stopped, frowning, squinting into the dark right at me.

174

I knew how I must look, bedraggled and bed-headed in yes-terday's clothes, holding a random plant in one hand. One *bare* hand. What I didn't know was how he'd react. He was a tall, broad-shouldered, austere-looking stranger.

"Oh," he said, quietly, then a little more loudly, "Hey, kiddo. You're up early. What've you got there?"

Kiddo? Really? I felt a spurt of entirely disproportionate anger. What made him think he could give me pet names? Pet names were for people who spoke more than twice in a month, for actual fathers, not strangers who paid the bills and slept with your mother and pretended you didn't exist.

"It's a tree," I said flatly. "I need a new mattress."

"Ah," he said, as if that wasn't weird at all. "I'll call on lunch, get one delivered, okay? Leave a note for your mother."

"Okay," I said, for lack of anything more intelligent to con-tribute.

"Gotta go, kid." I could almost buy the easy way he spoke, the deliberate cheerfulness, if it weren't for the fact that he still hadn't asked where I'd gotten the tree. I mean, it wasn't like I ran around sprouting trees out of nothing (from pollen I'd had in my hair, maybe?) on a regular basis. He knew that. He had to know that.

Maybe he didn't have to know that. He was already leaving, pulling a smartphone out of his pocket and tapping away as he headed for the front door.

"Bye." I shivered a little as the door opened and closed.

I went into the kitchen. He'd left the light on, and the room smelled like coffee. I frowned. Why would it smell like coffee? My parents didn't eat or drink in here, right? Too much chance of contamination with me around, using the dishes, touching the counters, generally being a walking public health hazard. But the aroma was unmistakable. As I watched, a fat drop of water dripped from the faucet, dropping with an audible *plink* into the Tupperware tub full of bleach water. It was empty, but the sponge sitting on the ledge just behind it, I realized, was wet. It was dripping off the edge of the counter.

The sponge shouldn't be wet. My mother used a new one every day, and she would have thrown out last night's after she washed my dinner dishes. She wasn't awake yet. There shouldn't even be a sponge there.

I don't know why I needed to figure this out—did it matter, really? I tried to tell myself that it didn't—but I nudged the nearest cabinet open, careful to touch as little as possible, trying to just prod it with the edge of a fingernail. I didn't feel much of anything there that could grow, but still. My hands felt cold and weird and too sensitive, and about half of me wanted to run back upstairs and pull on a pair of gloves as quickly as I could.

That only made the other half of me want to run through the house touching as many things as possible.

I compromised, and only touched the coffee mug that sat at the front of the lowest shelf, not arranged quite so tidily as the rest of the mugs. It was still warm, and faintly damp. Just washed. I jerked my hand back as if it had burned me. My eyes slid down the counter to the coffeemaker I'd thought no one used.

The round glass pot had dripped a little, just a little, onto the edge of the still-warm heating element. It made a little fan of condensate climb up the side of the glass.

My father had made himself coffee. Here, in the house, in the kitchen that I used. It seemed entirely possible that he did this every morning. I wondered if my mother even knew, thought of that not-so-carefully put away mug, and decided she must.

If I wanted to be stupid, I could have felt good about that. I'm not that stupid—close, I think, some days, but not quite there. Because I still hadn't even seen him in two weeks, and before that, it had been more than a month. I hadn't had a real conversation with him in longer than I could remember, didn't think I could ever remember him picking me up or playing with me or anything at all when I was little. My mother, I knew, avoided me because I terrified her—if Dad wasn't scared, all that meant was that he just plain didn't care.

My handful of tree was shedding little crumbs of decayed mattress onto the pristine marble of the counter.

I was careful, despite the way my hands were shaking and my eyes kept trying to go blurry, as I set the tree down—right there, on the counter, in front of the coffee pot. It wobbled, and I let it tip back against the microwave. I rubbed at my still sleep-encrusted eyes. My fingers smelled like earth and green things, and the hot-then-cold of smeared tears was shocking to skin that was used to feeling the world through a thin layer of cotton.

I went over to the cabinet, pulled out Dad's coffee mug, slammed it down on the counter, then plopped the little tree into it. Then I stood there, looking at it, one hand all covered in dirt.

I suddenly couldn't stand it anymore and scrambled over to the sink, knocking the tap on with an elbow and plunging my hands into the frigid water. I watched little flecks of decayed mattress fall down into the bucket of bleach and float, rise, overflow as the water kept running, and wondered what my mother would think when she saw that.

I wanted not to care. I wanted not to care so, so bad.

I crept back upstairs on shaky legs with dripping hands, dried them with one pair of gloves, and then pulled on another. The sensation of warm, dry cotton wrapped around my fingers was gut-level comforting. I hated that, *hated* it, but I cupped my hands beneath my chin for a moment anyway, fingers between each other to pull the gloves on as tight as they would go.

When I felt steadier, I got dressed for school, despite that it was just past 5 a.m. I paused in the hallway, listening. I heard the low thrum of the heating system working, but nothing else stirring. Mom was still asleep. Satisfied, I gathered my books up, then checked the fridge—there was a plate of eggs waiting for me, cooked up last night and laid out neatly.

It suddenly occurred to me that I had no idea how to cook eggs—heck, I had no idea how to cook *anything*. I was a master at microwave reheating. I wasn't sure that was really a life skill. I bet Nate knew how to make eggs, probably Mackenzie did too.

I ate my eggs cold and drank a glass of milk, then took my tree from the counter and the biggest spoon I could find from the drawer. I couldn't leave it here. I knew, objectively, that it was just a tree, but I didn't care—it was *my* tree, there was no way my mother was tolerating a live plant in the house (it needed *dirt*), and I was not going to let it be thrown away.

The walk to the bus stop seemed longer in the near darkness. The sun wasn't even thinking of coming up yet, but the sky wasn't entirely black. I decided I liked it out there, in the haze and the hush. I'd stayed up to 5 a.m. plenty of times, but I'd never gone outside.

The bus stop was at the end of the street, where our secluded little residential road opened up onto Route 232. It was pruned and sprayed and theoretically perfected for a little rounded space around the sign with the Old English lettering that proclaimed that I lived in Hart's Hollow. Normally I stood on the edge of the pavement, as far from green stuff as I could get without actually being a traffic hazard, hands stuffed into my pockets and trying to ignore the calling of all the unwanted things struggling to live beneath the manicured grass. I made a point of not getting there too early so I wouldn't have to stand there too long.

Well, today I was nearly two hours early, and I walked out onto the grass. The dew soaked through my sneakers. It was the exact opposite of comfortable, but I was determined to relish it. This was what normal people did; they walked through grass. They got their socks wet. I dropped my backpack off my shoulder, ignoring how many germs it'd be picking up on the ground, things I might accidentally set off later, at school, where they might get some of those normal people sick.

The normal people would just have to deal, I decided, sucking in a heavy breath full of cold and the smell of last night's rain.

Beyond the tidily tended entrance of the development the close-cropped grass gave way to taller grass interspersed with weeds, then brambles and trees. The road was wild woods as far as I could see in both directions.

As I stepped out into the weeds, I discovered a weird thing. I felt suddenly and inexplicably better the moment I was outside of the mowed area. This place, despite being outdoors and full of distinctly nonsterile, living stuff, didn't pull at me the way the weeded and pruned and insecticide-drenched lawns of my neighborhood did. Using the bathroom at school without rotting the walls was a million times more of a struggle than standing here.

I was too tired to feel anything more than grateful that this was going to be easier than I'd thought. Maybe later I'd wonder what that meant, but for now, I couldn't think about it too hard. I stopped at what I thought was a safe distance past where the lawnmower would go, then knelt down, careless of the wet patches I was leaving on my knees, took the spoon out of my pocket, and began digging.

When I'd carved out a respectable hole, I carefully pried my little tree out of Dad's coffee mug and set it into the earth. I was getting my gloves dirty; I couldn't make myself care. The entire lack of temptation here was making me feel sort of floaty. It was hard to worry about much of anything. I'd change into my spare gloves when I was done—no big deal. I tucked the tree in carefully, and wished I'd thought to bring water—but the ground was pretty damp. It'd be okay. It looked okay. It looked happy.

I don't know how the hell a tree can look happy, but it did.

That left me with the mug and the spoon. I considered that I had time to take them back to the house, wash them, even dump out the bleach water and replace it. Wipe the counter. Mom and Dad would never know. Also, I'd forgotten to leave Mom a note about the mattress, and I had only the one pair of spare gloves in my bag. I wasn't so out of it that I didn't realize that heading off to school without a spare pair of gloves left was probably not a good plan. It was too risky. Downright stupid.

I felt a faint twitch of movement on the back of my hand.

I looked down and sucked in a breath. For a few seconds, I thought I was going to hyperventilate.

There was a beetle crawling across my glove—a little yellow beetle with black spots. It was smaller than a pea—I don't know how I even felt it there. It was just wandering around, probably trying to figure out what it had gotten itself into. In the dim light I could just make out its antennae twitching. I didn't want to hurt it—it was just a bug, but it still didn't deserve to get turned into a rotting glob just because it had the poor judgment to crawl onto me. But my gloves were wet and dirty and my fingers were starting to tingle. I was exhausted and bugs aren't exactly sterile, and I felt my control slipping.

And . . . nothing happened. The sense of it there, felt as much in the back of my mind as on the back of my hand, sort of flared—it wasn't warm, like Nate had felt. It was bright, though, tiny and very bright. Its antenna had picked up a piece of lint, and it was trying to get it off with one stubby, segmented leg. It wasn't having much luck.

It wasn't rotting, I realized slowly. My gloves weren't even rotting. The bug and the dirt were just there, and the tingly electric sensation I usually associated with rotting something was there . . . and I didn't feel the need to do much of anything with it.

I just stood there for what felt like a long, long time, and all I could think was, *huh. Weird.*

Eventually the beetle headed toward the edge of my glove and the patch of bare wrist exposed before the start of my sleeve, and that wrenched me out of my daze. Letting it walk on my bare skin was probably really pushing my luck. I held my hand up to a nearby weed and let the beetle crawl away. It vanished off into the tangle of green within seconds.

I stared at the weeds and tried to imagine how many more beetles and spiders and things might be right there—maybe even mice or toads or things like that. The weeds were so dense I could be standing within a foot of anything and never know it.

And I wasn't hurting any of it.

I knew that meant something; that meant something *huge*— but I really didn't know what.

For right now, I just took Dad's coffee mug, the spoon, and my dirty gloves, and threw them as hard as I could off into the woods.

The balled-up wad of gloves didn't get very far. The spoon went farther. The mug sailed clear off into the distance, far enough that it vanished into the gloom before it even started a downward arc. I didn't hear it land.

CHAPTER

Fifteen

Two hours is a long time to sit in the cold doing nothing. By the time the bus came my shoes had soaked clear through, I'd reread most of my Western Civ textbook, and I'd texted Mackenzie half a dozen increasingly incoherent apologies for ditching her last night. I got no reply, but that didn't worry me too much—she was probably still asleep, like a sane person. By the time the bus got there, the romance was long gone from my little rebellion, and I was happy just to be somewhere marginally warmer. I lay down sideways on the bus seat. It didn't matter if I was taking up an entire seat myself, no one ever sat with me anyway. I was asleep in seconds.

The noise of everyone exiting the bus woke me up, sort of, when we reached the school. I dragged myself to homeroom, then Calculus, mostly on auto-pilot. Nate was there before me, for once, already in his seat. He frowned when he saw me come in. I hitched one shoulder and sat. He didn't look so great himself. Maybe that would have worried me more if I'd been closer to conscious.

Then I fell asleep in class for the first time in my life.

I woke to a hand on my shoulder shaking me—it was gentle,

but it still sent adrenaline spiking through me. I jerked back flailing. My chair teetered as I blinked, struggling to focus. The hand retreated, and Nate's ashen, worried face stared down at me.

He still looked like hell, I realized, my pulse hammering and refusing to settle. He should have been better today, and he wasn't. He was worse. I could smell the wound even through the bandages, and his whole body radiated a sickly heat.

"You okay?" he asked me.

"Am *I* okay?" I blurted. "Did you take—"

"Yeah," Nate said and shrugged unsteadily. He was shivering, I realized, trembling all over. He swallowed twice before answering, like his throat was dry. "Guess it'll take a day or two for it to work."

"Or it's the wrong thing," I argued, pushing myself up out of my chair and hoisting my backpack. I hadn't even gotten my notebook out, and Mr. Wagner hadn't said a word. "Why are you here? You should be in bed, like, sipping chicken soup or something."

He didn't answer for a long moment, then muttered, "We've got that Western Civ quiz." He turned and walked away. His shoulders were more hunched that usual, his steps heavy and deliberate. "See you at lunch," he tossed over his shoulder.

I blinked at his back as he disappeared around the doorway. We had a Western Civ quiz? Crap. I'd forgotten all about it.

But since when did Nate even care about some quiz? He ditched school more than he showed up. I hurried after him. The crowd in the hall was thin; most of the kids were already in their next class, so it wasn't hard to spot him. It helped that people got out of my way.

"Hey!" He turned toward me, and he was breathing hard just from walking down the hall. There were two spots of bright red high on his cheeks. The rest of his face was dead white. "Lemme take your bag or something. Seriously, you look like—" I almost said *the walking dead*, but I caught myself. "Like you're gonna keel over," I finished awkwardly.

"You're gonna be—" He had to pause to breathe, swallow, breathe again. He was shaking harder. "Late for class." Swallow. Breathe. "Your class is the other way."

"Like I care!" My voice wobbled. I felt like I might cry, *again*—I was so sick of crying, of looking pathetic in front of him all the time, of everything going to shit. "Like *you* care about some Western Civ class. Seriously, let's just go, I know you don't want to go home, I'm sorry, I know you probably don't want to talk about that but you're really, really sick and you shouldn't be here and you don't give a shit about some quiz so—so let's go to my house."

My mom would be home—I'd deal with that later, when we got there, whatever.

Nate was just staring at me like I'd lost my mind.

"I can drive," I babbled, "I don't have a license, but you shouldn't be driving like that, and I've been out driving a few times and it's not that far and—please? Can we just go?"

"What if your mom's home?" Nate asked. I wanted to stomp my foot and scream. Why did he have to think of it too?

"I don't care."

"She'd freak out." He was swaying on his feet in time to his labored breathing and he could barely get the words out. "Right?"

"I don't know what to do!" I could feel my eyes filling up and my nose closing off, tears hovering. We were nearly alone in the hallway now, sharing space with just a few stragglers meandering toward class—the stoners, the wannabe gangstas, some Goth kid with headphones in—all the freaks.

"I'll be fine." Nate gave me a sickly smile and brushed my hair behind my ear. I didn't freeze or pull away this time. I was getting used to him touching me.

His fingertips were so hot they almost burned.

"I don't wanna be a thing that makes you cry," he said quietly, smile slipping, fingers lingering on my cheek. "Smile, okay?"

So I smiled for him, queasy and tearful.

"See you at lunch." He turned and headed for the stairs.

I wanted to follow him, but what would be the point? I started off in the other direction. The bell rang, but I didn't hurry. I was already late. I brushed past the Goth kid, and he looked up as if startled to see someone else there. A teacher I didn't know gave me a disapproving look as she pulled her classroom door shut. A group of boys in pants dragging around their ankles stood in the alcove by the door to the janitor's closet. They eyed me speculatively as I stomped past, as if they wanted to heckle me but weren't quite brave enough. It was tempting to flip them the finger, but I didn't need to go asking for trouble like that.

Then I heard the crash from the stairs.

It was a muffled sound, down the length of the hallway and through the closed stairwell door. I still felt it like a physical blow. Something thumped, rolled, landed with a heavy slap and a crack. There was a cry, weak and strangled and barely human. The boys by the janitor's closet looked up with interest.

I dropped my backpack and ran.

Nate lay at the bottom of the stairs. His backpack had skidded off into the corner and split open, spilling books and papers. He was on his side and trying, with difficulty, to struggle up onto one elbow—he was trying to look at his legs.

From the knee down, his left leg was twisted, his foot lying at a grotesque angle. The leg of his pants had ridden up so that I could see his ankle—it didn't look like an ankle so much as a sock filled with Legos, just a bunch of jumbled, wrong shapes. The sight of it made my head swim. I had to grab the railing as I went down to avoid ending up lying in a similar heap. I heard someone following me, but I didn't know who and I didn't care.

"Oh fuck," Nate whispered. If I'd thought his face was white before, it was nothing to now. "I fell."

"Yeah." I knelt down next to him, hovering. I was afraid to touch, afraid of making the sickness worse but also terrified I might sense him like I'd done before. I felt like the worst coward in the world, but I didn't want to feel what his leg felt like right now. It was hard enough just looking at it.

"I think my leg's broken," Nate observed, utterly devoid of emotion.

"Yeah, I think it is." I heard exclamations from the stairs—the group of boys from the hall, sounding somewhere between nauseous and impressed. I ignored them, even as one of them clattered down the stairs and edged past me and out the door, hitting the downstairs hallway at a jog—probably going for a teacher.

"My leg can't be broken," Nate said, an edge of panic creeping into his voice. "I can't go to the hospital."

"I don't think you're going to have much of a choice." He shook his head rapidly and struggled harder to sit up. "Stop it, don't move!"

"I have to get up, I can't go to the hospital!" Nate snapped. "I can't, they'll find us, they'll put my name in their computer and they'll find us and besides that there'll be police and social workers and all that crap and I can't—I can't let them—ah!" He fell back flat to the floor, panting, tears running down the side of his face. "I can't." I didn't know if he was talking about going to the hospital, or getting up, or maybe just existing.

"Your leg's broken," I said helplessly. "You have to."

"Fuck!" Nate squeezed his eyes shut, mouth twisting. "Why'd I have to fall?" He pounded the floor beside him with one fist, the gesture furious but weak, barely making a sound. "Fucking goddamn—"

"Shh," I said and grabbed his hand. I couldn't not. I could feel the ghost of his pain like the edge of a knife—sharp and cold but not quite cutting into me—and I could feel the swirling hot potential of infection. It wasn't just in his face now; it was everywhere, all through him, in his blood.

"Shh, it'll be okay." My voice was hushed and wobbling. Nothing was going to be okay.

His fingers clutched at mine. "They'll think—they'll send police to my house."

"No they won't," I argued. I could hear footsteps approaching rapidly from the hall. "The school doesn't have your real address, remember? You're not going to tell them, so they won't know—unless, damn it, where's your driver's license?" I dropped his hand and scrambled over him to his backpack and his scattered possessions.

"Don't have one," Nate rasped, lifting his head. He could barely manage that, but he looked suddenly more determined than despairing. "But—" He struggled, face screwed up in pain and shaking hard, to get a hand in his pocket. "Phone."

Right—his phone, that his mother called all the time, from their totally traceable home number. Nate pulled his hand back out of his pocket just as the stairwell door swung open.

Mrs. Gibson skidded into the small space. I had her for English last year. She was young and stern—and at the moment, bug-eyed with panic. Half her class was behind her, and Amber was among them.

Mrs. Gibson swore under her breath and dropped to her knees next to Nate just as he shoved his phone and his keys into my hand. The teacher didn't seem to notice. Her eyes were drawn to his mangled left leg. She sucked in a hissing breath. I pulled my hand up into my sleeve.

"What happened?" Before Nate could answer, Mrs. Gibson turned and shouted, "Go to the nurse, tell them to call an ambulance!" Way more kids than necessary went running—but not Amber. Amber stayed and stared.

"What were you doing on the stairs and not in class?" Mrs. Gibson demanded, like that made it all his fault.

"Was going to class," Nate objected.

Mrs. Gibson gave him a very unimpressed look, but she didn't push the point. "Did you hit your head when you fell?"

"Just tripped, I don't know." Nate tried to shrug, and winced. "Happened really fast." Mrs. Gibson looked pointedly up at me.

"I didn't see; I was going to class the other way, I just heard— I heard him fall."

She looked back down at him—at his bandaged face, his sunken eyes, the bruises on his arms. She had to be able to feel the feverish heat pouring off of him. I could practically see the gears turning in her head, her expression going wary and suspicious. It was, I suppose, pretty obvious that there was more wrong here than a simple fall. It was apparently too much to ask that she not notice.

"Why were you both late for class?"

I shrugged awkwardly. "Just talking."

The look she gave me clearly said that she wasn't buying

it. "He was hurt before he fell. He's got a raging fever. What's going on?"

I couldn't think of a good lie. Her entire class was staring at me, wide-eyed and solemn.

"Whatever you were doing, whatever you're afraid is going to happen if you tell, I promise you, it's not as bad as what will happen if the EMTs don't know what they're dealing with," Mrs. Gibson said. "If you want to help him, you'll talk to me."

She was wrong, unfortunately—so, so wrong. I shook my head mutely.

"How did he get hurt?" Mrs. Gibson pressed. "The first time. His face."

"I can't," I said. I didn't mean to say it, didn't mean to admit that I knew anything, but I had to say something.

"If he hit his head before, or if someone hit him, the doctors are going to need to know that. If he fell because he passed out, for whatever reason, they need to know that. What you're not telling me could kill him."

"I can't," I repeated miserably.

"I just fell," Nate insisted, sounding weak yet angry. He wanted to defend me, even lying broken on the floor. "Tripped. That's all."

Mrs. Gibson didn't even look at him, her eyes still on me.

"If you—" She paused, and her spine went straighter, as if she were steeling herself. "Ellie, if something happened, if you were— you weren't as careful as you should have been, and he got sick or hurt or—"

"No! No, I didn't, it's not like that! He just—he just fell!" I wanted to sound indignant, but what I sounded was small and miserable and guilty. I wouldn't have believed me if I were her.

"He gave her something," Amber called out from the crowd. I stared, jaw dropping. Mrs. Gibson turned to give Amber her attention.

"It's up her sleeve."

I should have done something about her, any one of the millions of times she's tripped someone in front of me, thrown things at me, called me a freak—I hadn't wanted to hurt her, but I should have.

"What did he give you?" Mrs. Gibson demanded of me. "For God's sake, Ellie, if he's been taking drugs, I need to know that! The EMTs will need to know that!"

"It's not!" Nate tried to twist around to glare at Amber. Mrs. Gibson put a restraining hand on his shoulder. It was all too easy for her to keep him down. "It's not drugs, I'm not on fucking drugs." He was breathing even heavier and sweating from just that little effort. "I just fell, that's just—" He scrubbed at his face with one wobbly hand. "That's all, okay?"

Mrs. Gibson didn't comment on his language, she just looked expectantly at me. "What did he give you?"

"It's just his phone," I hurried to say. "And his car keys."

"Don't wanna take them to the hospital," Nate said.

Mrs. Gibson didn't look convinced. "Give them to me."

Over her shoulder, Amber gloated, her eyes catching and holding mine. She had no idea what she'd done, only that she'd done something to hurt me. To hurt Nate.

"Ellie, give me the keys and the phone," Mrs. Gibson repeated, sharp and stern, holding out her hand.

"You bitch," I whispered, eyes on Amber. "You fucking little *bitch*. I should have given you the fucking plague. I should have given you fucking herpes, if you don't already—"

"Ellie!" Mrs. Gibson snapped. I shut my mouth so hard my teeth clicked. "Ellie, you will give me whatever is in your hand."

"No." I shook my head. "It's just a phone." I could hear sirens in the distance, approaching. The hospital wasn't all that far from the school. I needed to get out of there, to get the phone with Nate's home number on it out of there. I glanced over my shoulder out the window, to the parking lot—I couldn't see the ambulance yet—then back down to Nate.

"Love you," he mouthed silently.

It should have been some big, special moment, that I had time to process, that didn't involve so many spectators and so much potential disaster. I should have had a chance to say it back.

Instead, before I had time to answer him, Mrs. Gibson said, "Ellie, whatever you've got there, you're either going to give it to me or to the police—you might as well save yourself some trouble." She stood. I was still crouched at Nate's side, so she loomed over me. She gestured impatiently for me to hand the phone over.

I brought my left hand, the one not clutching the phone and

keys, up to my face. I tugged the glove off with my teeth, then let it drop to the floor. "No."

Mrs. Gibson froze; everyone froze. The stairwell was suddenly silent except for the rasp of Nate's pained breathing. I rose out of my crouch and slowly stepped around Nate, toward the door into the hallway. My bare left hand just hung at my side, but the other kids started scrambling out into the hall anyway, getting out of my way. Amber was one of the first to go.

Mrs. Gibson didn't run. She got between me and the door.

I wanted to scream. Why couldn't she have been just a little more scared, just a little less responsible? I didn't want to do this.

"I have to go," I said. I didn't look down at Nate, now behind me—I couldn't think of how I was abandoning him. I was doing what he'd want.

"No." Mrs. Gibson shook her head, but she sounded much less confident. "No, you can't."

I raised my hand, fingers splayed and elbow tucked against my body. It shook. I was terrified that she wasn't going to move, and I was going to touch her—I was going to do whatever I had to in order to get her out of my way.

"Move," I said, my voice cracking.

Mrs. Gibson shook her head. She took a step back, but she was still between me and the door. Her class had all fled to the hallway. The sirens were louder, sounding like they were right outside. Behind me, Nate breathed, loud and ragged.

I took a step closer, reaching my shaking hand out toward her.

Her eyes were very wide, and I could see her shoulders shaking. "Move," I repeated, then, "please?"

For a long, terrible moment, I thought she wouldn't. I reached closer, closer, closer to her face—bare skin. Bare skin would be better, more of a sure thing than trying to reach through clothing. I needed her to drop fast.

Something in the back of my head was screaming at me, trying to tell me that I couldn't do this, but I was ignoring it. I *had* to do this.

My fingertips were inches from her face when Mrs. Gibson darted sideways, out of my reach. Gasping and shaking, I let my hand drop. She wrapped her arms around herself as if she were cold.

"I'm sorry," I choked out. Then I hit the doors and ran.

Amber was standing midway down the hall.

I skidded to a stop, feeling all the adrenaline in my body condensing into a sharp, hot spike of hate. I'd been ready to hurt, maybe kill Mrs. Gibson, who wasn't guilty of anything worse than trying to do her job—but Amber? I would *enjoy* hurting Amber, and from the look on her face, she knew it. She shrank back until she was plastered against the wall, shaking her head as if her denial could change anything. We were far from alone, half the class hovering a careful, fearful distance away. I knew some of them were her friends. None of them were intervening.

"I didn't mean—" she began.

"Yes," I cut her off, "you did."

She said nothing else, just kept shaking her head. I liked that I'd shut her up. I could shut her up *permanently*. I could reduce her to nothing but a smear on the floor, and it would be so damned easy. It would feel so good to just let go. I knew she didn't deserve *that*, not really, but it was very hard to care.

Outside, the muffled sound of sirens stopped; the ambulance was here.

"Please," Amber whimpered.

"I don't have time for you," I told her and took off running again.

made it as far as the back end of the parking lot—around behind
the building, and away from the police cars and the ambulance—before I threw up. I'd left my backpack, with my own
cell phone and what little money I had, in the upstairs hallway. I
didn't even have my house key. My left glove was lying on the
stairwell floor, and I didn't have another. I'd threatened a teacher.
I'd threatened Amber. I could never go back to that school, ever.

I had to keep moving, or someone was going to see me.

It was still cold outside, and gray. Getting to Nate's car without being seen involved cutting through the gap in a hedge and
creeping along the narrow space between two fenced-in backyards.

Nate's car wasn't hard to pick out. It was the one that wasn't
shiny and new and expensive. It had manual locks that opened
with a key rather than a button. I let myself in just as the cloudy
skies finally opened up. I sat on the driver's side, and I tossed the
phone onto the passenger seat next to me. I put the key in the
ignition, but I didn't turn it. The rain poured down, deafening on
the metal roof over my head, turning the view out the windshield
into an impressionist blur of blues and grays.

I had no idea what I was supposed to do next. Now, I thought, would be an appropriate time to have a total breakdown—this was a nice, quiet, isolated place, good for sobbing. I didn't sob, though the steering wheel began growing a fine layer of pink mold where my bare left hand clutched it. A few tiny, rather demented-looking mushrooms pushed up between my fingers. I felt utterly blank.

Then Nate's phone rang.

I glared incredulously at it for the space of two rings before picking it up. "'Lo?" I croaked, then cleared my throat and tried again. "Hello?"

There was no response.

"Hi? Who's there?"

There was more silence—then, voice high and dreamy, Mrs. MacPherson said, "Nathaniel?"

"He's—he's not here." I swallowed hard, and my pulse picked up step. I'd known it would be her—who else would it be? That didn't make actually hearing her any less terrifying. "It's Ellie, Mrs. MacPherson, remember me?"

"Oh," she said. "Yes, yes I remember you. Such a pretty girl."

I cringed, waiting for her to ask where Nate was.

"I'm hungry, Ellie," Mrs. MacPherson whimpered. "Tell my Nathaniel I'm hungry. I ate everything, I didn't mean to but I'm so hungry—he has to come home, he has to bring me more."

Oh God. Oh God, oh God, *oh God*.

"I, uh—" I had to stop and swallow, my throat suddenly too dry for speaking. "How about I bring you something, okay?" I offered. "Nate's—Nate can't come home right now."

There was another long pause.

"Where is Nathaniel?" Mrs. MacPherson finally asked, her voice rising and wobbling. "Why can't he come home? I need him to come home, I'm *hungry*."

"Nate had to go to the doctor," I hedged. "He's going to be okay, but he can't come to the phone now."

"I'm *hungry*," Mrs. MacPherson repeated, with the edge of a growl in her voice, followed by a hiccuping sob. "Please?" I could hear her crying, ragged and totally uncontrolled, like a child. "Where is Nathaniel, please, I'm hungry!"

Nate dealt with this every day. This was his life. I wanted to throw up again.

"I don't want to get so hungry I forget, please, I'm sorry I ate everything, I'm sorry, please come home, Nathaniel, please come home!" Mrs. MacPherson sobbed.

"It's—it's Ellie—"

"Please!" she all but screamed into the phone, loud enough to make me jump. "Please, Nathaniel, you have to come home, you have to bring me more!" Then there was just incoherent wailing.

"O-okay!" I agreed. I couldn't think of what else to say, what else to do. "Okay, I'll—okay."

Then I ended the call and threw the phone away from me as if it might bite. It bounced and skipped off the cushion to fall down clattering between the seat and the door. I huddled against the opposite door, as far from it as I could get, arms wrapped around myself and trying to stop shivering. The cloudburst overhead had tapered off to a trickle, and my breathing was far louder than the rain.

I had no money. I'd been to Nate's house once; I didn't remember the way; and my phone with its GPS was in the upstairs hallway back at school. Going home and getting money and doing a reverse search on his phone number and plugging the address into Google Maps and going out and buying meat—that was all going to take time. By then, Mrs. MacPherson was going to be in a state where she'd probably just as soon eat *me* as whatever I brought her.

I really hoped Nate had locked all the doors. I hoped she got too mindless to unlock them before she got too hungry to remember why she shouldn't. I hoped their neighbors were all out at work, and wouldn't call the cops when she started screaming.

I had a sudden, awful thought—were they going to call the cops on *me*? Would there be police waiting at *my* house? They'd call my parents at the least, but maybe they wouldn't have time to do that until they'd dealt with getting Nate to the hospital.

I took a deep breath, then pried myself away from the door to sit properly in the driver's seat. I adjusted it for my legs and found the lever that worked the windshield wipers. Foot on the brake and holding my breath, I turned the key in the ignition. The engine rumbled to life and the radio blared.

I slapped the music off and focused on remembering how to drive.

I took a couple corners much too fast, got honked at for going much too slow, and skidded halfway into one intersection, but I made it home in one piece. My mother's car was in the driveway, which, weirdly enough, was actually a good thing. I don't know how I would have gotten into the house if she hadn't been home. I fished Nate's phone out from under the seat and stuffed it in my pocket, then trudged up to knock on my own door, pulling my gloveless hand up into my sleeve.

Mom opened the door in jeans and a jersey with an apron over them and one rubber glove on. Her bare hand held a phone. Her hair was falling messily in her face. She looked like she'd been crying. For a moment I just gaped.

"The school called." Her voice was impossibly high and barely audible. She hadn't moved to let me in.

My shoulders slumped and my stomach dropped, but I just said, "I know." I started walking forward. She moved, stumbling backward in her haste to get out of my way.

There was something bitterly ironic about the fact that my own mother was more afraid of me than some teacher who barely knew me, but I couldn't dwell on that. Inside, the aura of bleach was so strong it burned my eyes; I couldn't think about that either. I just kept walking, heading for the stairs.

"What happened?" my mother demanded behind me. "Ellie, why would you—why—" She couldn't seem to finish the question. I stopped at the bottom step. I didn't have time for this. I really, really didn't have time for this. I turned anyway.

"Why would I threaten someone?" I asked, my own voice rising to match hers. "Why would I act like a monster? That's what I am, isn't it? That's why you can't even talk to me without sounding like you've been sucking down helium, that's why this place smells like it's the Clorox factory, isn't it? Because I'm a monster."

She stood halfway across the room, hands clutched together until the knuckles on the bare one turned white. The door was still open, letting the rain blow in, and her hair was starting to curl up into knotty spirals.

"You're not a monster, Ellie." She was barely whispering, and not coming any closer. "You don't have to be that. You don't—you don't understand, I've tried so hard—"

"Yeah." I flung a hand out at the house around me—the perfect, sterile, bleach-drenched house. "I get that."

"No you don't!" she shouted, coming half a step closer. "You *don't* understand; I'm keeping you safe!"

"From *what*? Myself?"

She shook her head silently, her face twisting up like she was going to start crying again.

"Whatever," I said, my voice cracking. I turned and ran up the stairs.

I had a new keyboard, and my mattress and box spring were both gone but not yet replaced. The bare metal of the bed frame stretched between the headboard and footboard like blackened bones, and it smelled even more strongly of bleach in here than it did in the rest of the house. I knew my mom came in and cleaned daily, but I wasn't usually around to see the process, and I'd gotten used to ignoring it—until today. Today, all my habitual numbness, my ability to just accept that this was my life, had evaporated. I didn't want to be here. I pulled on a fresh pair of gloves and turned on the computer. I wanted to get what I needed and then get out.

I didn't turn on instant messenger, but I emailed Mackenzie. There were too many things to explain and not enough time, but I wanted to say *something* in case things didn't go well with Mrs. MacPherson—but I wasn't going to think about that. It'd be okay. I'd just throw some steaks in the front door, and then . . . and then I'd figure out everything else.

Sorry about last night—I really wish I had time to tell you what's going on, but I don't, I wrote to Mackenzie. Let's just say I'm having a Hogwarts-letter moment. Yay me, right? Right. You've been the best—screw that, you've been the only real friend I've ever had. Besides Nate, anyway. Stay awesome. Don't try to dye your hair black again. Love you. Bye.

I wanted to roll my eyes at my own drama, but if you can't be dramatic when you might get eaten by a zombie, when can you?

Nate's home phone number was listed, thankfully (though still under the previous tenant's name), so finding his address and directions to it was easy.

And then I started packing.

It didn't feel like a decision—it just felt like what had to happen. Like something had broken, or maybe I'd just realized it was never going to be fixed. This was not my life, this bleached, gloved excuse for an existence. I refused to let this be my life.

I didn't have another backpack, but at the bottom of my closet I had an old toy suitcase full of doll clothes. I dumped them out and began loading in as much real clothing as would fit—some socks, some underwear, a pile of clean gloves, and a spare hoodie, and then it was full.

I had some cash and a spare credit card in my jewelry box, along with the keys to my own car. I considered those keys for a moment, but then decided to stick with Nate's. His car would stand out less, and besides, it was his; I didn't want to leave it in my parents' driveway. I took the money and the little keychain-sized card that matched the one I'd left in my backpack in the hallway at school. I had no idea what the limit was. Dad had given it to me for emergencies only. I'd never used it before, though I figured it would buy a bunch of steak. Then I went back downstairs.

My mother was sitting on the sofa waiting for me. She'd lost the one rubber glove and pulled her hair back into a tight, uneven bun. Her eyes darted from the tiny suitcase to my face.

"We need to talk." The words tumbled out in a rush. "Obviously." She gave a strained, half-hysterical laugh and shook her head at herself. "Obviously, we should have talked sooner, and I'm sorry, sweetie, but I just thought—I wanted you to get to have a childhood. A normal childhood, that's all I ever wanted. For you, I mean. That's all I wanted for you, and I know I waited too long, I know that—but we can talk now. Please." She patted the sofa next to her. Her hand shook.

I didn't answer her, and I didn't move.

"You need to know what's out there, why I—you need to know why, I understand that. I know it hasn't been easy for you, Ellie, I know you're lonely," Mom babbled. "I'm lonely too, you know, I can't talk to anyone but your father, and I'm terrified all the time that I'll say the wrong thing to your grandmother and she'll figure it out and—and I didn't know what to do with you, how to train you, anything. I just knew I wanted you to have the chances that I didn't—" She stopped. Swallowed. "I just wanted you to be safe. To be older before you had to face any of this."

I stared at her. She couldn't be trying to say what it sounded like she was saying. She just couldn't.

"Please, honey, sit down." She patted the sofa again, then wiped at her eyes. "Give me a chance to explain."

"You didn't know how to train me," I repeated back, hearing my own voice as if from a distance, utterly devoid of emotion.

"I thought maybe you'd figure it out on your own. I had hoped so." She sounded so pitifully frail and sorry, like the fainting heroine of some fairy tale. I didn't know what to do with that, what it made me feel—didn't know whether I wanted to hit her or reassure her.

I did neither. I just repeated back what she hadn't *quite* said. "You knew I could be trained. You know there are other people out there with powers like mine. You know what I am. You've always known."

Maybe, I thought, she'd deny it. Maybe that wasn't what she'd meant at all, and I was just hearing things, reading into things, because I'd had the morning from hell and I wasn't thinking clearly.

"Please let me explain," she whispered. She didn't deny anything.

"You had seventeen years to explain," I said and walked past her out the door. She didn't stop me.

CHAPTER

Seventeen

I parked in the empty back of the lot of the first supermarket I drove past, car awkwardly angled between two spaces because it was the best I could do, and tried not to think about my mother. I didn't have enough time or enough mental stability left to delve too far into what she might have known and when, what she was protecting me from, why the hell she'd thought that she could give me a normal childhood. What my grandmother had to do with any of it. It was impossible not to think about all the vague but terrifying things Nate had told me and put that together with my mother's delusional overprotectiveness.

Would she have explained, if I'd been willing to stay and listen? She loved me. I knew that. My mother loved me. She hadn't meant to hurt me.

But she had.

I didn't have time to figure any of it out now. Parked in the far back corner of the Stop & Shop lot, I really didn't have time to collapse and start sobbing, second-guessing everything I'd ever thought I knew about my life. I did anyway, just curled around myself in the front seat and trying to remember how to breathe.

The engine rattled and clicked as it cooled and people walked past with their shopping carts and not one person stopped to ask if I was okay. Not one.

Then I scrubbed at my eyes, got out, and went in the store. If my face was blotchy and people stared, well, it's not like people staring was anything new.

When I'd more or less cleaned out the Stop & Shop's supply of steak, I got back in the car and headed toward Nate's house. I stopped at the next grocery store too, and the next. Somewhere between the odd looks the cashiers gave me when I stacked the conveyer belts high with piles of meat and the realization that I was going to run out of gloves before I even got to Nate's house (packages of meat *leak*), I stopped bursting into tears every ten seconds.

The whole situation was really absolutely hysterical from a certain perspective—not from *my* perspective—but I could see the humor. There's a seriously fine line between crying and laughing. I was too drained to do either anymore by the time I pulled into Nate's driveway. It was nearly noon and the rain had stopped, though the day remained overcast and cold. It didn't feel like spring. It was the sort of miserably gray day where it didn't feel like it would *ever* be spring—or maybe that was just me.

I knocked on the door—force of habit, I guess. I knew no one was answering. I waited anyway, watching the neighborhood around me twitchily. My only observers were a few skinny squirrels and the cat in the window across the street. It stared at me. I turned my back and fit Nate's key into the lock with shaking hands. It stuck, but then gave way with a heavy clunk. The door opened maybe two inches. It was dim inside, the curtains drawn on all the windows and no lights turned on.

"Mrs. MacPherson?" There was no response. I looked back out to the street, afraid that someone was going to call the police and report me for breaking and entering, even though I *wasn't*. I had a key. I was invited.

"Mrs. MacPherson, I brought you, um, lunch?"

The house remained utterly silent. Inside it smelled sickly sweet, of mildew and raw meat. I pushed the door open a few more inches, letting a wide swath of gray light spill over the carpet.

There were shredded Styrofoam packages all over the dining room, some of them with scraps of meat still twisted up in the plastic. More meat lay scattered across the carpet in gnawed-on bits and pieces. Little drops of blood were splattered everywhere, heaviest by the entryway to the kitchen but spreading out into the living room, toward the door where I stood—like someone had been pacing. Dripping.

The little dining room table and chair lay in a broken heap beneath the back window, as if they'd been thrown against it.

There was no broken glass on the floor, so she couldn't have broken the window. The curtains still hung closed—they didn't exactly look like they belonged in *Better Homes and Gardens*, but they were *closed*. They'd be shoved aside if she'd gone out the window, wouldn't they? She wouldn't have the sense to put them back in place. Right?

I didn't know. I didn't know what the hell I was *doing*, but I stepped into the house and closed the front door behind me.

My glove stuck to the knob. I looked down.

It was smeared with red. There were bloody handprints all over the door—pounding, struggling, clawing handprints, overlapping and smudging clumsily around the knob and the lock.

I jerked my hand away and stumbled two steps backward, further into the house.

The blood hadn't gone through the glove. It was no different from the thin red that oozed out if you cut a rare steak, I tried to tell myself. It was just exactly the same stuff that I'd been getting on my gloves all morning from the leaking packages of meat—gross, germy, and tempting, but not horrifying. There was no reason to feel like I was going to lose my mind if I didn't rip that glove off *right now*.

All the spare gloves I had left—all two pairs of them, and I was *so screwed*—were out in the car. In my toy suitcase.

Apparently I hadn't *quite* exhausted my ability to be hysterical for the day, because I was making a sound that wasn't really a giggle and wasn't really a sob. It had something in common with gagging, that sound. I wanted to stop it. I couldn't.

I could make myself move, though, and I did. With my stained glove curled into a fist so that I couldn't see the blood, I marched myself across the tiny living room. I refused to look at my feet as I crossed the dining room. Things squished under my sneakers. I wasn't going to think about that. I jerked the curtain open, realizing I'd done so with my right hand—my bloody glove—only after it

was done. I refused to think about that either. It wasn't like the curtains weren't already splattered.

The windows were whole, locked, and relatively clean—free
of blood, anyway.

Mrs. MacPherson had never even gotten the curtains open,
much less the windows or the door, and that meant she was still
in the house.

I let the curtains flutter shut again.

"Mrs. MacPherson?" My voice was shaking and small. I swallowed hard, swallowed hard *again*, then righted the table. I set the
grocery bags down on the tabletop and pulled out a particularly
juicy-looking London broil. I thought of going into the kitchen
and looking for some manner of utensil, but decided there was
very little point. I stuck my thumb through the plastic. "Mrs.
MacPherson, I have food!"

The house echoed.

Something moved upstairs.

"It's Ellie! I'm—" I had to swallow again. My hands kept slipping on the plastic as I tried to pull it away from meat and Styrofoam. "I'm downstairs!"

More movement. I heard creaking at the top of the stairs.
Then nothing, not even the sound of anyone breathing but me—
but then, there wouldn't be.

I finally got the plastic loose enough to pull the piece of meat
free. Its thin blood had soaked all the way through my glove by
now, and I could feel something beginning to grow in the sodden

material despite how I tried to rein it in. The steak flopped and dripped in my fingers exactly like a piece of something dead. I had no doubt that any living person who tried to eat that steak now wouldn't be a living person for long, but that didn't really matter under the circumstances.

I was making that not-laughing, not-gagging sound again.

There was another small noise from the stairs, no closer than the first.

"Mrs. MacPherson, come *on*, please, I brought you steak!" I shouted, then flushed. Hiccuped. Closed my eyes and tried to remember that I should be polite to my boyfriend's mother and also, I should breathe.

"Please come down here?" I called in the general direction of the stairs. "I need to be sure you're still here and you're okay and stuff. Please?"

Nothing.

"Come on, please?" I walked myself and my piece of soggy dead stuff over to the base of the stairs. I was half convinced I was just hearing the house settling and that she wouldn't be there at all, that she was upstairs in bed or something and I was talking to myself.

I was wrong.

Mrs. MacPherson stood at the top of the stairs wearing a pair of blood-splattered floral pajamas. Her feet were bare and blue. Her hands were red up to her elbows, painted in smears and swirls like she'd been clutching at her own arms. There were stripes of

deeper red that didn't look like the thin juice you get from pack-
aged meat. In the dim light they looked almost purple, like thick,
old blood—like she'd dug her nails in. Her pale hair hung loose
around her face.

Lightning shot up my spine at the sight of her, hot and cold
all at once, spreading out through my limbs to the tingling tips of
my fingers. I wasn't afraid. I was so, so far past afraid. I'd been
afraid before. Whatever this was, I'd never been this before, and I
never wanted to be in this state again. I couldn't hear anything but
my own pulse. Every single instinct I'd ever had screamed *run*.

"Mrs. MacPherson?" I locked my knees. I wasn't shaking anymore. *Run*, screamed my hollow guts, *run, you moron, run!* "R-
remember me? It's Ellie. I brought you lunch."

I tried to hold the steak up to show her. I saw my arm rising
jerkily at the edge of my vision and realized that what I was holding didn't look much like a steak anymore. Wrong color. Wrong
texture. Probably shouldn't be covered in crawling white things.
I suddenly remembered that there'd been a fly buzzing around
the meat section at the back of the dirty little corner market
just outside Nate's neighborhood, landing here and there on the
packages.

Huh. Maggots. Insects. I'd never done anything that complex
before.

I flung the writhing thing away from me and scrambled in the
other direction, choking and gagging, tasting bile in the back of
my throat. There was nothing in my stomach, which is all that

saved me from being sick all over the floor.

At the top of the stairs, Mrs. MacPherson began to make a high, unearthly whining sound.

My head shot back up to stare at her. She was one step lower and swaying on her feet—forward and back, forward and back, her glazed eyes staring into mine. There was intelligence there, something aware.

That something was in no way human.

"Mrs. MacPherson?" I whispered one more time, and my body wasn't telling me to run anymore. My hands were raising defensively without any volition on my part—my feet shifting apart, my stomach muscles tensing, bracing for an impact. I couldn't form a single coherent thought, much less a plan, but some animal part of me was still thinking—and it was thinking *too late*.

She spilled down the stairs in a tide of limbs that twisted and lurched in ways that arms and legs shouldn't, but *fast*, so fast. She was screaming when she fell on me. I wasn't. I didn't have time.

Her cold hands closing around my upraised arms propelled me back. My head hit the floor with a hollow crack. She followed me down. I tried to kick but she crawled over me, keening, her knees digging into my thighs and my stomach. My arms were pinned to either side of my head, her hands tightening until it felt like my bones would snap. I couldn't breathe. The weight of her was crushing my ribs, though she'd looked so small before—so small, and pretty, and nothing like the feral creature crouched over me now.

"No, get off!" My feet scrabbled on the carpet. My back tried to arch. My fingers curled into helpless claws as they went numb from lack of circulation. "Stop it, you're hurting me, let go!"

Her eyes held mine, hovering over me, still wailing. Rocking. Glaring accusingly, as if this was my fault. And it was—I never should have come in. Her bloodless lips curled back from white teeth and blue gums as she snarled, her whole face twisting. The pitch of her keening rose, went more desperate.

"Please, it's Ellie," I choked out. My chest burned. The edges of my vision were going gray. I could barely feel my hands. "Remember? Nate's girlfriend. Remember? You're hurting me. Please—"

She gave an anguished shriek and lunged. Her teeth sank into my shoulder, just to the side of my neck. I did scream then; the lack of air didn't seem to matter.

Things get very, very clear when you think you're going to die. I had one last clear thought: *Mackenzie is going to be screwed up for the rest of her life over me disappearing. They'll never find me. There's going to be nothing left to find.*

There was surprisingly little guilt to go with the thought, as Mrs. MacPherson's teeth gnawed through my skin and I felt whatever little bits of sanity I had left drowning in the hot rush of pain—just blank realization. There was a wet slurping noise in my ear, something hot and wet running down over my shoulder. The pain peaked and changed, went strangely distant, as if someone else was feeling it.

Then the wet sounds stopped. I felt more than saw Mrs. MacPherson raise her head. My vision had gone funny, gray at the edges and feeding me only still-frame flashes of what was going on. I hadn't passed out, but I wasn't really all there anymore either. Probably that should have worried me. It didn't.

She made a sound, a different sort of sound—something like a gasp, or a sob. A far more human sound than she'd been making before. Then her weight was gone.

I lay there. I felt the carpet under my shoulder getting wetter. I was cold.

"Oh God, oh Jesus no, no, no nonono*no*!" The anguished whimpers came from somewhere beyond the narrow tunnel of my vision. I stared up at the ceiling, my hands tingling and burning. My stomach hurt. I was really very, very cold.

The whimpering lurched and stumbled off. There were tiny brown spots on the ceiling. Just a few of them. Not as many as there had been on the floor, I thought. When had I seen stains on the floor? I was somewhere that there were stains on the floor. I wasn't really sure where. I thought maybe that was important, like the increasingly insistent feeling of wrongness in my shoulder, or the spasmodic way my gut was twisting itself up, or the thick smell in the air. Copper? I stared up at the ceiling.

Footsteps approached again, faster now, and steadier.

Something was pressed hard against my shoulder.

It *hurt*, and it dragged me back into brutal clarity.

I sucked in an enormous, aching gulp of air and scrambled

backward, fumbling on still half-numb hands, slipping in the wide wet stain of my own blood. Gagging, I grabbed my bitten shoulder, trying to press on it, head swimming at the sudden urgency of the pain. Just *breathing* hurt, my chest aching and bruised.

"I'm sorry!" Mrs. MacPherson knelt where I'd been a moment ago, crying. "I'm so sorry, I didn't mean to, I'm so, so sorry!" She had a bloody dishtowel in one hand—that was what she'd been pressing to the bite.

Her lips were painted bright red. There was blood smeared across her cheek and all the way down her chin.

I couldn't answer. It took me several shaky tries before I could hold my hand out for the towel, which she gave to me. I pressed it to my shoulder, and oh God, but that hurt.

"I'm sorry," Mrs. MacPherson said again, choking on a sob. "I didn't mean it. Oh Jesus help me, I didn't mean it."

I slowly began to register other things, like that most of the slipperiness I'd felt hadn't actually been blood. It was the thick layer of mold that had overtaken the carpet where she'd pinned my hands. Mushrooms had sprung up through it, along with some kind of red-orange fungus that looked like coral and the thin green starts of weeds. There were no maggots left. They were already flies, buzzing around in lazy confusion before drifting toward the dining room. An earthworm, thin and sinuous pink, twisted in the lack of earth.

"God wants to punish me," Mrs. MacPherson whimpered, eyes trained on the worm. "He sends plagues to show me what

I am. Corrupt. Abomination. I didn't mean to, I didn't mean to, I didn't—"

"That wasn't God," I interrupted, as firmly as I could, which wasn't very. My head swam as I tried to stand. Somewhere in there, I'd kicked off a shoe. It was lying halfway up the stairs. I considered retrieving it, but decided that would require way too much effort. And balance.

Mrs. MacPherson blinked her wide, pale eyes at me.

"That's just me." I nodded jerkily down at the patch of her floor that suddenly belonged in some dank cave. "That's my wonderful gift." I leaned down very, very carefully and scooped up the worm with my free hand. My gloves looked like toxic waste, but I figured a worm shouldn't mind. I focused as hard as I could on its little wriggling, blind life, on not hurting this thing I'd accidentally called into being out of . . . what? A misplaced worm egg, a stray worm cell that had come in on somebody's shoe with the dirt? I didn't know, I didn't care. I just didn't want it drying out and dying there in front of me.

My other hand was still pressing the towel to my shoulder, though I had the sickening feeling that I didn't really need to anymore—that it'd probably stick on its own.

"What're you—" Mrs. MacPherson began.

"I'm taking it outside," I said. "It can't live here."

She said nothing, just watched as I wobbled my way back over to the door, opened it, tossed the worm into the damp lawn, and shut the door again. I didn't remember the bloody knob until then, and when I did, I started giggling, staring at it. Right. That had freaked me out, what, five minutes ago?

Mrs. MacPherson was still sitting where I'd left her, hands folded neatly in her lap.

"I'm going to go wash this." I pointed at my shoulder. "There's steak on the table. If you can't open it—" I stopped. I tried to think of something useful to tell her, like—what, where the knives were? "Just figure it out," I said flatly, heading up the stairs. I was guessing as to the location of the bathroom, but it seemed like a good guess. I clutched the railing as hard as my rubbery-feeling hands would let me and prayed not to fall.

It occurred to me that Mrs. MacPherson did a lot of praying too, most of it for things she wasn't going to get. But I didn't fall.

CHAPTER

Eighteen

I didn't know the bloody, round-eyed person in the bathroom mirror.

I pulled my gloves off and flushed them. There wasn't enough coherence left to the material to worry about the plumbing. I washed my face and neck in the sink, the water as hot as I could stand it. The mirror, thankfully, fogged over.

Washing the bite out hurt like all hell, but it wasn't as bad as I'd initially thought. The bleeding was already stopping on its own. It remained just torn flesh, not swelling or festering despite prodding at it with my bare fingers. The faucet and the sink, on the other hand, were quickly decorated with modern-art swirls of mold and bacteria. Zombie bites didn't seem to affect me the way they did necromancers—my abilities and my immunities appeared to be intact. Lucky me.

I heard Mrs. MacPherson's footsteps come up the stairs and tensed, but she kept going past the bathroom, shuffled around a bit somewhere down the hall, and returned downstairs. I exhaled shakily and started looking for Band-Aids.

The medicine cabinet's supply of first-aid materials was

depressingly complete, and made me think of Nate. I hoped he was okay, that some ER doctor had figured out what antibiotic he needed, and that they'd knocked him out before they set his leg. *I'm trying*, I thought at him. *I'm trying so damned hard and I don't know how you do this every day.*

I sat down on the toilet seat and pulled Nate's cell phone out of my pocket. I stared at it. My fingers hovered over the buttons. My neck throbbed.

I put it back in my pocket and went downstairs, shivering a little in my now damp shirt.

It smelled worse downstairs after having been in clean air for a while, and my empty stomach flipped over. Mrs. MacPherson was back to kneeling on the floor, but now her head was bowed, her hands clasped. I could hear that she was murmuring something, but the words were too soft and quick for me to catch. It wasn't hard to guess what they might be. I stopped on the last step, hovering uncertainly.

"I'm sorry," I said. "I didn't mean to snap at you."

She stopped and looked up at me. "It's my fault," she said.

"I'm pretty sure none of this is your fault," I told her. "I need to go out to my car and get some stuff, okay? I'll be right back. Don't try to rush the door when I open it, okay, please?"

She nodded agreement like an overeager child. I tried to walk calmly past her, I really did, but I couldn't help the way my pulse picked up and my breath went a little uneven, sharp pains shooting down my shoulder and my head swimming with a remembered dizziness. I sprinted the last few steps to the door and slammed it behind me.

Outside I stopped. Turned. Pressed both my hands flat to the door. I let my forehead fall forward against it. The paint peeled and the wood darkened beneath my fingers while I stood still, breathing and trying to steady myself. It felt freezing out there, but the grayness had lifted a little and thin sunlight warmed the top of my head.

I could leave.

I didn't want to think it, but I did, the idea taking hold so hard it made me shake. My fingers curled away from the rotting door. I could go home. We'd move. I'd transfer schools. I'd never see Nate again. There'd be nothing to remind me that I'd ever done such a cowardly thing. I'd be safe. I'd make up some story for Mackenzie, and she'd believe me, and everything would be just like it was before. I would never have to be this terrified again.

My teeth were chattering.

I forced myself away from the door and made my unsteady way to the car. My fingers stung as I unlocked the passenger door and reached for the suitcase zipper. I managed to get it open with only a faint haze of green on the zipper pull to show for it. Go me. I pulled on another pair of gloves and slung the hoodie over my arm.

That hoodie was the only replacement I had for my sodden, bloodstained shirt. I was down to a single spare pair of gloves. I was cold and I hurt and I was starting to get really, really hungry.

This wasn't some epic adventure. The world did not depend on this—just one dead woman and a boy I thought I might love.

I closed the car door so slowly it didn't catch. It took everything I had just to push it, as if it weighed a thousand pounds. I bumped it the rest of the way shut with my hip, harder than necessary, and marched back up to the house.

Mrs. MacPherson was standing just inside the door, clutching something small in both hands. I couldn't see what it was; I didn't especially care what it was. I walked around her into the kitchen, just around the corner and out of sight, and changed into the hoodie. Leaving the wet shirt in a heap on the kitchen floor, I went back into the living room.

"You should probably eat something else." I tried to make my voice gentle. "I think maybe you should eat *before* you're hungry? So you don't get . . . hungry." I was trying to be kind. Saying *so you don't turn into a rabid zombie freak* probably didn't fall into the category of "kind."

"You have to tell Nathaniel I'm sorry," Mrs. MacPherson said. "You have to tell him it wasn't his fault. It was mine."

"You'll tell him yourself." She still hadn't asked where he was or what had happened to him. I hated her for that, just a little.

"No, I won't," she said, as calm and sane as I'd ever heard her. "I—I hurt him." Her voice wavered. "I hurt him very badly. He's . . . he's fading. I can hardly feel him at all."

"He's fading? He's—dying?" I felt a rush of electric shock go through my body all over again, my stomach plummeting. "No, he's—he can't be—he's at the hospital, they'll—they'll know what—"

"Not him," she interrupted my babbling. "Me."

"Not—" I stopped. I ran her words back through my sluggish brain. "I don't understand."

"You love him." She nodded, satisfied. "That's good. That's very good."

"You need to tell me what you're talking about," I insisted.

"He's losing control of me."

Oh. *Oh.* Oh *crap.*

"Will you—" I had to stop and lick my lips. I was already backing up a step. "You're going to lose it again." That's what Nate had told me, I remembered, that a bad enough bite from the undead would render his powers null. Without his power to keep her alive, Mrs. MacPherson would die—but not right away, he'd said. Not right away.

"That's what should happen," she said, still so calmly. "What always happens. But it won't."

I blinked at her.

"It won't?"

"God promised me." She held out the thing in her hand. It was a tiny glass perfume bottle, filled with something swirling and dark—too thin to be just blood, too red to be perfume. My stomach twisted and flipped at the sight of it.

"God promised me it'd be okay, if I gave you this," Mrs. MacPherson insisted earnestly, gesturing for me to take it. "But

I'm scared." Her voice dropped to a whisper. "I'm scared to be judged. I've done terrible things."

"It's not your fault," I repeated; the words seemed to have become automatic. I took the bottle of bloody perfume and shoved it into the front pocket of my hoodie, out of sight. "But you have to—you have to lock yourself up somewhere or something, in the basement maybe, or a hall closet? Somewhere with no windows. You have to do it *now*."

"I killed my husband," she confessed.

I stared.

"I told him I'd leave him. I told him I couldn't live with it, I'd take Nathaniel and leave if he didn't stop, didn't get out, so he did, and they killed him. I killed him. It's my fault that they killed him, and I couldn't—I couldn't live with it. I tried. I tried to be strong at first, for Nathaniel, but then I just—I just wanted to forget, and I did, for a while, I'd get so drunk that nothing mattered at all anymore but then . . . then I'd remember. And I couldn't—I couldn't anymore."

Oh God, she could not be telling me this.

"I thought it'd look like an accident," Mrs. MacPherson sniffled, scrubbing at her face with the back of her hand like a clumsy toddler, smearing the tears and the blood. "Like I fell down the stairs by accident, I—I drank so much, I thought—he'd think I just fell. He wouldn't know."

"Don't tell me this," I said, almost inaudibly. "You shouldn't be telling me this, you need to tell *Nate*—"

"But he brought me back." She shrugged and sniffled, and wrapped her arms around herself and began rocking back and forth. "He didn't mean to. It wasn't his fault. He just found me and he grabbed me and I woke up and he was shaking me—shaking my shoulders, screaming at me to wake up, and . . . and I woke up."

Oh God oh God oh GOD, my brain repeated, over and over and over again.

"I shouldn't be scared," she moaned. "I shouldn't be scared, I should have faith, and I'm sorry—tell him I'm sorry." She sank back down to her knees, fingers digging into her own arms, still rocking.

"I confessed. I confessed, so it's okay now. It'll be okay. God will forgive me. But I'm still scared." The words seemed to burst out of her, and then she was sobbing, keening incoherently.

I took one heavy step toward her, and another, and another. I more fell to my knees than knelt, teeth clenched. I did not want to touch this—this thing, this shuddering, bloody dead thing that was somehow also a person. Shouldn't be a person. A person shouldn't ever, ever be a thing like this. But she was, and she was terrified.

"It'll—it's—it'll be okay." I put a hand on her shoulder. "God—"

Had a lot to fucking answer for, letting this happen—assuming He even existed, which seemed like a pretty big assumption under the circumstances.

"God'll forgive you. You'll—you'll go to Heaven. Okay?"

I thought that sounded right. I'd never been to church, never so much as cracked the cover of a Bible or a Torah or a Quran. What I knew about religion, I knew from sappy Christmas movies.

"I'm sorry," she begged.

"I know." That, at least, I could say honestly.

Maybe she heard that—heard that I meant it—because it quieted her. She gave a last, shuddering sob, and then just cried quietly. I stroked her shoulder, my glove dragging awkwardly on her sleeve.

And then she was entirely still.

"Mrs. MacPherson?" I whispered.

There was no response.

I shook her shoulder a little. "Mrs. MacPherson?" I repeated, more desperately. "Mrs. MacPherson?" I begged, shaking her harder.

She fell to the side and rolled onto her back, her blank eyes fixed on the ceiling. Gone.

I sat there and stared. And stared. And stared. I'm not sure when I started crying, my arms wrapped around my knees, and I'm not sure how long I cried. Eventually I stopped, and I stood, and I drifted back up the stairs in a daze. I found the room that must have been hers, full of girlish floral prints and piles of cosmetics and a heavy Bible on the bedside table. There were more perfume bottles on the dresser, like the one she'd given me, but they contained only clear liquid. I didn't look in the mirror. I pulled the comforter off her bed—a cheap polyester thing printed to look like a brocade, full of badly drawn ribbons and mauve roses.

I dragged it down the stairs and covered her.

Nate's cell phone started ringing in my pocket. The phone didn't recognize the number. I flipped it open and croaked a tentative, "Hello?"

Silence. Then, nearly as strange as my own, Nate's voice. "Where are you?"

"I'm at your house." My voice was a fragile, wobbling thing. "How are you calling?"

"The guy in the bed next to me is still knocked out," Nate said tightly. "His cell."

"Oh."

"She's—" I heard him swallow thickly. "She's gone, isn't she?" he asked, voice cracking.

"Y-yeah. I'm sorry. I'm so sorry." I meant it, so much, but the words still sounded trite and hollow.

He didn't say anything for what felt like forever. I could hear sounds—horrible, muffled choking sounds, like he was trying not to cry, like he'd forgotten how to breathe.

"It's—it's okay," he finally managed. "It's not your fault. Did she—are you—"

"I'm fine."

The silence on the other end of the line didn't sound like it believed me.

"I'm fine, really. Are you—?" I didn't know what to ask. He was *not* fine, not even close.

"I'm—" he began. I heard another voice in the background. The call disconnected.

I looked down at the phone and then at the shrouded lump of his mother's body, and went searching for the back door. I found it at the far end of the kitchen and let myself out into the tiny backyard. It was surrounded by a tall, faded wooden fence. There was a dilapidated set of swings in one corner. The grass needed mowing. I went to the swing set and sat on the swing with the least rusted chain, cell phone still in hand.

I flipped it open and dialed home.

"Hello?" It was my father's voice, rough and anxious. My father had come home? In the middle of the *day*?

"Hello? Who's there? . . . Ellie? Kid, is that you?"

I heard my mother in the background, then shuffling. "Sweetie? Ellie?"

I should say something. I didn't think I could.

"Sweetie, where are you?" my mother demanded. She sounded like she was on the verge of falling apart. "Are you there? Ellie?"

I snapped the phone closed. Stared at it. Opened it again, once I was sure it had been long enough that the call had disconnected.

I started to tap buttons, scrolling through menus looking for the text message function. Then I stopped, tapped until I was back on the main screen, and racked my brain to remember Mackenzie's number. I wasn't sure that what I typed in was right, but hell, potentially calling a wrong number wasn't even close to the biggest risk I'd taken today. I hit SEND.

It rang three times before it picked up, and a voice I'd never heard before said, "Hello?"

Of course she wouldn't recognize the number—I wasn't calling from my phone. I swallowed hard. "H-hey, Mack? It's—it's me. It's Ellie."

There was a beat of silence, then, "Oh my God, Elle, you're *calling* me? And what the fuck was that email? Way to give me a heart attack!"

And it sounded so very much, so just *exactly* like I'd thought she'd sound that I started crying again.

"Elles?" she said worriedly. "Spill. Now. Seriously."

So I did. I told her everything.

"Okay, *wow*," said Mackenzie, perhaps an hour later. The sun was fully out now, but the wind had also picked up, and my teeth were chattering as I huddled on Nate's swing set in a hoodie with no shirt under it. "That's . . . wow. I'm gonna go with wow."

"So, going to call the men in the white coats?" I laughed, because I just couldn't cry anymore. I wiped my nose on the back of my glove and nothing happened, that's how used up I was.

"No. Really, Elles, no. You're not crazy. I don't think you're crazy. *You* don't think you're crazy, do you?"

"Working on it, maybe?" I offered.

"Well *yeah*," she agreed. "Seriously, right? But I mean, you're functioning in reality. Too much reality. Über-reality. Karma owes you like, three years of pointless smutty fic and a never-ending supply of massages."

I laughed, and it wasn't quite so strained this time.

"But Elles, my life's not what you'd call normal either." She was abruptly serious again.

"It's not?" It was downright pathetic how hopeful I sounded.

"Yeah. Not. So very not." She sighed. "But we're gonna skip the parts about me for the moment, because this is your breakdown and I need to wait my turn, yeah? When's the last time you ate?"

"Um," I said intelligently.

"Pretty much what I thought," Mackenzie responded. "Okay, so, here's what you're going to do. Go back in the house."

"I don't want to—"

"No, really, you're going to go back in the house. You're going to take little cell-phone-me with you, okay? I've got your back."

"You're in Massachusetts," I argued. "I'm in Philadelphia. Some ass-end-of-nowhere suburb of Philadelphia. My back is nowhere near South Hadley, or you."

"Details. I've got your virtual back. You need to eat or you're going to go all hypoglycemic and crap, which is approximately the *last* thing you need, so get your ass back in that house and check out the fridge."

She kinda had a point.

"I'm going."

"That's 'cause you're brave and awesome, and also *I'm* awesome, and you know I totally didn't think that was going to work. Go dominatrix me, with the orders and stuff."

"Opening back door," I narrated. I choked and coughed at the smell as I went back inside. "Walking across kitchen. Checking out fridge that has been hanging open for the past several hours, so everything in it is probably all warm and gross. There's not much here."

"Well, what've you got?" she demanded.

"Milk that's probably bad now? Remains of lots of meat? It smells like dead things in here. Oh God, I can't believe I said that," I groaned.

"Yeah, yeah, you're a horrible person, whatever, what else?" Mackenzie pressed.

"Jar of peanut butter?"

"Eat that," she ordered.

"The jar?"

"Yes. I want you to take a great big bite out of that jar, especially if it's glass."

"Thought so. You should be a dietician." I took out the peanut butter, found the silverware drawer and a spoon.

"Are you eating?" Mackenzie asked.

"Working on it. I need to—" I tried to balance the phone on my shoulder so I could use two hands to open the jar. It didn't go so well. I hissed at the renewed stab of pain from the bite and almost dropped the phone.

"Ellie? What's wrong?"

"New plan," I said, a bit shakily. "I need to put the phone down to open the jar."

"Tell you what," Mackenzie suggested. "How about you hang up for now, eat some peanut butter, go upstairs and get in your boyfriend's bed, and have a nap before you just tip over. We'll talk again in a few hours, and we'll figure everything out then."

I felt a lurch of panic at the idea of ending the call—of being disconnected. Of being alone. Now that I'd started thinking about food, though, my stomach was rumbling and twisting almost painfully, and she was right. I was somewhere way past exhausted. Lying down (upstairs, away from Mrs. MacPherson's corpse, behind a door I could close and lock) sounded pretty tempting.

"Okay."

"It'll be okay," Mackenzie insisted. "You're strong and awesome and ass-kicking, got it?"

"Um, yeah, whatever."

"Good," she said, and hung up.

That spike of panic came back, but I did my best to ignore it. I shoved the phone back into my pocket, got the peanut butter open, and I ate half of it right out of the jar. Before today, just that would have been almost impossibly strange. My eyes started drooping as my stomach started to feel full. I hauled myself up the stairs, refusing to look at the living room as I passed.

I found Nate's door, opened it, went inside, closed it, locked it behind me. Fell onto his bed. It still smelled like plastic packaging, but also like sweat and old books and Nate. I dragged the comforter up over me, still in my clothes.

For maybe a minute and a half, I lay there wide-eyed and numb and thought that I was never, ever going to fall asleep.

That's the last thing I remember.

I woke to the doorbell ringing. The room had gone dark while I slept, which meant I must have slept for a lot longer than a few hours. I twisted frantically around to find the bedside alarm clock. 9:42 p.m.

Who was ringing the door at 9:42 p.m.? And oh God, there was a body lying in the middle of the living room floor, in plain view from the door.

Then the doorbell stopped. I waited. It was quiet.

I expelled a huge breath. If it was the police or my parents or the supernatural mafia, they wouldn't give up that easy. It had to have been someone selling something, or a neighbor with a lost dog. It was okay, I told myself. I had to keep it together.

Also, I had to pee. I swung my legs over the side of the bed and teetered to my feet and out into the hallway. My mouth tasted like stale peanut butter and lint.

The doorbell rang again. I froze halfway down the hall.

Someone started pounding on the door and hit the bell again, three times in rapid succession.

It couldn't be Nate, could it? He couldn't have been released from the hospital that quickly, and how would he have gotten here?

Nate's phone rang. I jumped halfway out of my skin and rushed to answer it. I didn't want whoever was outside hearing the noise. It didn't occur to me until I had it to my ear that it might have made more sense to just let it ring, as if there was no one around to answer it. Too late now. "Hi?" I said, my voice as loud as I dared.

"Elle, answer your door," said Mackenzie.

"What?" I said blankly. How would she know . . . ?

She sighed. "Okay, let's try it this way."

And then I heard her voice from outside, muffled through the walls, shouting, "Lemme in already, it's cold out here!"

I turned and ran down the stairs. Her tinny voice still emanated from the phone as I stumbled around Mrs. MacPherson's body. The room was dark, but I could hear buzzing; the flies had found her.

"Elles? Did you hear me? Ellie?" Mackenzie asked as I struggled with the lock. "Oh, okay, guess you did. Aren't old doors a bitch? My house is like, about a thousand—"

I got the door open, just a bare crack. "—Years old," I heard in stereo. Mackenzie saw me, grinned, and, with the hand still holding her phone, waved.

"Hi!"

I gaped.

Her hair was a black-cherry red with streaks of pink in it.

Apparently she'd been serious about dyeing over the black in stripes. She was shorter and curvier than her pictures had suggested. She was *here*.

"What?" Mackenzie demanded. "You thought I was going to let you have all the adventures without me?" Then she coughed and grimaced. "Okay, man, wow—dead thing. Major eau de dead thing, yeah. We need to do something about that."

"You're . . . here?"

"No, I'm a figment of your imagination." She winced at my expression. "All right, removing foot from mouth now. You worried me. You shouldn't have to deal with shit like this on your own and what'm I missing—a bunch of classes I could flunk and still graduate? This is more important."

"How did you *find* me?"

"And there's the other half of why I wanted to see you in person." Her shoulders slumped. "I didn't know how to tell you this and have you believe me—which is possibly really unfair, but sue me—so, anyway, showing you."

The phone in my hand beeped. I stared down at it. I had a text message.

From Mackenzie.

So, here's your free demo of why I'm a freak, said the phone.

I looked back up at her, standing there with her phone closed in her hand, fingers nowhere near any buttons.

"Just in case you're considering the possibility that I'm some not-me imposter, and that's the real me texting you from some-where else, it says, 'Here's your free demo of why I'm a freak,'" Mackenzie repeated back. "So. I mean, it says, 'So, here's your'—yeah. You get the idea." She giggled nervously.

I looked down at the phone, back up at her, back down at the phone.

So after I got the heart-attack-inducing email and then the even-more-heart-attack-inducing phone call, I kinda hacked your computer and nabbed your browser history and found this address, said the phone.

She couldn't have typed all that out that fast on a phone key-pad even if she had been typing—which she still wasn't. She was just staring at me, waiting for my reaction.

I wondered if it would be rude to tell her I was all out of reac-tions for the day. Probably.

I'm good with computers, the phone told me. Like, good with computers the way you're good with germs. You so got the cooler superpower. It's really not fair.

"Ellie?"

"I dunno," I said slowly, still staring down at the phone. "This? This is really pretty cool, and nowhere near as gross as what I got."

I looked up in time to see her enormous relieved grin. "Yeah?"

"You totally signed me in to IM that time, didn't you?" I demanded. "Like, a couple weeks ago?"

"You were killing me!" she protested, flailing her arms for

emphasis. "It was four in the afternoon!"

"Nate said he could tell what I was."

"Yeah?" Mackenzie asked. "Huh."

"So you couldn't . . . ?" It seemed too weird, too much of a coincidence.

"Maybe?" she offered. "You were like . . ." She scrunched her face up. "Just . . ."

"Different."

"Like I knew you'd get it," she said.

"Kinda automatic recognition of one of your own," I suggested.

"Exactly! I sorta thought it was a fangirl thing? I didn't figure it meant—you know, this. 'Cause, crazy, right?"

"Huh," I said. "The way he talked about it, I thought it was more kinda . . . glowing neon sign."

"That would be *easy*. You so don't do easy, Elles."

I laughed. "Would you get in here? Um, sorry about the decor." I moved out of the doorway.

Mackenzie followed me in and stopped, her hand still on the half-open door. There was a light just outside—apparently motion-activated, because I hadn't turned it on. Then again, maybe Mackenzie had turned it on. I didn't know if her abilities extended to things that simple. It spilled a yellow swath of illumination through the doorway, across the bedspread-covered lump of Mrs. MacPherson.

Mackenzie went very pale.

I walked carefully around her and pushed the door. Mackenzie let the knob slip from her fingers. If she'd noticed that it was
crusted with dried blood, she hadn't commented. The door closed.
I found the switch next to it and flicked on the inside light.

Mackenzie made a gagging, choking sound and brought a fist
to her black-painted lips.

"Sorry?" I offered weakly. I'd already readjusted to the smell.
It occurred to me that that was probably really not normal, and
maybe I should be worried about my own mental state.

"S'okay," Mackenzie choked out. She lowered her still-
clenched fist to her side and squared her shoulders. "It's okay," she
repeated more clearly. She nodded, as if that would make it so.
"I'm fine. I'm here to help."

"You're seriously the best friend ever."

"I so, so am," she agreed, staring at the body. Then she shot
me a grin. She still looked a little green, but mostly she looked like
Mackenzie, here, and that was amazing enough to compensate for
a lot.

"So. Plan. We should get one of those," Mackenzie suggested.

"Gibbering in a corner isn't a plan?" I asked.

"Not so much. Oh! I forgot, I have food in the car for you!
Chipotle Grill—you like guac, right? Be right—" She turned back
to the door, saw the knob, and stopped.

I could actually see her back spasming as her diaphragm
clenched. Her hand dropped back to her side. She sucked in several deep, audible breaths.

"Maybe food later?" I said, cringing.

"Food way, way later," she agreed.

"Cleaning now?" I proposed. "Um, hauling body to the basement now?"

"Real friends do help you hide the bodies."

———⁂———

Two hours later Mrs. MacPherson had been placed in a corner of the basement with as much reverence as possible, still wrapped in her bedspread. Mackenzie had thought to retrieve the Bible from her nightstand and set it on her chest.

We'd made a half-hearted attempt to pick up the mess and scrub the carpet, just enough so that it wouldn't smell so bad—all but the part I'd rotted, where the weeds had filled out and the molded polyester fibers were starting to resemble earth pretty closely. Mackenzie pronounced that *too damned cool for words* and wouldn't let me touch it. She also did her best to catch the flies alive and usher them outside. It was cold enough out that I thought she was probably just dooming them to a slower, more freezing death, but I left her to it. I hauled myself upstairs and into the shower, first collecting a pair of Nate's jeans and socks. The jeans were going to be too big, but I couldn't go out in the blood-splattered pants I had on now.

I wouldn't let myself think about where I'd be going once I left this house, but I knew we were going to have to leave, and sooner rather than later. It was somewhere between miraculous and really depressing that no one had called the cops about all the screaming earlier in the day.

I pulled on my very last pair of clean gloves as I emerged from the shower.

Mackenzie was waiting for me in Nate's room, his computer propped open on her lap. For a second I was annoyed. That was *Nate's*, and private. Then I mentally slapped myself—so was the bed she was sitting on that I'd slept in earlier, and the shower I'd just turned into a showcase of exotic mildews, and the pants that fit me better than I'd expected.

"I don't think they have Internet," I told her, wringing my hair out with a towel that smelled faintly of perfume and cheap shampoo. I thought that probably should have creeped me out, but it didn't; the past twenty-four hours had seriously raised the bar on what bothered me.

She lifted an eyebrow and smirked at me. "Oh please. They do now."

Oh. Right.

"Did you see a washer and dryer anywhere?" I asked.

She scrunched her nose. "Basement." Then she turned her attention back to the computer. Her one hand was flopped carelessly across her stomach, the other fidgeting with the edge of a sheet. Neither was anywhere near the keyboard, but I could see things flickering and changing in the glowing reflection the screen cast across her.

"That's really cool," I said quietly.

She gave me a brief, pleased smile before waving me off. "Yeah, yeah—go wash things or whatever. This hospital's digital security actually doesn't suck. This is taking concentration."

My stomach did a flip. "You're looking for Nate?"

"No, I'm looking for evidence they're conducting alien experiments."

"Oh bite me," I shot back.

She snapped her teeth together sharply, twice. I giggled. She flipped me the finger.

I went outside and retrieved my suitcase and the grocery bag I'd been stuffing full of dirty gloves. There were lights on in the windows scattered all up and down the street. I could see flickering television screens and the silhouette of a person or two sitting near the window or walking by it, doing who knows what. Normal things. Everyday things. Watching sitcoms. Having a beer.

I shivered, my wet hair an icy blanket down my back, and hurried back inside.

I'd never operated a washing machine in my life, but it seemed pretty self-explanatory. I dumped in a good quarter of the bottle of bleach I found sitting on a nearby shelf and a full cup of detergent. The machine started churning, and the basement started smelling less like corpse and more like bleach.

Like home.

I clomped noisily back up the stairs, stopping at the top to stare at the bundled shape of Mrs. MacPherson over in the opposite corner. It felt disrespectful somehow, the way we'd just taken over her house, but what else could we do?

I still had the little bottle of bloody perfume she'd given me in the front pocket of my hoodie, and my hand slipped in to close around it. It felt warm—from being carried around next to my stomach, I told myself. It was gross; it creeped me out; and I really wanted to get rid of it—but it had been important to her that I have it. I didn't know whether I believed she could be looking down on me now or not. Even Nate, who could raise the dead, couldn't tell me that. I didn't know where she'd gone, or whether she'd still care about any of this.

"I hope you're okay," I told the lump of comforter. "I hope you're not scared or sorry or anything, anymore."

The washer churned. Other than that, it was quiet. The smell of bleach wafted up the stairs and burned my nose and my eyes. I went up the last step, closed the basement door behind me, and headed back upstairs to Mackenzie.

She was frowning hard at the computer screen. I didn't say anything, not wanting to interrupt her, and sat on the end of the bed. She jerked and inhaled sharply when the bed shifted under my weight, blinking up at me.

"Sorry, I was trying to let you—" I waved at the computer.

"This isn't good." She nodded down at the computer, frowning. I shimmied up until I could see. The screen looked like so much gibberish to me, layers of boxes showing a bunch of ever-changing lines of text and numbers that might as well have been in Swahili for all I understood them.

"Okay?"

Mackenzie slapped the lid shut and flung herself off the bed, scrubbing at her eyes. "Somebody else already hacked it—the hospital's records, I mean. There's a worm in the system feeding someone data, and it started transmitting like crazy whoa about twelve hours ago."

"When Nate—" I began, my insides going abruptly cold.

"Bingo," Mackenzie nodded along. "Who, incidentally, doesn't exist so far as the hospital's records are concerned, as of about two minutes ago. I just found him in the system and then poof. No more record that he was ever there."

I scrambled backward off the bed and to my feet, adrenaline already pumping. "We have to—"

"Take you into a hospital? You think you can handle that?"

Oh. Oh God. Oh *goddamnit.*

"Yes," I said.

She just stared hard at me, crossing her arms over her chest.

"Like I've got a choice?" I threw my arms out. "These people killed his dad! We need to go, now!"

For a moment longer she just kept looking at me, weighing and judging and worrying.

"Please?" I begged. "I'll go myself if—"

"Oh like hell you'll go yourself! You think I drove all the way here to let you go by yourself?" She shook her head at me and smiled.

I looked down at my feet. "We need to go *now,*" I repeated.

"Do you, um, mind driving? Because I suck."

"No probs," she said. "You know it's going to be way past visiting hours."

"We'll sneak in through the back or something?" I hovered uncertainly in the bedroom doorway—I didn't want to rush in unprepared. "Could you go back online and find maps and floor plans and stuff?"

She snorted and brushed past me into the hallway. "We are so not doing the low-budget version of some bad heist flick. We don't need to. You clearly have no concept of your own powers."

"I don't?" I said doubtfully, following her down the stairs.

"Nope. When we get in the car, I'm going to dig out my makeup bag and sacrifice a mascara to the cause."

"I'm putting on mascara?" I asked, totally lost. "Um, why?"

"So it can smear." Mackenzie sighed in clear exasperation. "Duh?"

"Not duh?" I retorted. We went out the door and down the driveway to Mackenzie's car—a shiny red SUV that I couldn't recall her ever mentioning owning. Had she taken her mom's car?

"We are cute little girls," Mackenzie said. She pulled out her keys and hit a button to unlock the doors. "We are going to go march our pitiful selves up to the front desk and *cry*."

"That's going to *work*?"

CHAPTER

Twenty

"I cannot believe that worked," I said as we rode the elevator up to the Med/Surg unit where Mackenzie assured me Nate was—or had been half an hour ago, before his records vanished. I could only hope that it took longer to make a whole person vanish than a digital file.

"Why?" Mackenzie asked, squinting at her dim reflection on the steel wall of the elevator and trying to scrub away her smeared makeup.

"I dunno. I've just never done anything like that before."

"Adjust," she suggested flatly.

I sighed. "Yeah, I know." I watched the rising numbers on the box above the doors—three floors to go. So far, being in a hospital—another first for me—wasn't as bad as I'd feared. I'd thought of hospitals as places full of all manner of exotic germs just waiting for me to turn them into the next pandemic. Maybe that was the case inside the rooms, but the long, empty hallways mostly smelled of antiseptic and were considerably less germ-filled than the halls at school. It was a creepy, morbid place, but not an excessively tempting one.

The number above the door changed—two floors left.

"I *would* feel somewhat better about this if we had something that resembled a plan," Mackenzie observed in a very neutral tone.

"We're going to get Nate."

"Okay, yeah, I dunno about you, but I don't think I can be cute and pathetic enough to convince them they should let me just walk out with a patient," she pointed out.

"We'll figure it out." I stared hard at the glowing number 3 over the door so that I wouldn't have to see if she looked worried or scared or like she thought I'd lost my mind. If I saw that, I might start to feel guilty about dragging her into this, and I couldn't let myself go there. Not yet. Not until Nate was safe.

The floor number changed again—one floor left.

"You could wait with the car," I offered.

"And what exactly have I said or done in the three years you've known me that has made you think I'd *wait with the car?*"

I winced. "I'm just freaking out."

"Seconded," said Mackenzie.

The floor number changed. The doors dinged and slid open.

We were directly across from the nurses' station. It was empty. Carts stood abandoned outside of doors. There was no murmured conversation from inside the rooms. I didn't even hear a cough or a sneeze, just the quiet beep of machinery. There wasn't even a janitor or a security guard.

"Okay then, this isn't creepy at all," Mackenzie said faintly.

I stepped cautiously into the corridor. Mackenzie followed

me. The elevator doors slid closed behind us. I wished I'd thought to prop them open; their shutting felt ominously final.

"Shouldn't there be people around?" I asked. There were always people rushing around on medical dramas on TV, but maybe reality was different. Reality seemed to be different a lot.

"Uh, *yeah*," Mackenzie said. She walked around me and peered in the open door to one of the rooms.

"Is there someone in there?"

"Yeah," she responded quietly and stepped into the room. I hurried after her.

There were no lights on in the room, but the open doorway provided enough light to see clearly. An elderly woman lay on the first bed, hooked up to enough machinery for a shuttle launch and breathing slowly and evenly. A curtain divided the room in two so I couldn't see who was in the other bed, but I could hear another heart monitor beeping.

"Hi?" Mackenzie said, raising her voice.

"What're you doing?" I hissed.

"Seeing if she'll wake up," Mackenzie said, creeping closer to the bed. "Ma'am? Hello?" There was no reaction whatsoever from the bed.

"She could be deaf," I offered. "Or in a coma?" I shivered and rubbed my hands over my arms.

"Hey!" Mackenzie shouted, leaning directly over the sleeping woman. "Can you hear me?"

"You're going to scare the crap out of her!"

"No, I'm not, because she's not waking up," Mackenzie pointed out. She reached for the curtain and drew it back. The patient in the next bed over was a heavy-set, middle-aged man, his arm in a cast. He slept just as deeply, oblivious to the noise we were making. His bed was propped up, his head lolling awkwardly on his shoulder. His good hand lay across an open book.

"Think he's deaf too?" Mackenzie asked, walking right up to him and waving her arms around. "Hey! Hello?"

His chest rose and fell at the same steady rate, and he didn't stir.

Mackenzie dropped her arms and turned back to me. "So I don't think that's natural."

"Not so much," I agreed, feeling colder and colder, my heart thumping in my ears. "Can we just go find Nate and get out of here?"

"Yeah, I think that's . . ." Her eyes shifted to something over my shoulder and went very round. She swallowed hard. "Ellie . . . ," she began in a voice that sounded nothing like her, and couldn't seem to finish.

I turned around slowly.

The man standing just inside the door wasn't all that remarkable in outward appearance—dark hair, bland features, and about my father's age. He wore an expensive-looking suit and a dark red tie, and his expression was carefully friendly and unthreatening. I might have bought the act if every hair on my body weren't standing on end, my skin crackling with a cold energy just from sharing the room with him.

Here was as bright a glowing neon sign as I could have asked for. I knew in one look that this man was a necromancer, and a scarily powerful one at that. I would have bet my life on it.

"Ladies," he said, inclining his head in greeting.

I swallowed, and swallowed again, and finally managed a croaking, "Hi."

His lips quirked in amusement. "As you have already ascertained, no one on this ward will be waking for several hours. An . . . employee . . . of mine has made certain of it."

"O-oh," I said, for lack of anything more intelligent to contribute.

"Where are all the nurses?" Mackenzie asked, and I was damn impressed at how coherent she sounded. Then again, maybe she couldn't tell what he was. I looked back over my shoulder at her. Mackenzie's eyes were still wide and her hands were in trembling fists at her sides, but her chin was up and her back straight. She knew. She was just going to be a bad-ass about it, apparently.

"They all felt a sudden pressing need to be elsewhere," the man answered, and smiled. It wasn't an especially nice smile, and though it was Mackenzie he was answering, his eyes never left me. "Was it really wise to bring a mundane?"

I bit my tongue and did my damnedest to keep my face utterly blank. Mackenzie might be able to tell that he was something scary, but he apparently couldn't sense any such thing about Mackenzie.

"She drove," I said, thinking apologetic thoughts at Mackenzie as hard as I could for the haughty, if slightly quavering, tone that I managed.

It was the right thing to say. The man laughed and held out a hand to me. "Lucas Devarei."

"Elizabeth," I said and just stared at his offered hand. I didn't want this man calling me Ellie or Elle or anything else that might imply familiarity, I did not want to shake his hand, and I sure as hell didn't want him knowing my last name.

He raised a brow, but merely let his hand drop and said, "Well, just Elizabeth, you may call me just Lucas, then. If you'll follow me, I believe we have a common interest." He gestured for me to precede him into the hallway.

I wanted Lucas at my back about as much as I'd want a rabid dog in the same position, but I forced my shaking legs to put one foot in front of the other and march me forward, past him, out into the too silent corridor. He followed, gesturing again to indicate that we were walking to the right. I walked. I dared a darting glance behind to see that Mackenzie was following, white-faced and round-eyed and stubborn-jawed.

We stopped five doors down. Lucas indicated that I should go in, and I did.

It was dim in this room too, illuminated only by the light spilling in through the doorway. The patient in the first bed was an elderly man. I continued past the curtain, and there lay Nate. A small, thin figure in a heavy winter coat crouched at his side, hood up, its back to me. Nate wasn't unconscious, but from the confused, disbelieving way he blinked at me, he wasn't quite all there, either. Drugged, maybe—or manipulated in the same way as the nurses?

"Ellie?" His head lolled toward me. He frowned, slow and bewildered. "No, you're not here, you're not supposed to be here, can't be here—" His face wasn't bandaged anymore, I realized with a start, and there was no gaping wound—just a spiderweb of scars that looked years old. His legs, thrashing beneath the thin hospital blankets, moved normally.

"Shhhh," said the figure crouched beside him. It reached a thin, nearly translucent hand up to brush his hair off his forehead.

That figure radiated energy like a thick, pungent heat, something as heavy and liquid as Lucas's power was crackling and cold. Neon sign didn't even begin to cover it. For a second the air smelled of earth and rot and I tasted blood on my tongue, sharp and cloying. It was fleeting, not real, but I knew instinctively what it meant—here was another viviomancer.

Here was someone else like me.

"She's—she's not—can't—" Nate twisted on the bed in increasing agitation. His eyes locked on mine. "Can't be here!" he shouted.

"Hush," the viviomancer said more firmly, her voice childish despite the authority in it. Nate hushed, though his face contorted like he might cry and his eyes never left my face.

The viviomancer stood, her back still to me. "You," she said, "taste of ashes." And then she turned around to face me.

I forgot how to breathe.

She was older than she sounded, maybe a few years older than me—or at least she had been, at one time. I suspected she was much, much older than that now. Her skin was thin and clear like wax, laced through with visible veins. Her head was bald, though she had the finest wisps of eyebrows and long white lashes over eyes that were an opalescent pink, like a white rabbit's eyes. That was the only thing about her that would ever make you think of something gentle. I could see the red shadow of her tongue behind her translucent lips.

"Holy fucking shit," Mackenzie whispered reverently from somewhere behind me, near the door.

The woman's eyes focused over my shoulder, and her smile widened. She tilted her head. "How interesting," she said. She looked to Lucas, who had moved to stand at my side. "I believe I'd like a wig like that."

"This is Audra," Lucas said to me, ignoring Audra's request.

"No," Nate moaned from the bed. "No, no, no, can't be here—Ellie, go! Go!"

Audra turned back to Nate, murmuring too softly for me to hear and tucking his hair behind his ears. It made my skin crawl to see her touch him. I wanted to leap forward and shove her away from him, but I had the feeling that wouldn't end well.

I needed to think, not do impulsive, emotional things that were going to get us all killed—like, say, rushing to the hospital with no plan whatsoever. I thought silent but fervent apologies in Mackenzie's direction even though I knew, staring down at Nate, that if I had to do it over again I'd find myself standing in the same spot.

"Hush, hush," Audra murmured, her fingers lingering on Nate's cheek. "It's out of your hands now. It's already done. Rest." The gesture was almost maternal.

His eyes focused on her briefly, and he murmured, "Aunt Audra?"

"I'm here," she said.

His face twisted up again. "No—no!" he groaned, shaking his head in frantic denial.

I couldn't stand it anymore. "Why is he like that?"

"He isn't certain if he's awake," Audra said, still stroking his cheek, even as he tried to twist away from her. "I had to calm him. He was . . . distraught."

"His mother just—" I began indignantly, then shut my mouth. Damn it, I had to *think*.

"Died," Audra finished for me, her tone utterly devoid of emotion. "In a manner of speaking. We already know, just as we know who and what you are. There's really no use."

"No use in what?" I asked.

"Anything," said Audra, still so calmly.

Mackenzie made a frightened sound that wasn't quite a giggle, quickly smothered. Lucas cleared his throat. "Audra is tending to Mr. MacPherson's injuries, and I have handled the infection in his blood," he said. "I'm sure he's told you much about us, but as you can see, we are neither animals nor demons. We take care of our own."

He is not your fucking own, I thought furiously. "Who are you? I mean—you said 'we.'"

He gave me a long, measuring look. "There is something familiar about your face," he said obliquely, then shook his head. "And yet you ask that question. To put it in the simplest terms possible, we are businesspeople. That's all. The MacPhersons have a long history with the company—back to a time when men were expected to keep their word, and a son was expected to honor his father's contracts."

Nate made an inarticulate sound of protest; Audra began humming tunelessly to him. It might have been a particularly trippy variation of "London Bridge Is Falling Down," but it was difficult to be sure with the way her voice dipped and wavered, high and then low, unearthly. Mackenzie's shoes squeaked on the floor. I looked over and saw that she'd backed herself against the far wall, as close to the door as she could get without being outside of the room.

"What—" I had to stop and swallow, my eyes shifting back to Lucas. "What sort of contract? What do you want him to do?"

"I wish him to take up a position in . . . let's say 'human resources,'" he said. "We're a textile manufacturer, Elizabeth, a series of factories that make shirts and shoes and such. That's all." He spread his hands in a gesture of confusion. I had to admit, that didn't sound so bad.

"You can't hire some other human resources person?" I asked. "He doesn't want to work for you. And he's *seventeen*—why would you want to give that job to a seventeen-year-old?"

"Mr. MacPherson is uniquely qualified for the position," Lucas insisted. "He would be compensated accordingly, if he would only cooperate. You and he could have a very comfortable life."

My pulse jumped at that *you and he*—when had this plan started including me?

When I walked right into this sleazebag's hands and let him find out what I was, I guessed. I wanted to kick myself.

"Uniquely qualified *how*?" I pushed.

Lucas smiled tightly. "I hope you are aware that I'm answering your questions only out of courtesy."

"Murdering bastards," Nate muttered from the bed, words slurring. Audra didn't hush him. "Leave her—let her—Ellie—"

"Audra," Lucas said sharply.

Audra hummed more loudly, the smell of upturned earth hovered briefly in the air, and Nate subsided into silence again.

"Look, it doesn't matter; he doesn't want to work for you." I moved so that I stood between Lucas and Nate. It put Audra behind me, but frightening as she looked, I wasn't as worried about her as I was about Lucas. "Thank you for helping him. If you—" I licked my lips and swallowed and racked my brain for what someone sophisticated and confident and not scared to death would say. "If you require compensation, I can arrange that."

He laughed at me. It was not a nice laugh.

I flushed, and I felt adrenaline shooting through my limbs, but I said, "This is a private room. Nate doesn't want you here. Get out."

"No," Lucas said simply, still grinning.

I stood there. Out of the corner of my eye I saw Mackenzie edging further into the shadowed alcove created by the curtain that separated the room, toward the old man's bed.

Lucas raised a questioning brow. "Did we not think of what came next?" he taunted. "When you issue an order, Miss Elizabeth, it's best to be able to enforce it."

"She's strong," Audra's voice suddenly came from behind me. "Very strong. But untrained."

Lucas made a humming sound of vague interest, still watching me with vindictive amusement.

He's just like Amber, I thought. *He's just the grown-up, superpowered version of Amber.*

"Who said I couldn't enforce it?" I asked. My voice shook. My hand didn't as, for the second time that *day*, I brought it to my face, bit the fingertip of my glove, and dragged the glove off. I let it drop to the floor.

"Am I meant to be impressed?" Lucas snorted. I felt the chill of his power suddenly flare.

And Mackenzie, half-hidden behind the curtain, made a high, pained sound.

I whipped around toward that sound. She was standing by the old man's bedside table, one hand curled into a fist on the tabletop and the other clutching at her chest. I could see the veins standing out on that hand and in her neck. Her skin was going blue and her eyes looked strangely dark—burst blood vessels. Her eyes were filling up with blood. Her face twisted up in an expression of agonized confusion, as if she couldn't understand what was happening, only that it hurt.

"Stop it!" I cried, and rushed toward her, jerking the curtain back. The old man's bed got in my way, and Mackenzie's eyes focused on me as I was stumbling, panicked, around the end of it. She shook her head—just a tiny, almost convulsive movement. *No.* I stopped at the end of the bed. No what?

No, don't try to fight him? Or no, please don't let him kill me?

"Consider this a bit of free education," Lucas said. "A properly trained necromancer, or viviomancer, need not be limited to power over what they touch—which makes your threat somewhat less impressive and more pitiable, really."

Mackenzie dragged in a gasping, gulping breath and lifted the hand on the table just a fraction of an inch.

There was something in her hand.

"Don't," I said, and hoped Lucas thought I was still talking to him.

"I suggest you come back over here and sit down quietly," Lucas replied calmly, "if you're at all fond of your mundane friend."

Mackenzie sucked in another horrible, drowning breath. Her eyes lost focus, but she still clutched whatever it was she had in her left hand. She began pulling that hand in toward her chest, slowly and jerkily, as if it were very heavy.

I could see what it was now—a phone. The old man's cell phone. I had no idea what good that would do her—but she had a plan.

"And then?" I asked, turning to face Lucas and praying between talking to me and choking the life out of her, he wouldn't see what Mackenzie was doing.

"And then, when Mr. MacPherson is well enough, we're all going to leave here without a whole lot of fuss," Lucas explained. "You will be coming with us, and so will your mundane. If you cooperate, Audra will simply erase her memories and we'll leave her at the nearest rest stop. Now, isn't that generous of me?"

"You don't want just Nate," I said. "You want me too."

I should have chosen my words more carefully, I thought, as Lucas gave me a very different sort of appraising look. I wanted to vomit all over him.

"Nate said viviomancers are a lot more rare that necromancers," I babbled on. "I'm worth more than him, aren't I?" Lucas looked somewhere between incredulous and amused, but I made myself plow on ahead anyway. "So take me. I'll come with you all nice and quiet if you let them both go."

"No!" Nate gasped, apparently coherent enough to have understood that. "No, you can't—"

Audra shushed him quickly, throwing a look over her shoulder at me—I thought I saw pity in that look.

Lucas chuckled. "Brave girl, but, no. There is no negotiation occurring here. You and Mr. MacPherson will both be coming with me; the only question is whether your mundane is going to survive the evening. That makes no difference to me one way or the other."

Behind me, Mackenzie breathed, the sound awful and lurching and strained.

I swallowed hard. I didn't dare look back to see what she was doing—what, if anything, she was planning. Maybe there was no plan. Maybe she just grabbed the nearest bit of technology like some sort of cold, digital security blanket. I clutched at the end of the old man's bed, trying not to panic, trying to *think*, damn it, *think*. There had to be *something* I could offer, or threaten.

And there was, I realized queasily. It was right there. They got rid of all the nurses. Put all the patients to sleep. If they let Mackenzie go at all, they were going to erase her memory of them. They needed me to come *quietly*.

Could I do this?

"You're trying my patience, Elizabeth," Lucas said. Mackenzie choked and moaned. "Audra, dearest," Lucas called out pleasantly, "how long does it take for oxygen deprivation to start causing brain damage?"

Audra just kept humming, though the tune wobbled momentarily.

Could I do this? Yes, I realized, yes, I very much could.

"Let her go," I said, my voice a low, shaky rasp, "or I'll kill him." I jerked my head at the old man on the bed. I didn't look at him. I couldn't look at him.

Lucas laughed and shook his head incredulously. "And what is that to me?" He gave a negligent wave in the direction of the bed. Mackenzie's breathing was a constant, struggling whine at my back. "Have at it."

"I'll kill him," I repeated, and had to stop to swallow, to work some moisture into my tongue. The bed creaked as I clung to it and shook. "I'll kill him by reducing this entire bed to a bacterial culture, and rotting his skin, and bursting his lungs when the little grains of pollen inside them grow into trees. It won't be quiet, and it sure as hell won't look like a natural death."

Audra stopped humming.

The smile slipped from Lucas's face. I felt cold power crackle over me.

"Do you think you could, little girl, if I wanted to stop you?"

"Yes." My voice cracked, but I meant it. "You think you can be sure you sucked the life from every single grain of pollen? Every germ? *Every one?* I don't think so."

"You have no idea what I can do," he said. "Do it and your friend still dies."

"You're going to kill her anyway," I said levelly, though everything inside of me was wailing in denial at the very thought of Mackenzie dead. My best chance to keep her alive was to pretend I didn't care.

For a moment he just glowered, and that cold energy swirled around me, biting at me, seeking purchase against my skin and sliding off again. It wasn't pleasant, but he couldn't hurt me.

"I could simply drag you out of here by force," Lucas pointed out. "Leave Audra behind to alter the impressions of anyone who sees."

"Do it and I'll rot everything I touch the entire way," I shot back. "I think it might be hard to alter people's impressions of random forests springing up in the middle of hallways, or walls turning into dirt, or this being ground zero for the next black plague."

I let go of my own power just a little—just enough to make fine swirls of virulent red shoot out from where my hand was wrapped around the rail at the end of the bed. I didn't let it get as far as the sheets, and the human being lying beneath them.

"Idle threats. You won't do it—I can see how attached you are to this thing." Lucas nodded past my shoulder to Mackenzie, and she made a horrible, gargling sound of renewed pain. I flinched. I couldn't help it. Lucas's smile was triumphant.

"You won't endanger a whole hospital full of innocents," he said.

"What innocents?" I rasped out, shaking.

He just sneered at me, and Mackenzie moaned, and the rail under my hand turned black and the threads of red started creeping out over the blanket.

"*What* innocents?" I repeated, my voice raising, going stranger. "What'd you call them—mundanes? You mean the people who have made my life *hell* for seventeen years? The people who throw rocks at me and call me Typhoid Mary and make me have to wear gloves and sit at the back of the room like some sort of dangerous freak? You mean those people?"

I couldn't even recognize my own voice anymore and at some point I'd started crying, but I wasn't bluffing. A part of me meant every word I was saying, and from the look on Lucas's face, he knew it.

"There are two people in the world, in my whole life, who haven't treated me like shit, and you're sucking the life out of one of them and threatening to drag the other off into indentured servitude, so yeah, actually, I'd do it," I said. "Maybe I'd lose sleep over it. Big fucking deal. It'd still be done and you'd still be all over the evening news, so try again."

Lucas wasn't looking amused anymore. His expression was hard and cold as he said, "I'd simply burn the place down. Fire, you'll find, hides a multitude of sins—and no one would ever know how big a tantrum you threw."

And that was it. I had nothing to say to that. I was done. All I could do was just stand there staring, crying helplessly, because I knew he wasn't bluffing either, and it wouldn't even give him nightmares.

"Hey," Mackenzie managed to choke out.

I spun around. She had the cell phone open, the lower half of it stuck into the waist of her jeans so that it didn't rely on her blue and trembling fingers. The little camera light blinked red.

"Who—" She coughed and choked and tears ran down her gray cheeks. "Who're you—" She gagged, gasped, *fought*. "—Calling mundane?"

The room's two television sets, mounted high on the walls opposite the beds, suddenly burst into static-filled life. Lucas jumped, eyes shifting between the TVs and Mackenzie as the static slowly resolved itself to a grainy, waist-level perspective on the room in which we stood. Lucas stared up at his own shocked expression for a moment before he regained control of his features.

Audra stood, slowly and carefully, giving Mackenzie an appraising look. Behind her, I saw Nate's eyes clear, but he remained still and said nothing. Smart plan, I thought.

"Those're—" Mackenzie had to stop and clear her throat, but she was obviously breathing a little easier. Her eyes were still a bloodshot, opaque red, but the color of her skin looked a little more normal. Apparently sucking the life out of someone took concentration, and she'd interrupted the hell out of Lucas's. "—Patched through to every security—" She coughed again. Reached a hand up to rub at her throat, then her sternum, and gave her head a hard shake. "—Camera in the place. And a few video blogs, and every news station I could think of, and, oh yeah, the first three numbers in *your* phone's address list."

Lucas reached into his jacket and pulled out his phone. I could see from here that its little LCD was glowing—transmitting. He jabbed a button—presumably the POWER button.

The LCD still glowed. He jabbed the button again. Again.

The image on the TVs fuzzed out momentarily, then came back, only now it was a close-up of Lucas's panicked face—the view from his own phone. Apparently it was showing on the phone's screen too, because he jerked back as if it had slapped him, then threw it away from him. It bounced and skittered across the floor, spewing bits of plastic and a battery as it went, and the TVs reverted to the perspective from Mackenzie's waist.

Lucas stared at Mackenzie with wide, furious eyes.

Her answering grin was vicious. "Smile for the camera," Mackenzie concluded, and her voice echoed in surround sound from both TVs over our heads and, faint and tinny, up and down the hall as all the other TVs in all the other rooms repeated her.

Then she doubled over coughing and retching—but it was just reaction. Lucas's power was pulled in so tight I could barely sense it at all. He swallowed hard, once and then again, his expression murderous but also afraid.

"Killing her won't stop it," I said quickly. "It'll take some IT guy hours to undo what she's done."

Lucas looked at me, and I think if his power had worked on me, I would have died right then, cameras or no. Instead he barked, "Audra!"

Audra was suddenly at his side, as if he'd jerked a leash. Her eyes were still on Mackenzie. Then they slid slowly to me.

Lucas turned and stalked out of the room. As soon as his back was turned Audra reached out, the tips of her fingers just brushing my wrist.

"*Help me*," said a thin, echoing voice inside my mind. I jerked away in surprise. Audra gave me an unreadable look and followed after Lucas. I listened to the sound of one set of footsteps storming down the hall. Audra's feet made no noise at all. The steps stopped. The elevator dinged. Its doors whooshed open and closed, and then there was silence.

I crept to the door and peered out into the hallway. It was empty.

I walked back into the room in a daze. Nate was pushing himself up to his feet, looking entirely lucid, if not very steady. His hospital gown flapped around legs that shook, but looked whole and the right shape. He staggered over to the old man's bed and slapped a hand down on the thickest bit of mold and rot, and it shriveled. The rotted parts of the blanket just disintegrated. Bit of desiccated mold flaked off the railing and fell to the floor like ash.

You taste of ashes, Audra had said to me.

The TVs stuttered into static once more, and then silence. Someone in one of the other rooms coughed. The old man on the bed grumbled incomprehensibly and shifted onto his side, but didn't wake.

"Okay," Mackenzie croaked. She cleared her throat. "Did we seriously just pull that off?"

I couldn't answer her—my teeth were suddenly chattering too hard. I wrapped my arms tight around myself, trying to stop my shivering. I could feel bile rising in my throat.

"Hey." Nate took hold of my upper arms. I just blinked at

him. "Hey, you're okay."

"You wouldn't have really done it," Mackenzie piped in. "But it was a damned good threat."

I wasn't so sure she was right.

"You *didn't* do it," Nate said firmly. "You're okay. You're a fucking *idiot* and if you ever do anything like that again . . ." He trailed off, shaking his head and running his hands soothingly up and down my arms. "You're okay. We're all okay, but now we've gotta move."

"You're welcome," I managed through the clacking of my teeth.

He grinned, and then he kissed me.

My teeth stopped chattering. I stopped shaking. I may have squeaked, and my hands flailed until they found his waist, and when he pulled back, just seconds later, he looked very, very pleased with himself. Exhausted and half-dead, but very pleased with himself. My lips felt warm and strange, almost tingling.

"A-*hem*," said Mackenzie.

"We've got to move?" I reminded Nate.

"Right. Moving," And we moved.

Twenty-One

introduced Nate to Mackenzie as we went. We stole some scrubs out of a hamper and Nate changed into them. Despite her protestations to the contrary, Mackenzie actually had checked for alternate exits—we found an employee-only doorway to the parking garage and used it. The SUV was where we'd left it, and there was no sign of Lucas or Audra.

"You're sure the freaky chick didn't figure out where you live?" Mackenzie asked, for perhaps the 837th time, as we pulled out of the parking lot. She was up front driving while Nate and I shared the backseat. "Because she apparently pulled Ellie's entire Facebook profile out of your head."

"She didn't," Nate said.

"I don't have Facebook, I'd just get harassed," I grumbled. It's entirely possible I was still a little adrenaline high, and not really focusing on the important points.

"Because it would really suck if you were wrong, and we just handed ourselves right back to them," Mackenzie pressed.

"You can tell when someone's in your head," Nate snapped. "You can tell what they're getting, and no, she didn't even look, because they already had me. Probably she's gonna catch hell for that, but she didn't."

"Kinda weirdly sloppy of her," Mackenzie said doubtfully, as we pulled out of the parking lot.

"It wasn't sloppy, she meant—just, she didn't, okay?" Nate said. "You wanna let me out here and take off, your call."

"We're not going to do that," I interjected. "We're going back to your house. We are. Because—" I stared up at the back of Mackenzie's head and willed her to understand. We couldn't ask Nate to leave without giving him a chance to see his mom. To say good-bye. Even if it was a risk, it was one we just had to take. "Because we're not going to leave without doing that. We'll be quick. Okay?"

There was a significant pause.

"Okay," Mackenzie said, sounding more subdued. "All right. Just make sure they're not following us, okay?"

"Okay," I agreed, while Nate just glared out the window, shoulders hunched, knees drawn up to his chest.

No one said anything for a long stretch of dark road and one traffic light.

"So, Mr. Grew-Up-With-This," Mackenzie threw out into the awkward silence, "I'm kinda curious—what do you call somebody like me?"

"Honestly? If I hadn't just seen you do that I wouldn't believe it was possible," Nate said. He smiled weakly and deliberately relaxed his shoulders. "I'm pretty impressed, actually."

I blinked at him. "Seriously?" I asked. "But—the stuff you can do—and I can do—"

"Is all natural," Nate argued. "Death and life, spirits and bodies, everybody's a little connected to that stuff. Made up of that stuff. But to connect with mechanical things? That's a new one, so far as I know. Why'd you wait to grab that old guy's cell phone?" he asked Mackenzie. "You've got your own."

"Yeah, with a totally traceable number that gets billed to my house, where my mom and my pain-in-the-ass brother live, and however many times I may have told him to drop dead, I didn't actually mean it. These people you've got after you strike me as the sort who like to send messages in corpses."

"Oh. Right," Nate said. We pulled out onto the highway.

"I mean, I'd have done it if there was no other option, but given other options? No. Not doing that to them," Mackenzie said, and shot through a red light. The road was mostly empty.

"You don't have to explain wanting to protect your family," I said.

"Yeah, well, you're family too, Elles," Mackenzie insisted. "Which I guess makes you like family-by-extension or something, Nate. In that 'you hurt her, I beat you to death with a shovel' way."

"Mack!" I squawked, but Nate snorted a laugh.

"S'okay." He jerked his head in Mackenzie's direction. "I like her. And not just 'cause she just helped you save my ass."

"We are ass-saving and ass-kicking incorporated," Mackenzie pronounced.

"What does that even mean?" I objected, but she had me smiling, which was downright miraculous.

"I dunno. It sounded cool," she said and stuck her tongue out at me in the rearview mirror. "So who exactly were those assholes? I like to know whose gory death I'm plotting."

Nate's shoulders went tense all over again. He turned to the window and didn't answer.

"You called the freaky chick your aunt?" Mackenzie pressed. "Is she a vampire or something? She was seriously—I dunno. Seriously something. Wow, did she ever *not* sparkle."

"Wraith," Nate corrected her. "And her name's Audra."

"Wraith?" Mackenzie asked, sounding doubtful. "Isn't that like a ghost?"

"No," Nate said flatly, and nothing else. His hand curled into a fist where it rested on his leg, and he was still facing the window.

"Mack," I began cautiously, "maybe just leave it for now?"

"What?" Mackenzie said, and there was an edge to her tone that made me think maybe she wasn't taking this all as well she wanted us to believe. "We need to know." Her voice cracked on the last word, and she started coughing again. Nate flinched at the sound, and drew back from the window.

"She's right," he said, though he didn't sound happy about it. "You're right." He turned toward Mackenzie. "Lucas didn't actually lie to you—omitted a hell of a lot, but didn't lie. They really do make shirts and shoes. Actually—Mackenzie, could you pull the tag on the back of your shirt up so I can see it?"

She twisted an arm around behind her neck and did so. Nate leaned forward and peered at it. "Yeah, thought so," he said. "That's theirs."

"Would it be overkill to rip my shirt off right now?" Mackenzie asked.

"Yes," I said emphatically.

"They're everywhere, you can't help it," Nate said. "I don't even remember how many brands they've got—it was like two dozen when—" He stopped and grimaced. "When my dad worked for them. Smith-Valens Global. Lucas was my dad's superior, responsible for him—it's why he's so damned determined to bring me in. Losing my dad made him look bad."

"And . . . they make shirts?" I asked.

"Audra's not really my aunt," Nate said, which really wasn't an answer to the question, but at least it was more information. "I mean, not genetically. She just—" He had to stop again. "She was just around when I was little, y'know? So I called her—" He scrubbed at his eyes. "Whatever. It doesn't matter. Yeah, she's a member of the undead. She belonged to my dad."

There was a moment of awkward silence.

"Belonged?" Mackenzie finally asked incredulously. "Like . . . *belonged*?"

"Yeah," Nate croaked. "He didn't treat her like that, though, not like Lucas—oh, whatever, fuck it. Yeah, my dad owned a slave. He inherited her from his dad. My family are bastards who kill people for a living. Is that what you want me to say?"

"No!" I shook my head emphatically. Mackenzie turned her attention back to the road and made no comment. We blew through another red light. "You don't have to talk about it. You don't."

"Yeah, I fucking do." Nate leaned forward, pressing the heels of his hands hard into his eyes. His throat worked, swallowing over and over. I looked away.

"You don't have to—" I started to say, speaking to my own window.

"Just let me," he snapped. "Just—give me a minute, okay?"

"Okay," I winced.

There was another long span of quiet and then Nate murmured, "Sorry. I'm being a dick. I just—sorry."

"It's okay," I said.

We pulled off the highway, turning onto a smaller two-lane road. I twisted around in my seat, making sure no one was following us. There was a lone pickup truck some distance behind us. It reached the road we'd taken and kept going. I strained my eyes to see the driver, who was just barely silhouetted by the sputtering streetlight. I couldn't even tell if it was a man or a woman, but I could see that the person was too heavy-set to be either Lucas or Audra, and was alone in the vehicle.

I kept watching the highway long past the point where I had any hope of making out such details. No more cars went by. I only sat back in my seat when we turned another corner, putting the highway entirely out of view. We were alone on the road now, and the car seemed suddenly much too quiet. Nate still wasn't talking, just huddling against the far window and trying not to let us hear him trying not to cry. I tried to catch Mackenzie's eye in the rearview mirror, but she had her eyes glued to the road in front of her.

"They want me to raise workers for them," Nate finally said. "Like my dad did."

"Raise?" I repeated.

"Yeah," he said. "Raise and . . . prepare for raising." He gave a bitter laugh and shook his head. "That's how they say it, y'know? You *prepare* them. That's a nice way to say 'murder,' isn't it? You can't just go around robbing graves; you need whole, functional bodies. Young bodies."

"My shirt was made by zombies?" Mackenzie asked a little faintly.

"Yep," Nate said, popping the *p*. "Best work force in the world—never get sick, never get tired, don't need smoke breaks. Work 24/7. Of course you have to replace them periodically, but nothing's perfect."

"Are we *sure* ripping my shirt off right now is unreasonable?" Mackenzie asked.

"Hey, your call. It's the same damned shirt it was an hour ago."

"Yeah, that's the really disturbing part," Mackenzie objected.

"Where do they get the—the people?" I almost said "the bodies," and there was something really, really terrible about that. They weren't just bodies; that was the whole point.

"Homeless people," Mackenzie threw out. "Right? It's always homeless people getting kidnapped and experimented on and stuff like that."

Always? Where, on *X-Files* reruns? I didn't say that. She was dealing the best she could. We turned left into Nate's development. I gave the road behind us one more paranoid glance, but it was dark and empty. There were no streetlights here, so headlights would have shown at quite a distance. There were none, only the shadows of houses and cars and trees, undulating in the wind. I saw a flash of eyes, low to the ground, round pupils reflecting back the glow of our tail lights—probably a raccoon. It vanished into a bush before I could make out anything more. We were otherwise alone. I still couldn't shake the feeling that this had all been much, much too easy.

"Sometimes it's homeless people," Nate said. "But they tend to be sick. Mostly it's runaway kids, or people trying to sneak across the border. They'll go overseas—private airlines, of course—to where there are wars going on, take people out of refugee camps. There's always something. The world's not short of people who no one'll miss."

I couldn't think of a single thing to say to that—I remembered giving him a hard time about having hurt one of these people when they came after him and his mom. I'd questioned his morals. I wanted to crawl right under the seat just thinking about it.

"Okay, yeah, plotting gory death," Mackenzie said, and it startled a giggle out of me. "I'm going with 'plotting gory death' as a reasonable response to this."

"Just hope they can't figure out who you are," Nate said. "Seriously, you cannot take these people on, and running—" We were pulling into his driveway. He swallowed hard. "Well, you saw how well that worked for me." He flung himself out of the SUV the second it was stopped, leaving Mackenzie and I sitting inside as he stomped up to the house.

"I have the keys," I said to no one in particular. The light by the front door came on as he approached it. "Is that thing automatic or are you doing that?"

"That thing's a cheap-ass piece of shit," Mackenzie said. "Maybe it's *supposed* to be automatic?"

"Thanks." I hoped she knew I meant it for more than turning on a light. I got out of the SUV and walked up to where Nate was just standing on his own front step, staring at the rotted handprints I'd left on the door.

He was crying, head down and hands shoved in his pockets, shoulders hunched.

"I don't wanna go inside."

"You don't have to," I offered.

"No, I do."

"Yeah." I held out the keys. He took them and opened the door.

The smell wasn't anywhere near as overpowering as it had been. Really it was just a faint whiff of something wrong now, like maybe a mouse had died somewhere in the walls. He still choked and gagged. I suppose, in his shoes, I probably would have too. Behind us I heard Mackenzie getting out of the SUV, then the beep of it locking. I followed Nate into the house, and Mackenzie followed me, closing the door behind us.

"Where . . . ?" Nate asked.

"Basement," I said.

He nodded, and trudged off in that direction. Mackenzie exhaled, loud and shaky, the minute he was gone around the corner.

"So." I tried to make my voice light. "He meet your standards?"

"I want to give you a hug so bad right now," Mackenzie said.

"Me too." We waited as the house echoed with Nate's footsteps going down the stairs.

❧❧

Nate came back up the stairs twenty minutes later—his eyes red and his nose swollen—told me he'd put my gloves in the dryer, and went up to his room. I let him go. Mackenzie and I waited in the kitchen, sitting on the floor with our backs to the cabinets and eating the stale remains of the Mexican takeout she'd brought (separate bags, of course).

After ten minutes or so Mackenzie sighed and pulled out her cell phone. "Okay, and now the part where I risk my life."

"Huh?" I asked.

"I need to call home." She grimaced. "At least, I think I should. You think it'd be better to just show up with you guys?"

"Um, no," I said. "No, I don't think that'd be better."

"Yeah, me either." She stared at the phone like it was a dose of bitter medicine. "I mean, I'm just assuming you guys are coming home with me—you are, right? You're invited. My mom'll be fine with it once I explain. She's going to want to feed you. Like, you're going to gain thirty pounds in two days."

"That won't get her in trouble?" I asked. "Taking me in when I ran away? I'm not eighteen."

She bit her lip. "Well, your birthday's in, what, a month and a half?"

"Yeah," I agreed. I didn't know when Nate's birthday was, but I didn't think he was eighteen either.

"Eh, close enough."

I didn't think the law worked that way, but I had nowhere else to go. I wasn't going to argue.

She didn't press any buttons on the phone, of course. She just sighed and brought it up to her ear, and then I heard the tinny echo of it ringing at the other end of the line. A female voice answered with a frantic, "Mackenzie?!" that I could hear with perfect clarity from three feet away.

"Um, hi, Mom," Mackenzie said.

Then she jerked the phone away from her ear as her mother's shouting dissolved into feedback squeals of static, such that I could only make out a few words—words like "scared to death" and "better explain" and "so much trouble." Mackenzie squeezed her eyes shut and scrunched up her nose until the tirade wound down, then brought the phone very gingerly back up to her ear.

"It was an emergency," she began.

That was the wrong thing to say; her mother was off again. Mackenzie covered the phone momentarily and said, "I'm gonna take this outside."

"Okay," I agreed, a bit faintly. I couldn't even imagine my mother screaming like that.

"Right." She uncovered the phone and tried again. "Mom? Mom! Mom, listen—listen to me! I'm *trying* to explain!" she shouted right back at the phone as she jerked the back door open. "Because there wasn't time! No, I couldn't have! Because—" And the back door slammed shut.

I hoped the neighbors were all sound sleepers. I could still hear Mackenzie's voice through the back wall, though not clearly enough to make out words.

Nate came down the stairs with a stuffed trash bag in each hand and a little kid's Power Rangers backpack slung over one shoulder. He'd lost his bag back at the school too, I remembered.

"Wanna go to South Hadley?" I asked, and held out the bag with what remained of the tortilla chips.

Nate dropped one of the trash bags and dug out a handful of chips. "Where?" he asked, mouth full.

"Massachusetts. Mackenzie's house," I elaborated.

Nate chewed, staring at the floor. I waited. "I'm going to have to just leave her here. Mom." His voice broke. "I can't even bury her."

I had nothing to say to that.

"Somebody's gonna find her body eventually and then—I

don't know. I just don't know." He tossed the bag of chips onto the counter and leaned against the door jam, scrubbing at his eyes.

"I'm sorry." I seemed to be saying that an awful lot. I drew my knees up against my chest and felt something small and hard press into my stomach—the vial of blood. I fished it out of my pocket.

"She gave me this." I held it out uncertainly.

Nate glanced down at it, but made no move to take it. "Is that blood?"

"I think so?" I shrugged awkwardly. "She said I'd need it." I paused. "Actually, she was all talking about God and stuff. I dunno."

He just kept staring at it, expression blank and eyes red.

"Do you want it? Maybe you should have it. I don't know what I'm supposed to do with it." I regretted the words the second they left my mouth. They were true, but they sounded ungrateful.

His head fell back against the door jamb. "I don't know either." His throat worked. "I mean, undead blood, that's got to be good for something, right? You can't buy that at the drugstore. Probably it's one of the million and a half things Dad never got around to explaining and that she thought God would teach me. She was trying, I guess. I guess—I dunno. I don't know. Keep it; she gave it to you. Whatever. South Hadley sounds good."

Then he wandered off into the living room.

I tucked the vial of blood back into my pocket. This was going to be a very, very long drive.

CHAPTER

Twenty-Two

We decided that it would be better to all pile into Mackenzie's car (or rather, her mother's car, I suspected) and leave Nate's. None of us wanted to risk being separated. It was well after midnight and eerily quiet as we loaded the car with as many of Nate's belongings as would fit. There were no lights on in the houses up and down the street, no passing cars, no one awake but us, but I kept feeling eyes on the back of my head.

I tried to tell myself that I was just being jumpy. We'd had the road almost entirely to ourselves for the drive back from the hospital. We would have seen another car tailing us. Lucas and Audra could not have followed us. But by the time I shoved the last trash bag full of books into the backseat the feeling had gotten so strong that I whipped around, half expecting to find Audra standing just behind me.

There was no one, just the swaying shadows of the neighbors' trees.

"What?" Nate asked, slamming the trunk and coming to stand beside me. It was just the two of us for the moment since Mackenzie was back in the house. I hovered near the open passenger door and shook my head, straining my eyes trying to pick shapes out of the dark. It was cold and windy, predictable for the time of year but inconvenient for trying to discern if something was moving up in the tree at the end of his neighbor's driveway. I thought I caught the glint of eyes, just briefly, but then it was gone and the feeling of being watched with it.

"Nothing." I shuddered and shifted half a step closer to the car, planting my feet more firmly in the little puddle of brightness cast by the SUV's dome light. The air tasted like rain again. What I saw was probably just a raccoon checking us out, I told myself, maybe the same one I'd seen earlier. Those eyes, if they had even been eyes and not just a flash of reflected light on a wet leaf, were very high up and out at the edge of the branches. Those branches couldn't hold a person's weight.

I tried not to think of how small Audra had looked, in her oversized coat, or of how she wasn't precisely a person. It was a raccoon, I repeated to myself, just a raccoon.

"I'm just creeping myself out," I told Nate.

"Understandable." He stared out into the dark in the direction I'd been looking.

The door to the house creaked open and slammed, and Mackenzie came down the driveway. "Anybody else need a last bathroom trip before we head out?"

"Let's just go," Nate suggested, still frowning at the trees.

"Okay, what'd I miss?" Mackenzie turned to look in the direction Nate was looking.

"Me being paranoid, hopefully," I said. "But just in case, maybe we should leave? Like, now-ish?"

"Now-ish works," Mackenzie agreed, and climbed into the driver's seat.

I ended up in the front passenger seat watching for exits while Nate and his worldly possessions took up the back. According to the GPS, the trip was about six hours. Mackenzie said that her mother wanted us to stop halfway at a hotel and get some sleep, but Mackenzie was determined to push on through. I wasn't sure further annoying her mom was the best plan she'd ever had, but she was the one driving, and I had little to no concept of how her family operated.

Within an hour we were in New Jersey, which seemed to be made up entirely of long stretches of nearly deserted highway. A handful of other cars shared the road with us, coming and going as we drove by the exits for other major highways. The rhythmic passage of streetlights and reflective mile-markers was hypnotic. Despite Mackenzie blasting My Chemical Romance at deafening decibels and singing along nearly as loudly, I started to nod off.

The GPS said something that was drowned out by the music. Mackenzie reached out to turn the volume down. "Crap, is it telling me to exit?"

"Uh?" I leaned forward and squinted at the little glowing box. "Uh—yes? I think so? If that's Route 287."

"North?"

"North," I affirmed.

"Got it, go back to sleep." Mackenzie shifted into the right lane. I leaned back in my seat, wide awake now. My mouth was dusty dry, and I was hungry, but I didn't want to complain.

"Hey." Nate tapped my shoulder. I jumped. One of these days, I was going to get used to the idea of casual physical contact, but that day was not today.

"What's up?" I twisted around in my seat.

"Sorry I'm being a big emo freak," Nate shrugged at me. He grabbed my gloved hand and squeezed it. "Don't know what I'd do without you."

"You're not—I mean, it's not emo when you've just—it's fine," I finally settled on saying. Mackenzie swung the car off onto the exit, slowing as we went into the sharp curve of the narrow access road. It was wooded to either side and unlit such that we plunged into sudden blackness. The only light came from our headlights and the glow of the dashboard.

"Love you," he said—quietly, but aloud this time.

We still weren't alone, and it still wasn't exactly romantic. The car kind of smelled like three people who hadn't showered in a while, but his hand in mine was warm and alive. If I had to have a witness to this moment, well, at least it was Mackenzie. I could just look at it as saving me the trouble of having to relate all the details later.

"Love you too," I said. I could just make out his smile in the dark. I think I was grinning back.

That's about when I saw the headlights behind us, approaching much, much too fast.

"Mack!" I managed to scream before they slammed into us, the force of the impact jerking my hand out of Nate's as I was thrown forward in my seat.

It wasn't quite enough of a jolt to set off the airbags. Nate shouted in wordless alarm. Mackenzie began swearing, high-pitched and frantic as she tried to regain control of the vehicle, but the car behind us didn't stop when it hit us. It was another SUV, just as big as we were, and it had momentum on its side. With a crunching, grinding screech of metal on metal it pushed us forward, off the edge of the pavement, until the front half of the car slid into the ditch at the side of the road and we could go no further.

"Oh my God, oh my fucking God, oh my—" Mackenzie was babbling.

"Out of the car," Nate suddenly barked.

"What?" I was too stunned to move. I heard two doors open and then slam shut behind us—not ours. The vehicle that hit us. Someone was getting out. Was that bad?

"Get out of the car; run back toward the highway!" Nate shouted and shoved me in the direction of my door so hard my shoulder hit the glass. Then he turned and flung his own door open—and stopped.

"Nate?" I asked.

Someone rapped on the glass behind my head. I jumped and

twisted around. Audra was staring in at me. Her eyes glowed faintly red in the dark, reflecting the scant light just like an animal's—just like the eyes I'd seen outside Nate's house. We'd never really gotten away at all.

"Out," she said.

I shook my head frantically no. Her translucent lips compressed into a thin line, and she backed up, looking out over the roof of the car to someone on the other side.

Mackenzie had gone very quiet, I realized suddenly. I turned.

Lucas stood to the other side of the car, and he was holding a gun. It was pointed at Nate.

"Out," Audra repeated.

My hands shook so hard I had trouble operating the door handle, but I got out. She gestured for me to walk around the car. I did, tripping and stumbling through tall weeds. Lucas had Nate and Mackenzie lined up against the side of the car, Mackenzie looking pale and terrified, Nate murderous. I went to Nate's side.

"Hello again, Miss Elizabeth," said Lucas.

"Go to hell." My voice shook but my chin was up. I was pretty sure I was going to die, might as well do it with some style.

"Eventually," Lucas agreed, sounding entirely untroubled. "Now, this is much better, isn't it? Of course, modern technology being what it is, we still must take steps to assure our privacy even in such a remote location as this. Your phones, if you please—just toss them on the ground."

"F-fuck you," Mackenzie said.

The sound of the gun firing was deafening. The SUV's window shattered behind Mackenzie's head. She jumped and screamed, her hair and her shoulders glittering with shards of glass.

Then there was only the hushed sound of traffic passing on the highway behind us. It continued on uninterrupted, around the curve of the road and out of sight, as if she'd never screamed at all.

"Your phones, please," Lucas repeated pleasantly.

I pulled Nate's phone out of my pocket and threw it at Lucas's feet. It took Mackenzie three tries to do the same, her hands shaking so hard she had trouble getting them into the pockets of her tight jeans. She was crying and not bothering to hide it, just shuddering and sobbing like a scared little kid.

"I don't have one." Nate nodded at the phone I'd already thrown on the ground. "That's mine. Hers got left at school."

"Check him," Lucas said, and Audra glided over to him without hesitation, her hands running perfunctorily up and down his sides. She was shorter than him by nearly a foot and kept her eyes trained on his stomach, never looking him in the face.

"It's not your fault, Aunt Audra," Nate murmured, holding his hands out and letting her pat up and down his sleeves.

"What's fault?" Audra wouldn't meet his eyes. "Silly words for silly children. He has nothing," she turned and said to Lucas.

I curled my arms around myself and shivered. I felt a hard lump in the front pocket of my hoodie. The bottle of bloody perfume, I remembered—the one that God had supposedly told

Mrs. MacPherson I needed. Maybe I could throw it at Lucas, I thought. Maybe I'd hit him in the eye and he'd just topple over like a bad cartoon.

Audra picked up both cell phones and snapped them in half with her bare hands, then tossed their remains into the woods behind her.

"Now," Lucas said, "let's try this again. You are all going to be coming with us—most especially you, young lady." He nodded at Mackenzie. "What an interesting talent you have—so potentially useful."

"I will die," Mackenzie said, her voice guttural low and determined, "before I ever work for you."

"Likely," Lucas agreed, and smiled at her. "Audra? If you'll handle Miss Elizabeth, please?"

I had a horrible moment to wonder, tense and prepared to fight, what exactly "handle" meant. Then Audra produced a pair of heavy rubber gloves and a set of handcuffs from the pocket of her voluminous coat.

"Audra can simply render these two unconscious, but she tells me you are too strong for her," Lucas said, tilting his head at me as if this was all just fascinating—not terribly important, but fascinating. "But since your abilities are limited to touch, well, we'll just have to limit what you may touch. Audra?"

She walked forward two steps and stopped, staring hard at me. I stared back, and her red eyes bore into mine. I could easily imagine that she could see right into my skull.

"Audra!" Lucas snapped, and Audra's expression went disappointed and resigned. She'd been trying to communicate something to me, and she'd failed.

What had she wanted me to know? Could she help us? I didn't think so. She seemed to be completely in Lucas's thrall.

Audra took another step toward me, and got a strange glint in her eye. She tossed the gloves and the handcuffs on the ground at my feet.

"Pick those up," Audra ordered. "Put them on."

I didn't get it. I was sure that she was trying to help as much as she could. She was giving me something, but I didn't know what it was. I bent slowly, racking my panicked brain for any hint as to what she intended me to do. What could I do with a set of cuffs and a pair of rubber gloves?

Help me, I thought—at Audra, at Nate, at the God who hadn't answered Mrs. MacPherson, at any power out there that might be listening. *Help me, please, tell me what to do!* I reached down as slowly as I could—and as my gloved fingertips touched the earth, something *answered.*

It was like the weeds and the trees and the ground beneath my feet were speaking to me. I understood immediately that it wasn't the gloves or the cuffs that Audra wanted me to use. She'd wanted me, shaken and desperate and open to anything, to touch the ground. To feel *this.*

Something that wasn't quite a voice whispered around me, over me, in the back of my head.

It said *let go*, and I did.

It was like jolting out of a dream—that moment when the dream world goes hazy, stops making sense, and the real world is too sharp, too bright, too loud. I could feel every living thing around us, from the trees to individual bacteria, each of them singular and unique and bright, blinding, discordant, and deafening for less than a breath—and then they began to pull together.

Sparks, turning into a single blaze. Voices forming a harmony. I was the tuning fork, and this, this was my symphony. Nothing in my life had ever felt so right, so *easy*.

Lucas gave a shout, Mackenzie was screaming again, and the air was choked with dust—I didn't understand why at first, didn't connect my sudden kinship with the roots of the trees with the way the ground all around us was churning. Nate scrambled back up onto the hood of Lucas's car, and Audra . . . Audra just stood there, smiling grimly, as vines shot up out of the earth and saplings grew and twisted in fractions of a second, all of them bent toward Lucas.

All of them tuned to my desperate prayer: *Help me.*

Lucas swung the barrel of the gun toward me and fired, but a vine grabbed his wrist and the shot went wide. More vines twisted around his arms, his legs; the branches of the trees caged him. Ants swarmed up out of the ground, pouring over him. Other insects flew around his head, unidentifiable in the dark. Some sort of fungus began sprouting out of his expensive suit and his face reddened with something that shriveled and crackled his skin. His furious screaming went hoarse and choked. I saw larger things gathering back in the trees, though I couldn't quite see what they were—just eyes, dozens of eyes gleaming out at me in the glow of the headlights.

A bright red fox broke from the cover of the undergrowth and dashed in to snap at Lucas's ankles. Blood ran down over his shoe and painted the fox's muzzle. It turned and looked at me, licked its lips, and whined like a dog.

I rose slowly out of my crouch, breathing deep and feeling the blood pumping through my heart, the breath in my lungs, every inch of my skin.

I could feel all of it, flowing and entwined and rushing in my veins like liquid light, so much life, so much power. What I was doing didn't require effort or concentration or force of will—all I had to do was stop holding back. I smelled earth and storms and pennies, copper pennies on my tongue and something wet and burning running through my hands like silk, all around me and in me. It was amazing and ecstatic and as natural as breathing. I still had my gloves on. It didn't matter at all.

Lucas had gotten over his surprise and started fighting back. Branches blackened and cracked away dead where he grabbed them. Ants fell from him like dust, and I felt each one of them like a light going out, a tiny firecracker burst of hot and cold, and then nothing. It didn't matter. There were more. Lucas's cold power lashed out toward the fox that still sat there begging my approval. I reached for it, heat crashing into cold, the impact jarring up my spine. The fox yelped and danced away. It hovered a few feet back and growled, and Lucas couldn't touch it. I pushed forward, pushed Lucas's power back.

"Oh my God," Mackenzie was whispering, not crying anymore, just standing there staring in paralyzed shock. "Oh my *God*, Elle."

"Keep going," Nate said from behind me, though he didn't need to tell me that. I couldn't have stopped if I wanted to—not that I wanted to.

The branches were bearing Lucas down to the ground, roots reaching up and growing in a thick tangle over him. The gun had fallen from his hand. "Audra!" he managed to call out before a vine wrapped itself around his throat. His head jerked backward, and he was silent.

"Finish it!" Audra said, and something in her tone made me turn and look at her. She didn't look so calm anymore. She was standing with her hands in shaking fists at her sides, her eyes tight shut. "He's trying to compel me to fight you. He's not dead yet. You need to break the bond, or I'll have to do what he wants. It's taking everything I have to hold back."

I heard the words, but my brain refused to make sense of them. Kill him? "No—no, I can't—" I tried to protest. I wasn't going to kill anyone. I couldn't do that, not like this, not when he was already on the ground, defeated. But I could recognize in a very distant, detached sort of way that Lucas was going to be very dead, very soon, if I didn't stop—and I really didn't want to stop.

"Now!" Audra shrieked, stumbling toward me in a way that didn't look voluntary.

I stumbled away from her. The perfume bottle in the front pocket of my hoodie swung and thumped back against my stomach.

And I knew what I needed to do.

The tangle of new trees that surrounded Lucas twisted and groaned out of my way as I approached. I knelt on his vine-covered chest and grabbed his nose with my left hand. With my right I pulled out the perfume bottle and flicked the cap off. He gasped for air, mouth opening. I poured Mrs. MacPherson's dead blood down his throat.

He choked and struggled and tried to spit, but he swallowed some of it, and I felt his power die away almost instantly. There was only the pungent heat of my own energy around me, settling into a contented lull.

Lucas blinked up at me, too terrified to try to charm or snarl, just wide-eyed and utterly at my mercy. He was struggling to breathe, probably because there was a vine around his throat and I was still crouched on his chest. He said nothing—what was he going to say? He was a monster, and I knew it, and it would be so, so easy to just *end* him. To reach out, just a little, and let all the simpler things around him and in him take my power and feed and grow. Bacteria or fungus or insects or weeds—they were inno-cent. They'd helped me. They hadn't threatened people I loved. Why shouldn't I reward them with this piece of meat, this thing that didn't deserve to live?

I pulled off my gloves and felt the power washing over my bare skin, and it was glorious. Lucas saw it, tracking my movements with wide-blown pupils, his lips starting to go purple. I liked that.

I *liked that.*

There was something wrong with that, wasn't there? It was hard to remember. It felt so *good.*

"Elle?" Mackenzie's voice came, soft and scared, over my shoulder. Was she scared of me?

Why was she scared of me?

"You don't have to do it," Nate said, squeezing between the trees and crouching down, putting himself in my line of sight. He nodded down at Lucas. "I'll finish it. It doesn't have to be you."

But I *wanted* it to be me. I could do it. I was strong, powerful—I didn't have to justify myself to anyone.

Lucas was still watching me silently with round eyes, his lips going ever paler. Maybe he couldn't get enough air to speak. I'd never seen someone look so afraid—not my mother, not even Mrs. Gibson or Amber, who I'd threatened.

Maybe they hadn't really believed I'd do it, that I'd kill someone. Consciously. Intentionally. They hadn't believed that I could be that evil.

Lucas believed.

Lucas recognized a fellow monster.

I crawled backward off him.

"No." I shook my head hard and looked around for my gloves, but they'd fallen into the weeds and I couldn't see them in the dark. "No, you're not going to do that. We're not going to do that, none of us. We're not monsters. We're not. We'll—we'll just leave him here. I'll—I'll just—" I lurched forward and grabbed the vine at his throat, pulling until it broke.

Lucas sucked in a frantic gulp of air. "Thank you," he rasped out. "Thank—"

"Shut the fuck up!" Nate snarled. Lucas shut up.

"Someone will find him." I was backing away. "We're not going to kill him. We're not monsters."

"Ellie—" Nate began, sounding like he wanted to object.

"No!" I shouted, and the trees rustled ominously at the sound of my voice.

"Okay," said Nate, his voice low and soothing. He followed after me, walking around Lucas, between the trees—they didn't get out of the way for him. "Okay. If that's what you need us to do, okay." He didn't look like he liked it, but he wasn't arguing. "You're not a monster, Ellie. You're not. We're not."

"Really," said another voice—Audra. I'd forgotten all about her.

She had the gun in her hands, pointed at Lucas's head.

"You may not be a monster," Audra said, "but I am."

She pulled the trigger. The sound of the gun going off, so close, was so loud it was like a physical blow. I staggered back and my ears rang. Audra never faltered, just squeezed the trigger over and over and over until it made a hollow clicking sound and there was only a red smudge where Lucas's face had been.

Mackenzie gagged. Audra tossed the gun away, walked up to the corpse, and put a hand on its chest. The ground rumbled and roiled and I tasted power in the air again, familiar but not *mine*. What was left of Lucas collapsed into so much earth in the span of a few seconds. The roots that had bound him settled flat to the ground, and a thick green moss began growing over them.

Audra stood and looked at us, all of us, her red gaze assessing. Then she threw something at Nate—it jingled as he caught it. Keys.

"Our vehicle is in better condition that yours, I believe. It's rented in a false name. I'm sure this one"—Audra nodded at Mackenzie—"can turn such a thing untraceable without too much trouble, yes?"

Mackenzie stared blankly at Audra for a moment shuddering and swallowing convulsively. She nodded. "Y-yeah. Yeah, I can do that."

"I thought so." Audra nodded. She tilted her head at Mackenzie. "Do you know, you are the first new thing I have seen in two hundred years." She smiled, and it made her face oddly childish. Then she turned to me, and her smile slipped. She licked her lips. "Ashes."

"I don't understand." I was starting to feel very cold, used up, and possibly about to tip over sideways. Maybe what I'd just done *had* taken some effort, even if it hadn't felt like it.

"I look forward to seeing you burn the world down," Audra told me, and then was gone. One second she was there, and the next she wasn't—I never saw her move. She hadn't just vanished, though. I felt the stir of air where she'd passed by me.

"Okay." Mackenzie cleared her throat. "Okay. So. We won, yeah? It's okay. It's—it's okay. It's—did she just *fly away?*"

"Ran," Nate said. "And, really? That's what bothers you about what just happened here?"

"I'm processing what I can," Mackenzie said.

"What do we do?" I stared at the spot of wild roadside that had been Lucas. I felt like there was a similar spot somewhere inside me, some part of my soul that I'd left on the ground over there, overwhelmed and changed and gone. "What are we supposed to do now?"

Neither of them answered.

"I think," Nate offered after a long pause, "that we get in our stolen car and we keep on going to your house." He nodded at Mackenzie. "Like we were going to do before."

I laughed, and stared at that patch of ground.

"Ellie?" he said, approaching me. "Ellie, what do *you* want to do?"

I thought about it.

"I want to find my gloves."

Nate looked down at my hands. He stepped closer. "Nah," he said, and he reached out for me. I flinched, but he just followed me, until his bare fingers were wrapped around mine.

I stared down at our joined hands. I could feel his life, light pulsing in his veins in a steady, thumping counterpoint to mine. I could feel the dirt and the germs and the pollen and the spores on his skin, too, but it was okay. It was *okay*.

"You don't want that," Nate said.

"No," I said, very slowly. "No, I guess I don't."

"So," Nate said. "South Hadley?"

"Mom really doesn't mind," Mackenzie offered. "At this point, after what I told her, she'd probably freak out if I showed up without you. And she's going to freak out anyway because I wrecked her car, but, hey, best excuse ever, right?" Her laugh was very, very forced.

"Ellie?" Nate asked again.

"Okay," I was still just staring at our hands, mine and Nate's.

"We're gonna need to move all your stuff over," Mackenzie told Nate. "Toss me the keys, I'll keep driving."

"You think you're okay to drive?" he asked.

"I think there's something wrong with us if any of us are okay to drive, but somebody's gonna, and I'm the one who knows where I live, so gimme the damn keys." It was good-natured, except for the part where her voice shook.

"Right. Sorry," Nate said, and I heard the keys jingle as they were tossed, then caught. I couldn't seem to look away from our hands. I was clutching at Nate's hand rather hard. His fingers were going kind of purple. Mine looked very, very white.

I heard Mackenzie opening car doors and the rustle of bags

being moved.

"You should go help," I told Nate's fingers. "I—I don't know if I can. I'm not sure—without gloves—"

"It's okay; it's not that much stuff. You wanna just get in the car?" Nate offered. I nodded.

Then I had to pry my fingers out of his to go do that.

I wobbled. My legs felt like they were made of paper, ready to fold out from under the weight of me, but my head felt impossibly light.

"Hey—" Nate reached out to steady me. I staggered and flung my arms out, waving him off. I breathed. Stood there. After a few seconds I opened my eyes again. Nate was watching me.

"Go haul stuff, I'm fine," I ordered. I turned and walked very, very carefully toward the SUV and climbed into the backseat. Someone else was going to have to play navigator. I wasn't sure how much longer I was going to be conscious.

It smelled like earth and lightning inside, even with three doors and the trunk open—like Lucas's power and Audra's.

"You hanging in there?" Mackenzie asked, her voice coming from behind me. She dropped a bag full of something that made a heavy thud into the trunk.

I wedged myself against the far door, trying not to touch anything as I moved. The car was clean, but not sterile. There were germs on the door handle, the seat, the window—mold spores, some pollen.

Very slowly, very carefully, I lay my bare hand against the window. It was cold, smooth, strange under my enervated skin.

"Elles?" Mackenzie prompted. "Stop being spooky, Elles, we've reached our quota on that for the night. Are you okay in there or not?"

I didn't want any of what was on the window to grow. It didn't, and it didn't hurt at all.

"I'm fine."

"Right, 'cause you look it," Mackenzie pointed out. "You're not at all doing your best mental patient impression."

I let my hand drop away from the window. "I'm as okay as I'm getting, under the circumstances," I amended and leaned sideways, resting my head on the glass.

"All right, fair enough," Mackenzie allowed, and I closed my eyes.

A few minutes later Nate crawled in beside me. I didn't flinch this time when he brushed my hair away from my face.

"Hey," he said softly.

"Hey," I repeated back, blinking at him. "Shouldn't you be up front giving directions and stuff?"

"Mack says she's got it," Nate said. I felt momentarily amused that Nate and Mackenzie had apparently bonded such that she was now "Mack" to him. "She's got my winter coat and a bag full of books riding shotgun. I'm back here with you." His fingers lingered on my cheek, no longer making any pretense of rearranging my hair—this was just him touching me for the sake of touching me. Up front, Mackenzie turned the key in the ignition.

The SUV climbed backward up over the embankment, and I murmured, "I thought about what I want."

"Yeah?" Nate prompted.

"You think they'll leave us alone?" I asked, rather than answering. "With Lucas—" I had to stop and swallow. Audra had killed him, I told myself. Audra shot him in the head. Not me.

But I wasn't sorry he was dead, and I'd made it possible, and the fact that I hadn't actually pulled the trigger didn't seem all that important.

"With Lucas dead," I made myself say, "do you think they'll give up on you?"

"I don't know," Nate answered. "Maybe? If they don't, we'll handle it." He paused, and then he laughed—a quick, unsteady sound. "Okay, who the hell am I kidding? You'll handle it. I'll watch and clap. Maybe sell tickets. It'll be awesome."

"Good old-fashioned freak show." I smiled tightly. It wasn't funny, but he was trying.

"Good old-fashioned freak show." He smiled back at me.

I reached out and touched his face with just the tips of my fingers, carefully, cautiously. Nate's smile slipped, his expression suddenly going very intense. He didn't move as I ran two fingers down his cheek, feeling the faint roughness of stubble and the softness of skin, just brushing the corner of his mouth. I paused.

He turned and kissed my fingertips.

I pulled my hand back, heat rushing up my neck.

"What do you want?" Nate asked, his voice gone low and

302

strange in a way that tugged at things inside of me.

"I don't know," I admitted. "I guess . . . I want to figure it out. I want my own life, without a bunch of excuses and bleach and gloves and—I want to know what I can do."

"I'd say 'anything,'" Nate suggested, smiling softly. I flushed, but I didn't look away, didn't duck my head or hide behind my hair. "I'd like to be around to see that. If you want."

"I want," I said softly.

"I like this plan. C'mere."

I leaned toward him, and his arm came around me, and after some awkward shifting and misplaced elbows and me blushing until I felt like I might die of it, I ended up with my head on his shoulder and his head resting on the top of mine.

"I wasn't making it up—what I said at the hospital," I added, just softly, pressing closer to Nate's side. "You and Mack, you're—" There weren't adequate words. "No one gets to use you. I don't care how powerful they are, you guys are all I've ever had that's mattered, and they can't have you. I don't want to be a monster, but if they come after us again—well, that part I think I've got figured out already. I'll do whatever I have to do."

Nate's arm tightened around me. "That doesn't make you a monster," he said. "That makes you human."

Acknowledgments

There are more than a few people who I'd like to thank for everything they've done to make the writing and publication of this book possible.

First, I'd like to thank Michael Carr, associate agent at Veritas Literary, who spotted my query letter on a forum and thought it was worth a second look. He brought my manuscript to the attention of Katherine Boyle, who became my agent. She held my hand through my initial joyous panic and everything since.

Next I want to thank my editor, Lisa Cheng—who put up with me while I learned how this whole process works—and the entire creative team at Running Press. Your patience is greatly appreciated. Thank you so much for taking a chance on a newbie author.

This book got its first reviews and editorial comments from the Penwood Writer's Group of Langhorne, Pennsylvania. Every single member has my gratitude, from those with whom I always seem to argue to those who clap and squee when I say I have new material to read. Both things are useful. You have no idea how petrified I was of reading out loud that first day, but I'm glad I took the risk—because of how it's improved my writing, and because of the friends I've made.

Of course there are people who contribute to the making of a book long before the words hit the page. Mrs. Weber, my ninth-grade English teacher, tolerated a handful of fifteen-year-old would-be writers haunting her classroom after school. Mrs. Kay King was my elementary-school art teacher and remains my friend. Kay, you gave me a space to be myself, and you've always been proud of me. Even when I didn't do what you expected or wanted, you had faith in me. That's meant a lot more than I can express here; just know that it's been noted.

Sharon Haiduck has been the sort of friend who is basically family for what seems like forever—are you *sure* we didn't go to kindergarten together, Sharon? But really we met in junior high, and we survived being teenagers together. Can I thank someone just for existing? I guess I just did.

My parents and my sister are also deserving of gratitude—if not sainthood—for providing practical support and living with my "artsiness" and my mess. Thank you for giving me the chance to keep trying.

Last but definitely not least, I need to thank an amazing and diverse bunch of thoughtful, compassionate, creative people, who I feel privileged to know—the friends I found through online fandom. You know who you are. When I was at the fraying end of my rope, you were always at the other end to pull me up. You kept me sane. You made me a better writer. You are my Scooby gang, my team, my pack—whatever you want to call it, geeks are the best friends in the world. I love you guys.